Behold This Dreamer

For All True Believers

Behold, this dreamer cometh

I was sprinting for the trees on the other side of the Long Island Expressway, lunging madly for safety.

I remember thinking that it would be only a matter of seconds before they began shooting, and tried running a broken field pattern that I vaguely remembered from high school. And I thought I was doing pretty good. They'd never be able to hit me. Even with their long barreled .44 Magnum revolvers, with which they'd probably spent hours practicing with, down at the Suffolk County Police Pistol Range. And at places like Vic's, after hours, just to hone their skill.

Waiting for a chance to show their style on crazies like me...

But wait a sec—I never played football in high school. I played soccer, wrestled a bit. But never football. And I sure didn't know any 'broken field patterns.'

I stopped to ponder this on the grassy strip forming the median on the Expressway. I was also out of breath, and stumbled around, drunkenly trying to remember *where* I was and *what* I was doing there.

Cars screamed by on either side of the median, lights stabbing into the early morning blackness. They gobbled up the roadway in a flash, then disappeared into the murk.

I spun around a couple of times and finally fell face first into the cold brown grass. I looked up, facing the place from where I began my flight. There were three patrol cars there now, their red and white strobe lights grinding into my eyes.

And it was cold.

Really cold. As cold as it could get at four o'clock in the morning, this middle of November.

The cold helped. Things were coming back to me now.

I could see a few of them milling around, staring in my direction. One of them seemed ready to come across, his hand placed resolutely on his gun, all set for the headlong rush it would take to get across the three strips of concrete without being turned into hamburger by some erstwhile commuter, or some sadistic drunk blasting homeward after a binge.

And there was my car now. Lying low, the county vehicles dwarfing it, its ripped convertible top flopping in the vicious gale created by the seventy mile per hour traffic rushing by it. I could see Zeke's eyes glowing from where he still sat, waiting patiently in the passenger seat.

Stay there, boy!

I sure as hell didn't need him to jump out and try to find me now. He was a good dog, and at least I knew that he'd keep the cops out of the car long enough for me to get away…

Another patrol car pulled up, and one of the cops, the one who had been about to risk his intestines running after me, jumped in. They paused just long enough to shout instructions to the others before the car spun around and started coming across to where I was.

Just at this time, a woman in a Cadillac decided to hit the brakes. She was probably spooked by all the flashing lights, thinking there must be an accident, and inadvertently put her car into a perfect four-wheel drift. One Mario Andretti would have been proud of. She came sliding sideways down the road, skidding on all fours, her tires screeching like raped cats.

She seemed to look right at me as she flew past. I could see the look of fear in her eyes, hair standing on end and probably thinking that she should have mailed those lovely invitations to her daughter's wedding that were still in the glove compartment...and now were in danger of being spread all over the stinking road, and would never go out, and *then* what would happen?

I stuck my head in the dirt, or tried to. The ground was frozen.

The Cadillac, a peach-colored Sedan de Ville, bounced sideways into the patrol car just crossing the road. Both vehicles rebounded from the crash just as I looked up again. One of the strobe lights on the county car rolled down the highway, its opposite number still blinking. The two officers inside sat stunned and disbelieving.

The Caddy seemed untouched. Its driver sat stock still in her seat, eyes wide and unblinking. The car had bounced back, directly in front of me. She seemed to be staring straight at me again.

By this time, of course, all hell was breaking loose behind. Cars were piling up like coins in a winning slot machine. The cops along the edge of the highway were running around, frantically trying to light flares and direct traffic just managing to get through.

A couple of them were even on the median now, a few feet from where I was. But they were watching the road now.

I didn't feel that drunk and disoriented anymore. I must have been really blasted before, though. For the life of me, I couldn't remember what I was doing there—I didn't remember getting pulled over...

Zeke was at the driver's window in the car. At what is

actually called the side curtain, the car an Austin- Healy Sprite—his fiery eyes burning brightly. He was barking now. I couldn't hear him, but I could see the flash of his teeth and big tongue in the intermittent lights. He seemed to be saying: *Come on, you stupid fool! Let's go! NOW!*

Screw it. Either they got me, or they don't. The dog is right.

I got up, brushing the dirt and dead grass off me, and, walking as straight as I could, crossed back over the expressway.

Cops were everywhere now. The sounds of sirens were getting louder in the distance; blowing horns and shouted orders added to the din. To the west, the roadway looked like rush hour, though it wasn't due in this direction for another twelve hours or so. The cars and trucks were backed up as far as I could see. In the opposite westbound lanes the rubber-neckers were already slowing down to get a hopeful look at some real carnage.

I only looked once, then kept my eyes on the empty stretch heading east. The sky ahead was clear. One of the morning stars hung brightly there. Probably Venus. Or maybe Jupiter—

I was at the car now. Zeke was frantically nudging the side curtain window open with his big wet nose. I stuck my hand in, reaching down to release the door handle. On a 1959 Sprite, which this one was, there are no outside handles or latches. Zeke nuzzled my hand as I reached down, making it all the more difficult. I got it open though, and got in.

No one noticed me yet.

I had to beat Zeke back into his seat, of course. Labradors can be stubborn beasts, especially when excited. Then I fumbled for the hidden switch I had for the ignition. It wasn't securely attached to anything, so it took awhile.

Finding the switch, I flicked it on and then pulled on the starter, praying the little bastard would start. Sprites don't like cold weather; it hadn't been sitting there very long, however, for it roared to sputtering life. There was no muffler—long ago the victim of a few road dividers, curbs and other bothersome low-lying obstacles that seem to fall in my way.

I turned the lights on. The police car in front of me was very close; he couldn't have pulled in that close. He must have backed up on me. I could read his plate number: 666. Exhaust fumes filled the car. Time to leave. I put it in reverse.

WHAM!

The bastards had a car close behind, too. Why didn't I notice that before?

Cursing a bit, but glad that the Sprite was tiny, I maneuvered back and forth until I got out of the spot. We then rolled along the grass on the edge of the pavement, picking up speed.

Sticking my face back out into the cold, I looked back.

The bashed-in side of the de Ville looked like a piece of crumpled paper someone tried, unsuccessfully, to flatten out. There were two cops helping the woman out. Her hair was still standing straight up, and, in the light, she seemed to wear a halo.

I fumbled around in my pockets for a Camel, finding one in an old pack. It was bent in a u-shape, but I stuck in my mouth and lit it anyway. I didn't want to take a chance on straightening it out. It might break. My hands were shaking some, whether from the cold or whatever; I didn't know...

I pulled back the side curtain window again, and automatically looked once more for any oncoming traffic. There wasn't any.

With a soft *Adios!* I headed off into the night.

CHAPTER TWO

So, what's it all about?

Glimpy Fallon

There was a time I didn't get away. *That* had been years previous, and I thought about it now, going down the road.

I remembered talking about it:

"And what happened?" she asked.

"I got busted. DWI," I said, shrugging it off.

"That's when you called Cal?"

"Yeah."

Jeannie leaned back in her chair and puffed on her Virginia Slim. She blew neat little smoke rings. Her eyes were on me. They were dark, alternately soft or penetrating. I could never decide which.

She was my psychotherapist. My shrink.

She was also my former best friend's lover.

We didn't have an easy relationship, she and I. It had something to do with her thinking that I was sexually attracted to her, and though she said that she could handle it, she was sure *I* could not. Therefore, I had been searching for another one. Another shrink.

I felt it didn't help matters much that she always carried on her assignations with Cal immediately after our usual meeting, and told her so: "You know," I said, "it probably doesn't help matters much here, especially when you're thinking of Calvin when you're talking to me, and…"

She was waving her cigarette back and forth. "Excuse me for interrupting, Jonas, but we've had this discussion. You were arrested, then called Cal…"

Him again. "You see," I accused, "you can't forget him."

"Jonas. Would you rather we talk of *my* relationships, or yours? I'm sure you would prefer the latter," she went on, her Irish up. "After all, it's your time."

"My time. And my money."

"That's right," she said. "Your time and your money."

Silence while we regarded each other.

She got up suddenly and went out of the room. She called back in, "You want a beer, Jonas?"

I told her 'yeah,' and fingered the colored pebbles and rocks that were placed in little glass containers on the coffee table. They were all different colors. Lots of blues and reds together, bright yellows and hot pinks. I looked around the room, trying to fix it in my mind. I liked it. It was comfortable. But I didn't think I'd be coming back.

Jeannie came back in with two bottles of Michelob. She handed me one and I unscrewed the cap off, glad that she'd left it on. I had a nervous habit of grinding the beer bottle cap on the bottom of the bottle. It used to drive Cal Franks nuts. I would start doing it unconsciously while we were driving along, or even just talking somewhere. Cal would just say to me, "Hey, Jonas. Hand me that a minute, will ya?" And I would hand him the beer bottle cap automatically and he would throw it out the window, or into the water, or wherever.

I started grinding away now, and told Jeannie about it.

"It is an irritating noise," she said.

"Do you want me to stop?"

"Yes and no. It's only irritating when I think of it."

She thought a moment. "Jonas, hand me that thing."

I threw the cap to her and she caught it neatly. We both laughed.

It was the end of the session. We usually finished it with a beer and a joke. She supplied the beer and I supplied the joke. The jokes were usually true, too. They were painful, some of them. But then a lot of things that happened in rooms like that one were painful.

I made ready to leave.

It was past eleven-thirty and Cal would be coming in soon. For some reason I couldn't bear to see him after I'd just finished a session with Jeannie. I felt too raw.

She must have explained my feelings to him, for after the first few times we met there, we didn't see each other there again. He was always in evidence, though. I'd spy his car up the block, or hear him come in the backway at the end of my hour. *That* was irritating.

Their affair had been going on now, hot and cold, for about three years. Calvin Franks was divorced, no children; Jeannie was still married, with five children. He was in his early thirties, my age; she was closing fast on forty.

I had been coming to see her for eight months, once a week. Of course, it was the same night that Jeannie could get off to spend with Cal.

I started coming to see her when I began having the dreams of dread again. They weren't really dreams. I would have feelings of intense dread come over me in the middle of the night. I would wake up, and without particular thoughts I would feel desperately unhappy. I was sleeping alone then, either on the couch or the floor.

9

The feeling would come over me like a dark cloud covering a bright moon. I would actually tremble in the darkness.

Covering my head over more with the blanket, I would peer out at the shadows in the half-finished room I slept in. The dreams began while I was adding a wall in the house. The wall studs were up, and the formed shadows looked like bars in some places. Piles of material and tools lay about.

Maybe I just didn't like it being unfinished. But I was happy to be doing the work. It was winter still, and I was glad to be working inside. The wall I was constructing ran straight down the middle of what once was the living room of the house. Then, I started to curve the wall, putting a soft round turn to where the doorway would be. It was to be a proud entrance. I had a pair of French doors to hang there. I meant the room to be both a study and bedroom.

I began dreading going to sleep there. But, along with this dread, I felt almost a fiendish delight in being awakened by the dream. I wanted it. Somehow it was appealing to me, and for a long while I wasn't disappointed. Only when the dreams stopped did I call Jeannie and make an appointment. And that was the second time.

I remember being disappointed because she couldn't tell me why I was having those intense feelings of depressing dread. She told me I'd need analysis for that. She did say she could help me deal with it, though. I never did tell her I thought I secretly liked it—the dread feelings.

I suppose I haven't told her a lot of things. She asked me why I was sleeping alone:

"When you say you were in the room alone, where was Carol?"

Carol was my wife. We had separated, but were back together in the house we owned then. We had a child. A boy.

To try and cement the marriage back together I was doing work on the house to please her. I really couldn't afford it, either the money or the time. But it seemed worthwhile anyway.

"She was asleep, with the boy," I answered Jeannie. "In the boy's room."

"Why didn't you sleep together?"

"She didn't want to."

"Why?"

"She didn't want to have sex with me, I guess. And sleeping with the boy was impossible. I never got any sleep."

"How did you feel about that?"

"Not good."

"Weren't you angry?"

"Yeah, I was angry. I like to get laid once in awhile."

I was working on the bay all day, then come home; maybe go to class, then work on the house; then sleep, then get up and do it again—

"Did you tell Carol how you felt?"

And on and on.

I *was* pretty busy during that time. I was in a graduate study program, taking night classes. And trying to make a living digging clams out on the bay. It was hard work clamming in the winter. I didn't have a boat, so I would beg rides with different people. The work was brutal and tedious. We hand dug clams from specially designed boats, using wood-handled tongs.

Most of the men I went with were decent enough. They didn't mind taking me. But id did mean that their income would be slightly lower for the given day I was aboard. And in the wintertime this just made things more miserable.

I couldn't blame their resentment, if there was any. But sometimes it would come through, or seem to. One time I was culling clams from all the other bottom debris on the forward deck. The temperature was low that day, about fifteen degrees. The wind was blowing offshore at twenty-five knots or so.

My fellow clammer—his name was Shultz, everyone called him Shultzie—had finished cleaning up his catch earlier than I had. We still had plenty of time to catch the clam buyers on the dock. But Shultzie started the boat up and insisted on heading in before I was finished.

Clam boats, due to their special proclivity, have their decks very low to the water. This boat was typical of most of them. When Shultzie decided to go in on this day, he could have done slowly, as he usually did. Instead, he gave the engine more throttle than normal. Since I was working forward, with no protection, I got soaked in the freezing spray.

I remember looking back—aft—and seeing him standing there in the cabin, protected from the seas that were crashing over the bow and onto me. He just stared straight ahead, as though he was oblivious to my predicament. It was one of the first few days that I worked with him—maybe the very first.

Later on, we became friendlier. But I never forgot his disregard for me that day. I know that it was because he felt he couldn't refuse me. Most baymen, as the clamdiggers call themselves, have been in a similar situation, needing a ride when their own boat has broken down or some other catastrophic event prevents them from going out alone. It was a code they followed.

Shultzie sure didn't owe me anything, though. Later, after getting to know him better, I realized the extent of his personal problems. My own seemed infinitesimal in comparison.

It seemed a strange period of my life. Most of the baymen who helped me were strangers, more or less. I didn't go with the few, or had been, actual friends. One of them, a boyhood friend, flatly refused to take me out with him. I never received a satisfactory answer why, though I still saw him socially on occasion. I even asked Jeannie about him once, as she knew him also through other friends. But she never offered an explanation.

It was about this time that I started building a small boat of my own, a garvey. I had decided to try poaching clams full time. I wasn't getting anywhere doing anything else—I was about to be thrown out of the graduate study program I was in, my marriage was dying...

Poaching didn't work either, though. But the weather then was beginning to get nicer, the days longer, and I had the urge to build. I needed to.

But I can remember the day I realized that it wasn't working out for me—though the actual realization of *that* didn't come until much later. I was looking over a cove with another long-time poacher. It was a place way out east, near Moriches; a long closed area and looked promising. There was a small marina there, making access easy. An old hulk of a boat was tied up near the marina entrance. It was apparent, though, that at one time the boat had been beautiful. The name *BOOKIE* was on the forward bow.

"That's my old boat," my fellow bandit said.

"Not anymore?" I asked.

"No."

"Why?" I wanted to know, and wasn't sure then if he'd tell me.

But he did.

"Dreams—dreams," was all he said.

The final break came with Carol and in the ensuing settlement I got to live in the house and she got custody of the boy.

CHAPTER THREE

The sun was up and grinding its pitiless light into my face.

My eyes hurt. I didn't want to open them. My head began to hurt, too.

I had made it, though.

The car was parked, facing east. Zeke stirred in the seat beside me, grunting arthritically as he woke. He was a young dog no longer. He stuck his cold wet nose into my crotch in an effort to wake me.

I bent my head down out of the sunlight and opened my eyes. Zeke regarded me, then sheepishly put his big black head to one side.

I must be a pretty sight. Goddamn dog won't even look at me.

We were at Orient Point, on the far eastern end of Long Island's north fork. The ferry from Connecticut wasn't due for at least a couple of hours yet. On board should be the boy. I was there to pick him up.

Every other weekend I made this trip. The separation agreement spelled out the terms. My former wife had custody of our son, and, in return for my continued support payments, she would deliver him for a visit on alternate weekends.

I wasn't adverse to the arrangement. I looked forward to the visits; though, at times, like the incident that occurred just a few scant hours ago, it made life difficult. In order to meet the early ferry I had to leave extremely early in the morning from the house. And if I'd made the mistake of going out the Friday night before, like I had, going to bed meant I would never get up in time for the two hour jaunt to Orient from where I lived. So I would just stay up—or drive out to Orient Point and sleep there. Like I just did.

I loved the boy, little Jonas. Jonas Coffey. He was my only son, my only child, and would carry my name into posterity. He was too young for this bullshit—two and a half years old.

We're never *too* old, though. I remembered Doris Lessing, in the *Golden Notebook*, speaking of the love, joy, and delight of life being absent from being grown-up. So true, so true—

I looked around the ferry terminal parking lot. It was still too early for the shit-pot diner there to be open. The coffee was lousy there anyway. I felt crusty, beat, and terribly hung-over.

I felt around in my field jacket pockets for cigarettes. Nothing. There were a few crushed packs littering the floor of the car. I went through them. *Nada.* Jesus.

I suddenly remembered last night, and the fracas on the Expressway. God. That was where I had my last smoke, too. The Suffolk County cops must have my number by now.

Maybe.

A big maybe. I didn't remember giving them any information—but surely they had to have my plate number. There was only one license plate on the car, and it was on the back. But it wasn't the right plate. It was off a 1967 Rambler that was last registered to...let's see now...Julian? Nadine? I didn't know.

One thing I did know, though, was that they'd have a hard time tracing it to me. Julian and Nadine were halfway to Florida by now on Julian's boat. If the plate it traced to their last address it'll be the one they left months ago.

So far, so good.

Only trouble was that the little buzzbomb I was tooling around in wasn't exactly inconspicuous. It was once painted red, but had corroded into a rusty shade of ocher. And there were only a few of these cars around. It was nicknamed the Bug-eye Sprite, due to the headlights incongruously sticking up out of the forward hood. The car was a classic and was noticeable, all right.

I'd have to lay low, I guess. Maybe get another set of wheels for awhile...

I was suddenly too exhausted to think about it. I settled back in the seat, and watched the morning wind blow the salt grass back and forth on the dunes. Mesmerized, I fell asleep again.

And I dreamed:

I was on a dark desert, and far in the distance was a tiny figure, and the figure was shouting something. It appeared to be a man, dressed like an Arab, with flowing robes. I began walking towards the figure, thinking that it would get larger as I approached.

The ground was covered with stones. Some were larger than others, and I would continually trip on these as I made my way. It was hard going, but I wanted to hear what he was saying, or shouting, rather. I had trouble picking my feet up to clear the big stones. I would see my feet approaching one, and would make a conscious effort to lift my feet so as to clear it, only I was unable to do that. Again and again the stones would make me trip, and I began cursing my clumsy feet.

I must have made some progress, for I began understanding what the man was shouting. Only he didn't get any larger.

He reminded me of Saint-Exupery's Little Prince. He was about that size, wearing the same innocent look and loose clothing. And he had that little turban on his head. He was shouting at the top of his little lungs, and as I got closer I realized he wasn't speaking in English, but in Spanish. He was repeating a phrase, over and over again, from a poem I thought I had long ago forgotten: *Yo quiero que me ensenen donde esta la salida para este capitan atado por la muerte.*

The poem was by Federico Garcia Lorca, and the phrase meant: *I want them to show me where the way out exists for this captain shackled by death.*

The little man seemed to speed up his speech as I approached. He was shouting louder now, and the shrillness of his tiny voice began to hurt my ears. The ground was lighter-colored near him. But the stones were larger, and I was now stumbling over boulders that came up to my knees. I needed to get to him, but I was moving slower.

I was sweating now, and the sweat seemed to come down off my forehead and congeal in the creases of my skin. It made my face stiff, like a mask, and I knew I had a terrible look on me, a great grinning sardonic look that scared me as I thought of it. I couldn't move my features. They were stuck in this hideous mask. I was afraid of scaring the little man away—

As I got closer the figure looked more and more familiar. He was shouting faster and faster, the same phrase over and over again, watching me now as I approached. He didn't look afraid, but curiously troubled, like a child does when he's confused about whether to be scared or not.

I was almost within reach of him. He seemed so tiny. I was reaching for him, wanting to speak, to tell him not to be afraid, it was only me...But I couldn't speak. My mouth and face were frozen in this horrible mask.

I was almost there. One last boulder to crawl over. As I did so the boulder grew, and the figure was standing on top.

I felt crazed now by the shouting, and only wanted to stifle the incessant intolerable noise of it. The boulder was of a light sandy texture, and as I stretched out to grasp the little man and smother the sound, the boulder turned to sand, and I felt myself slipping backwards. And then I looked up into the figure's face.

It was my son, Jonas—the boy. And me...

***

I woke up sweating in the hot glare from the sun. It was higher now. Zeke was whining, and his breath was making the windshield fog over. I felt really horrible. My lips were dry and crumbly like burned bacon.

The parking lot was almost filled with cars. The ferry would be due any time that meant. I let Zeke out on his side and opened my door. The cold hit me with a rush. The sweat drops on my face felt like they were turning to ice.

I looked over towards the diner. There were people going in and out now. I had to take a leak bad.

A blue-and-white just then pulled up in front of the place. Uh-oh. I automatically cringed back down in my seat. The driver got out carrying his portable walkie-talkie and went into the diner.

I didn't know what I was so paranoid about. There was a car on either side of me now, and all one could see from the diner was the dead balloon tied to the top of my radio antenna.

Oh, yeah.

I got out and got rid of it. It was one of those advertisement balloons for a bar. Julian was with me when I got it. I remembered tying it on. I was so drunk that I made about fifty half-hitches to secure it, only backwards, so that when we took off the knots unraveled and we almost lost the balloon. And it did come off; I remember diving out after it, the top being off the Bug-eye, and sliding down off the back of the car. I hit the road in a forward roll, landing perfectly. The car was still in gear, and though I had hit the brakes, stopping it momentarily, it traveled on off the asphalt into the soft sand along Dune Road, with Julian frantically trying to stop the car by pulling up hard on the emergency brake, which of course didn't work.

I retrieved the balloon, only now we were stuck in the sand, and really too drunk to do anything about it except laugh. Julian tied the big balloon back on, making sure this time it would stay. We stumbled back to the bar where we'd been drinking. The balloon was from there, and was emblazoned with a joint-puffing Chinese dragon, with the name below, *Gold Dragon*.

The owners were friends of ours (or were). Business associates at one time, really. We used to run grass for them.

Calvin and Stephen Franks, the owners, weren't quite one's idea of big time saloon keepers; they were too lazy for that. The *Gold Dragon* was more of a local rock and roll bar; the beautiful people were invited, but they didn't hang out there. One reason was that the place was located in Hampton Bays, and not in Southampton or East Hampton where the celebrities did their serious partying.

The place had pretensions, though. Cocaine might not have been a staple of the customers, but they wouldn't turn it down if it was offered. It was a big place, with a certain style suggesting more of the open West than the closed-in stuffiness of the Eastern singles bar.

The Franks brothers had bankrolled the *Dragon* by ferrying huge amounts of pot up from the hinterlands of the

Mexican desert to the rich shores of Long Island. Julian and I had done some of the ferrying also; we didn't make out as well as the brothers. They had made the easy money and trying to go legit, as it were. So was I.

You could say that Julian and I did all right on our end, too. Or rather Julian did. He tended to live like an ascetic anyway. He was cheap. To him, if something cost a dollar there was no reason that he couldn't make it, do without it, or at least cut the cost in half some way. He was a genius at it. And he could fix anything. He was happiest when something broke and he *did* have to fix it. There were times that I'd swear he deliberately let things go to the point where something did break...

Julian never liked things too fancy, except for his boat. He had a basic distrust of things that were too clean. For years, he ran a one-man marine repair business that he impishly called *Quick & Dirty Marine*. When he had something new to deal with, such as an engine to install, or some other piece of equipment to work on, the first thing he would do would be to throw away any official instructions, labeling same as theoretical, vague, and misleading. He would then dive into the job on his own, trusting to his mechanic's intuition.

Most of the time he'd do all right, though there were times that this petulant attitude cost him. A fiery temper, which always seemed to erupt at the wrong moment, also plagued him.

He wasn't exactly a success. Somehow, people didn't appreciate his fuck-the-paperwork-let's-just-do-it cavalier approach to servicing their goods.

I met him one night to give him a hand re-installing a marine refrigeration unit. The boat owner was there, and I think Julian asked me to come just to handle the flak. The unit broke down right in the middle of a summer's cruise, and the owner, a Dr. Bradley, was incensed.

Julian originally installed the unit in such a way as to maximize its efficiency. But it worked too well, freezing itself up continually, and then the damn thing quit.

The good doctor had kept the thrown-away instructions, noticing at the time Julian's disdain for them. When the catastrophe occurred, Bradley read over the installation instructions and found a discrepancy in Julian's method. Though it was obvious, to me at least, that Julian wasn't at fault, the owner insisted that he was.

So there he was, in the middle of the night, trying to fix the thing. Dr. Bradley wanted no part of that, though. He wanted a new unit, and he wanted Julian to pay for it. The warranty, of course, would not cover the damage if the installation instructions were not carried out to the letter.

The doctor was adamant. Julian, however, just quietly sat there, trying to decipher the intricacies of the dead machine while I tried placating the good doctor. I had brought a bottle along, and was liberally sharing it with Dr. Bradley— ostensibly in hopes that he would go home or at least to his bunk below. But he had sworn not to leave there until he had 'obtained satisfaction.'

It was no use on both accounts, mine or Julian's. Along about two in the morning Julian had had it. He might have fixed the thing if he'd been left alone, but the constant whining, bitchy tone of the now drunk—thanks to me—and also viciously insulting Dr. Bradley was too much.

For the hundredth time, the doctor, looking down into the engine compartment where Julian was elbow-deep in oil, grease, and tiny parts, said, "I thought you told me you were an expert. Some expert. If I had done something like that in *my* business..."

He'd then turn to me, a look of superiority on his swollen face, "Why, I'd be *laughed* out of the profession." This last time, he added, "I thought one could still get decent work done today, but I see now that it's impossible, at least around here. Nothing but snot-nosed kids who think they're *experts* because they slapped together a few outboard engines for some low-life clamdiggers..."

At that, whether because the doctor mentioned clamdiggers, which was what I was doing for a living at the time (and so was Julian, though he didn't like to admit it, the marine repair business, under the aegis of *Q & D Marine*, not exactly providing much of a living for him; I like to think, though, that what he did, he did because of me) or that Julian was well past the eruption point anyway, a low growl came up out of the engine compartment.

I looked down and saw Julian grunting to lift the entire refrigeration unit over his head. The thing had to weigh over eighty pounds. Julian struggled up to the deck, the unit high in the air now, his eyes blazing in the drop light's glare...

The doctor's mouth dropped open. The bulky refrigeration unit, dripping oil, Julian held just over their heads. "You know what you can do with this *fucking* thing?" Julian cried, his voice straining. "You can take it and shove it up your pompous *professional* doctor's ass...after you go swimming for it!"

Over the side it went, high in an arc—it seemed from where I was seated—and landed with a depth-charge like splash which echoed across the quiet marina. The moment was punctuated by another crash, which was the doctor's glass of scotch—one I had just poured for him—breaking on the deck. Time for us to leave.

It's funny now that I think of it, but my feelings at that time were very confused. I had spent the evening being as pleasant as possible to the doctor. He was a pompous ass. And an insulting drunk. But after trying so hard to get him to accept the situation, I found *myself* unable to do so. I was mad at Julian for acting so childish in the face of that jerk, while at the same time delighted that the incident had ended in such an appropriate, given the circumstances, manner. In the doctor's intentioned slur about clamdiggers I was the victim, though he didn't know it. Julian didn't consider himself a clammer; so, if I accept the idea that the deliberately insulting remark of the doctor's was the initial spark for the explosion, I had been championed by Julian.

In thinking back about it, I should have been ecstatic. Fuck the rich doctor and his stinking boat. The insulting bastard got what he deserved; he was lucky Julian, or even I, didn't throw him in the water after the refrigeration unit.

I wasn't ecstatic though. I attempted to be, giggling with nervousness in the car: "Christ, that son of a bitch probably shit his pants—aheheh, heh, heh..."

I was drinking right out of the bottle then, too. We were lost somewhere on the back roads near Montauk, and I must have been trying to choke down my confusion. I was so goddamn angry at myself and trying to be happy at the same time that all I could do was utter stupid inanities. I was really ignoring Julian.

"Well," I said. "You had good intentions, Ju. Good fucking intentions."

"Good intentions mean sloppy shit," Julian answered me, his voice tired and ragged sounding. He was slumped against the door, his head resting on his arm.

"*What?*" I yelled at him, careening the car around a corner. I was driving way too fast, drunk myself now, and not giving a damn.

"Will you slow the fuck down!"

He was looking at me, his dark eyes full of bitterness and a gut-wrenching hate. One hand was on top of the windshield, the other clutching the seat, his fingers white-hot in the darkness.

I stopped the car.

The bottle was between my legs. I lit a cigarette.

Julian was breathing heavily.

I suddenly felt really drunk then, nodding almost. I finished the bottle; then gagged, retching horribly.

Inside I felt better though. Numb now, the conflict smothered in the smooth deadness, I was glad I was sick. I didn't have to care anymore.

Julian just said, "Let's go home now."

CHAPTER FOUR

It wasn't long after that incident that we started making runs for Cal and Stephen Franks.

Cal was a friend of a sort from the beach. I got to know him through a couple of lifeguard buddies of mine. They used to bring him along to parties.

I was living on my boat then at Oak Beach. Cal was recently divorced, so we had something in common. He had some money—a lot more than I had. It was rumored that he moved large quantities of grass up from the south. He always seemed to have good smoke with him, that was for sure.

Being my usual inquisitive self, I got to know a bit more about the operation. Cal and I soon trusted each other; or rather, he trusted me. We spent a lot of one summer getting drunk and high together on my boat.

The boat wasn't much, being wood and sixty years old. It was a Marblehead with a raised forward deck and had seen some service in its time. She was named *Confusion*, and had made her reputation two generations earlier by running in whiskey from offshore and never being caught. She'd been set up with twin engines and would still crank out across the flats, flying along in places where the Coast Guard still won't go. A damn good sea boat. But it was comfortable to live on, with a tumble-home transom and pretty lines. From a distance it was hard to take your eyes off her.

I was still in a high state then. I had a little money, and

wasn't working much, if at all. Carol had walked out eight months before, and had quickly filed for and would eventually get a 'well-earned' divorce.

I didn't give a fuck then, and I used to say so at every opportunity. So did Calvin Franks, my new running buddy.

It's funny, or perhaps sad, how quickly others tire of hearing the divorced-husband-bullshit rag. I've heard it before and didn't like it either, from someone else. But it gave Cal and I something to talk about. Both of us were bitter, and not really depressed yet. There were plenty of available women around at the beach whom we could alienate and psychologically abuse. That was our 'fun.' We were those two crazies on the antique boat.

Near the end of the summer I began running out of money. I was also going nuts. I was hot to make a move. Do *anything.*

One afternoon, Cal and I were lying around on the deck at the Oak Beach Inn, making cracks about the girls that passed by.

"I gotta get out of here," I said.

"You heading back to the boat?" Cal asked, his eyes following what must have been a sixteen-year-old as she sauntered back and forth on the deck, her eyes tauntingly fixed in our direction. She was much too young to know better...

"The boat, always the boat. No, I want to split. Go somewhere—anywhere. Africa. Europe. Tanzania. Just go."

"So go," Cal said, his eyes somewhere else.

The girl came over now and stuck her bikinied butt down on the end of the bench we were lounging on. She played with lighting a cigarette.

"Oh, good Jesus," I muttered. Another one ripe for the kill. Only she wouldn't be expecting the type of venomous response Cal was getting ready to spit out. He'd begin slow, tantalizing. Like the Cobra.

"You look like you need something," Cal said to her, his voice taking on a caustic edge; his eyes squinting as he sized her up.

He exuded just enough macho appeal to entice someone like her...someone young and unwary, looking for that 'fun and excitement' a place like the Inn promised.

"Well, I could use a light," she replied, her voice innocent and trusting, though she was obviously trying to make contact.

I suddenly felt afraid for her. Her eyes were large and blue, her face clear and, yes, sixteen-year-old beautiful. She looked too pretty to be there – *here*. At least she should be with someone. In a moment or two she definitely would feel very alone. Alone as Cal and I were.

She had her legs crossed, her pretty knees close together; her painted toenails the color of puce. Her skin a light delicious brown. I wondered where her father was.

"*Well*, come on over then, and we'll take *care* of you," Cal purred, mimicking her first word just enough.

He was going to be a real bastard this time.

She stood up and came over. I held one hand over my eyes. I didn't want to be a part of this for some reason. I usually saved my nastiness for older women anyway.

She started bending over to accept the flame from Cal's lighter, and with his free hand he grasped the back of one golden thigh and held on.

"Nice *hams*, honey," he said, his voice suddenly tough now as he quickly put the lighter away and grabbed her other leg also.

Cal's hands were huge, and the girl was small.

He had her.

The animal fear was suddenly in her eyes. The coquettishness gone, but she was trying to remain cool. She didn't move, but I could sense the tenseness in her body.

Her eyes were locked on his.

I glanced at Cal, but his snake-like gaze was cold, almost senseless.

His prey was bent over him, and she had to put a hand on his shoulder to keep from falling. There was sweat now on her upper lip.

I stupidly thought: *What possible pleasure is he getting from this?* Then I made a mental note *not* to ask him later.

Then I was suddenly disgusted with myself for being so detached. The girl was really afraid. I could *smell* her fear now, a sweet sex smell that actually began to arouse me. Maybe I was disgusted because I wanted her for myself.

I was still peeking out at them from between my fingers, the coward voyeur.

Cal dropped his malevolent gaze to her breasts. They were protruding to within inches of his face. She almost cried then; in fact, a small cry did come from her, a bleat almost. She broke from his leering and looked about wildly now, searching for help—

The deck was crowded, as it usually is that time of day. But there was really nothing amiss in her or even Cal's actions that could possible cause alarm. Just normal sexual by-play to anyone passing by. That's what a singles bar like the Oak Beach Inn was all about.

The girl was astute enough to know all this; she didn't want to cause herself anymore embarrassment or call attention to herself. Really. She was definitely underage, and easy prey. But she was scared. I felt her fear in the pit of my stomach. It formed a small, knowing knot there.

"Nice," Cal murmured huskily. "Very nice..."

He had his mouth open, and was pulling her closer, one quivering breast almost in his teeth. Her arms were taut and straining against him, her hands afraid to let go of his shoulders, her nails—those pretty little dark one-day-would-be *claws*...

She was still valiantly silent, her mouth stretched downwards though, the edges of her teeth visible, her breath quickening past her drying lips...and, at the last instant, just before Cal actually would have touched the thin fabric of her bikini top with his dripping fangs, he let her go with a raucous *Whoop!*

She reeled away, almost white in spite of her tan, shaken. Her bright yellow hair disheveled; like she'd been through a hurricane.

We watched her bounce off a couple of guys who tried to catch her too. She shook them off quickly, like a frightened—but newly wary—animal does a pair of inexperienced dogs out for a romp in the field.

I was glad it was over.

"*HA, AHA!*" Cal crowed. "Cunt doesn't know what a little fun is." He chugged down the rest of his Beck's, then sat back in triumph, leering about like an old pirate after a good score. But his eyes betrayed him. The cold blank stare was gone, the arrogant machismo buried again. He suddenly looked lonely and depressed.

I had the temerity to think that he was worse than I was—I thought I wasn't as bitter. About women, that is.

Cal had broken up with his wife, for the final time, just two months previous. There were no children involved; only a—as he described it—gnawingly cold and bitchy remembrance of the last few years of a sorry marriage. To say it was sorry was to put it in mild terms, for Cal was actively hostile towards women in general.

At the time he was, like me, incapable of sustaining a relationship with anyone—besides someone in a similar situation.

So we got along.

Cal had a house on the beach. He had shared it with his wife, but at the time I met him there was little evidence she had ever been there. He told me that she cleaned it out one weekend with the help of her new boyfriend.

The place was now furnished in late American Marlboro Man, replete with the obligatory male masturbatory magazines and pseudo-erotic pop art. The tone was almost asexual; especially in its screaming late twentieth century emphasis on empty sexuality.

There were personal touches in the place though. Like the big poster, hand-lettered in gothic German script, that greeted one while seated on the toilet. It read:

> After they had him captured,
> they tied a club in his
> mouth and transferred him to
> Innsbruck. They punished
> him and tortured him but he
> would not recant. They
> proceeded to put him in ice
> cold water until he could not
> move. From there they put him
> in a warm room and lashed
> him unmercifully. They cut
> wounds into his body and poured
> alcohol into the wounds, lit

it, and let it burn. But
still he would not recant.
After much suffering and torture,
he was sentenced and burned
at the stake alive.

When I asked Cal about the poster, he translated it from the German, telling me it was a description of Jacob Hutter's ordeal before he was burned at the stake in 1836.

"Oh," I said.

He then told me his wife had *made* the poster and used to keep it prominently displayed in their bedroom.

"Is she a Hutterite?" I asked.

Cal looked at me strangely then, gauging my interest perhaps. I *was* interested, but must not have shown it; or, maybe I showed too much.

"Not anymore," he finally replied, breezily dismissing the subject. "I just keep it in the shitter there for inspiration."

Cal kept quite an extensive library in the house. Besides the standard erotic literature, there were volumes of books and magazines on natural history. I was impressed, and being curious I naturally used to look over this collection whenever I had a free moment there. I would pick up a work such as Scheffer's *Seals, Sea Lions, and Walruses*, or Fox's *Behaviour of Wolves, Dogs, and Related Canids*, and leaf through it. Some parts would be underlined; other pages marked in various ways with slips of paper, unopened junk mail envelopes, or empty matchbooks. There was a whole section of the library devoted to the Hutterites: *Hutterite Society, The Hutteries in North America, The Hutterite Way*, etc. All had been marked, like the others, for future and quick reference.

Whenever Cal would see me perusing a volume, he

would launch into a discussion of the subject, usually going way beyond me until he would then apologize, seeing I was hopelessly lost. Sensing my interests, though, he quickly learned to point out interesting facets concerning whatever subject fell into my hands. This could happen at any time: Cal was a natural born lecturer.

One book was *The Spotted Hyena*, by Hans Kruuk. We had come back to the house from the Inn, drunk, and just after obnoxiously alienating some more innocent females. He had to change his shirt after one of the victims doused him with her drink. Coming out of the bedroom with three or four fresh shirts he saw the *Hyena* book in my hands and started on a leering, sinister-sounding lecture about spotted hyenas—all the time going through his shirts, flinging the rejects about the room: "The spotted hyena...yes, Jonas, quite a beast. *Crocuta crocuta,* known in legend as hermaphrodites. Wrongly, mind you. Even Aristotle pointed *that* out."

He was down to a military-style cut shirt, with button-down pockets and epaulets—very macho, which suited his mood now, and an almost feminine-looking embroidered garment, probably Haitian. He held out each in front of him, his eyes flicking from one to the other.

"Aristotle," he went on, "in his *Historica animalism* points out the falsity of the statement that the hyena has both male and female sexual organs...yes."

He laid both shirts down on either side of me, draping them over the back of the Chesterfield sofa I was seated in the middle of.

I knew he was off and running now. His eyes were on me, but were barely focused. He was really drunk. So was I, but I didn't care. I like hearing him talk.

"The legend, Jonas, though ole Aristotle was right, had arisen for good reason. And you know why? I'll tell you."

He touched each shirt, straightening them slightly, his eyes focusing in and out like camera lenses.

"Female hyenas, and I *know* you'll be interested to hear this, are virtually indistinguishable from males...quite unlike *our* species. Hey, Jonas?"

He played with the shirts again.

"The female hyena clitoris," Cal went on, "is enlarged and extended to form an organ of the same size, shape, and position of the male penis. And it can also be erected. Their labia have folded up and fused to form a false scrotum that is not discernibly different in external form or location from the true scrotum of males. It even contains fatty tissue forming two swellings easily mistaken for testicles."

He looked at me, his body swaying.

"I'm not *losing* you, am I?"

I hastened to reassure him. "No...no, go ahead," I told him. "Tell me about the fucking hyenas."

He went on then.

"*Fucking* hyenas...yes, do you know *how* they do it? They can't, you know, until they reach maturity. The goddamn slit just isn't big enough. Matter of fact, females grow to be bigger than males. Outweigh the bastards by twenty pounds or so, become the goddamn bosses of the pack even...regular *fucking* matriarchy...cunts."

He swayed there a moment, then roughly grabbed the macho shirt and put it on.

The lecture was over. He marched out of the house, leaving me still sitting there on the big sofa. The feel of the sea rolled in through the open French doors, and I remember its coldness on my legs and its smell. I could hear him outside, muttering *'fucking hyenas'* as he stumbled around in the darkness.

CHAPTER FIVE

When I first met Cal I thought he was just a rich kid going through his first painful divorce. I heard the rumors, of course, about the smuggling, but never paid it much. I just knew he had plenty of money, and if he did run a little grass around, so what? He seemed a dilettante to me. Much too intelligent—or educated, rather—to be anything as illegal as a *drug trafficker*...

I eventually found out, however, that, with his brother Stephen, he brought enough smoke up to Long Island annually to keep the whole township of Babylon, including Oak Beach, continually high.

That summer I met him though, Calvin Franks was going crazy. His old lady had jilted him for the last time and, subsequently, the last Mexican trip had almost ended in disaster.

Cal was the strategist. He was supposed to keep his head straight. That spring, just before crossing the border at *Ciudad Acuna* into Texas, Cal had insisted on stopping at Boy's Town, the Mexican playground set outside the city for the whores and honky-tonks to get theirs before the gringos went home. The local government was trying to keep their native attractions all in one spot for the benefit of male visitors and their considerable capacity for hell-raising. It wasn't a coincidence that just across the border in Del Rio was a large American Air Force base.

Having just received his final divorce decree the month

previous, with the finalized financial settlement, which was considerable, Cal was almost berserk.

He should have never gone on the trip, only there was no one else. Things had gone well so far, as it usually did, and the brothers Franks had their VW van packed with almost 800 pounds of quality Mexican green.

Their cover was impeccable. Cal had credentials from universities and wildlife foundations, government grants and stipends, authorization from the Mexican government, and whatever else he might need to pursue 'educational research' in the Mexican outback. His wife had formerly served as his research assistant, and for the last five years or so they had made these trips down into the Sonoran heartland several times a year without a hitch.

That Cal obviously had the education and connections to do right well by himself without taking the risks as he did was beside the point. He was crazy.

While still an undergraduate at the State University of New York at Stony Brook he began making these field trips, doing his research, then bringing back small loads of pot to supply his own and his friends needs. He quickly realized that the penalties were roughly the same for getting caught with one pound of the weed or a hundred—or more. And once his brother Stephen, a burned-out-biology-now-business major, caught on to how much of a market there was for good quality Mexican the brothers Franks had found their true calling.

And on one trip to their growers during the early part of that decade know as the Slippery Seventies, the brothers met one Gertrude Nadine Griffiths. She was to become Mrs. Calvin Franks, but at the time the boys met her, she was a budding ethnomycoligist from Yale who was also a devotee of R. Gordon Wasson of magic mushroom fame.

She had also been raised in a Canadian colony of Hutterites.

She was tall, thin, and had a cascade of blonde hair that she kept pinned up on top of her Modigliani head while she did her own research near the central Mexican village of Huautla de Jimenez.

Her specialty was *teonancatl*, the Aztec 'Flesh of the Gods.'

It was love at first sight for Cal.

For Nadine, as she preferred to be called, Cal at first seemed to be somewhat of a flake. She didn't understand just what he was doing there in the high Mexican desert, being barely supported by an almost non-existent research stipend, when the real fame and glory was in psychoactive plants. She wasn't interested in a low-life biologist studying the sex life of Mexican ground squirrels.

Besides, everyone knows there weren't any ground squirrels this high up.

But Cal pursued her, and finally won her over after she'd insisted that the only way they could ever have *any* relationship, personal as well as professional, was if they jointly participated in a divinatory rite involving the sacred mushroom.

The event was soul-shattering for Cal, but it did the job. For Nadine, anyway. Cal was the one converted, or so she thought. He gave me his lecture on it once:

"Nadine was then embarked on a personal crusade," he told me. "She wanted to obliterate culturally conditioned hostility to the fungal kingdom, especially its psychoactive members."

We were aboard the *Confusion*, and I was catching up on a bit of varnish work. I like it clean.

"Hey," Cal said. "This was serious shit with her. She's

a maniac, like I told you. Just because the controversy over magic mushrooms, morning glory seeds, peyote, and other natural hallucinogens had reached its zenith several years earlier did not mean that there was an end to serious research in her field."

I was slowly spreading some spar varnish on the cap rail, the stuff flowing along smoothly. I nodded to Cal, just to show interest. He had a beer in his hand, and I didn't want him any closer. He had a habit of getting right in one's face if he felt you weren't *getting* what he was saying.

"Like Leary and those guys, huh..." I put in, hoping he wasn't going to spill any Beck's on the portion of the rail I hadn't gotten to yet.

"Look," he went on, "forget the effects of such psychedelic visionaries like Tim Leary, Ken Kesey, Allen Ginsburg and other cult figures of the Sixties, whose well-publicized bullshit had made *hallucinogen* a house-hold word, and—mind you— just *intensified* the interest of law enforcement agencies around the world, even with all that crap, there were still members of the scientific community intensely interested in studying natural psychoactive plants."

"You sound like you're trying to convince the jury," I said, laughing. He was being a good boy, staying out of the way. I wanted a beer now.

"Listen," he said. "This is important!" He laughed too. "After all, the psychedelic revolution had fucking *begun* in that little town."

"What town?"

I grabbed a green bottle out of the Igloo cooler with one hand and set the brush in a can of mineral spirits with the other. This was getting interesting.

"*Huautla de Jimenez*, fool! When *Life* magazine published

Wasson's account of his extraordinary experience while under the influence of *teonanacatl*. The article unfortunately resulted in a veritable invasion of the Indian highlands by seekers of instant nirvana—you know who I mean. And when Albert Hoffman, the inventor of LSD-25, made the startling discovery a few years later that the principal psychoactive compounds in morning glory seeds were nothing other than lysergic acid alkaloids, the mind-blowing pattern of the Sixties counterculture began to gel. The drug culture picked up on the natural affinities of these hallucinogens as the path to a pure and simple life!"

"Right," I said, but shaking my head.

"*Yeah*," he said slowly. "But pot and hash became a staple and a symbol of the turn on-tune in-drop out lifestyle. And the media got hold of *that*, and the rest is history."

"What do you mean by that? She was bummed about it? I would think she would have been happy. At least people were turning on to something." I could sense something else now from this conversation—

"Listen," he said. "Listen well..."

And he told me about the psychedelic fervor dying down, and how Nadine's type of research, though once semi-respectable, became tinged with the desultory effect that the previous decade had put upon it. He considered her efforts to pursue her own research in the field incredibly naïve. To him, there was little or no market for hallucinogens anymore. The real money was to be made in pot. That her aim was pure research seemed intolerable to him—even though this was supposedly his aim also.

"Hey—there I was, trying to be straight with her, you know? But the amount of grants and stipends I got wouldn't feed the average Indian *there* for a month! She thought what I was doing was a joke. But she was in the same boat. No one gave a shit about psychedelics anymore in the universities—it fucking reeked of disrespectability. Besides, it was dangerous. The government didn't like it. You could get *busted*, man, just for the sake of educational research."

"I remember," I said. I had made my own sorties on that level—

"Anyway, the ganja trade was on an upswing, as you probably know. Everybody wanted a taste. It was becoming respectable again to smoke pot. Laws were being weakened. The cops wanted to bust people for heroin and coke, not pot. It was the time of the 'heroin epidemic'!"

He shouted this last bit out, and the words echoed over the harbor.

I laughed again.

He went on to tell me how he and his brother remained in business, quietly moving a couple of tons a year. That 'commercial Mexican' wasn't the high-quality smoke serious connoisseurs desired did not deter the brothers. They dealt in volume enough that they had a ready market. So what if they were the K-mart of the pot trade?

Nadine, of course, thought that she had convinced Cal of her personal goal: Delivering the civilized world from its pretensions and hostility in general by re-introducing the benefits of magic fungi.

She even approached him with the idea of joining her in her research. He had the credentials; he had only to write his dissertation for his Ph.D. in field biology. Together they could garner enough grant money to continue.

"Don't you see, Cal? Once the world comes back to its senses, dimensions that we've only begun to explore will be opened up for everyone. And it's all right here..." she told him, spreading out her lovely long and sun-tanned arms, encompassing the entire mesa that stretched out to the blue sky and gray mountains surrounding them.

They were resting after another all night Indian divinatory rite in which the 'Flesh of the Gods' played a major part.

Now Cal was well-versed in pharmaceuticals, having spent much of his undergraduate days experimenting with one form of mind-blower after another. But 'shrooms were new to him, it was true, but he felt that the real reason for his ecstatic euphoria was this golden goddess standing next to him. He wanted her, no matter her crazy preoccupation with saving the world through natural chemistry.

Her naiveté was also intriguing. She was a throw-back to the Sixties, a beautiful hippie-child lost in a time warp. The Indians adored her, carefully sharing their secrets, though they were anxious not to let her work become too publicized. They were still smarting from the previous invasion of visionary world-shakers.

Besides, many were involved in growing pot for the Franks' and others like them. They sure didn't need any publicity now.

"You're right, Nadine. It is all *right here*," Cal told her. He was thinking, of course, of his own little grass empire. "And we can do it, but we'll need help. More than those paltry university stipends provide."

"Do you think so, Cal? Do you feel we can do it together also? *I* do!"

God, I love her, Cal thought. She's so fresh, so willing, so...sexy.

"First," Nadine went on, "we'll conclude our research here." She skipped around him, her blue eyes focused on the sharp horizon. "It should take only another four or five years.

Then, we'll publish our findings, bringing it to the attention of all the world leaders first—of course—outlining our plan for the new order..."

Cal watched her cavort about like a high school cheer leader, her angular body shining and vibrant in the cool Mexican morning. He was enraptured. She was crazy, he knew that—probably something to do with her upbringing, somewhere on a religious commune in Canada, an experience she'd described to him one night with a taint of bitterness.

This also accounted for her childish naiveté, Cal figured.

"But we'll need money," Cal said—yelled, rather—as Nadine did cartwheels through the mesquite.

"I know," she called back, still spinning. "That's why it'll take so long. Good things..."

She flipped to a stop right in front of him, her golden hair now in lovely tangles hiding her face. She cast the mass of curls back, and looked deep into his dark eyes.

Cal melted.

"Good things sometimes take forever," she whispered, holding his face in her hands. And then she kissed him.

What the hell, Cal thought. She may be permanently spaced out, perhaps even *because* of the mushrooms, but she was fantastic.

Stephen was not fond of Nadine. Her presence in the Indian highlands could cause problems, and he was anxious to get the current load home. Besides, he made no bones of the fact that he felt Nadine *was*—with all her ingenuousness—freaked out permanently.

Reluctantly, Cal had to agree with his brother and they left.

But less than two months later Cal was back in Mexico alone. He had convinced Stephen to remain home, something

Stephen was only too glad to do. The actual smuggling part of the operation was the most dangerous, and brother Stephen the businessman was very careful to cut back on his own personal risk.

But he didn't realize how smitten Cal was, and was taken by surprise when Cal returned with Nadine as his bride. The pair had tied the nuptial knot in Nogales, and honeymooned through the South with almost a thousand pounds of Mexican green packed away in the inner recesses of the van.

Stephen wasn't overjoyed about having a third partner, but when Cal explained to him that he would still retain half the profits, brother Stephen gave them his blessing. He was even happier when they explained to him that he wouldn't have to make anymore trips. Cal and Nadine would take care of that end from now on, minus expenses, of course.

But Calvin Franks was to learn the truth of Stevenson's line, as many of us do, that 'Marriage is like life in this—that it is a field of battle, and not a bed of roses.'

Oh, yeah.

So it ended, but not without bloodshed and bile spilled on both sides. Stephen was pressed back into service, and, to his horror, found that now Cal—beforehand his cool and calculating semi-scientist natural historian dope smuggling brother—had become a raving lunatic at the sight of promiscuous woman.

CHAPTER SIX

Ah, you dirty woman. Oh, you dirty girl…

This was a condition that was determined to wreak disaster, for Cal now would go out of his way, much as the moth to his incineration, to encounter a wanton lady. And then only to denigrate and otherwise abuse such innocently hapless vamps as came onto his path.

This attitude did not go down very well in *Ciudad Acuna's* Boy's Town. The girls had pimps to protect them, besides the local contingent of *Federales*. These women were definitely not your local American singles-bar *habitues*.

That Cal would go berserk in a Mexican whorehouse was the farthest thing from Stephen's mind when his brother insisted on stopping at one. Stephen was only too much aware of the painful effect Cal's divorce was having on their business.

All the way down—and now on the way back—Stephen had to listen to a constant diatribe on matrimonial matters as Cal covered the subject in his routine natural historian's manner: it took the form of an intensely boring Socratic dialogue, with Stephen as reluctant participant.

Needless to say, the ride was excruciating.

Perhaps, Stephen had figured, they could both blow off steam a little by sampling some border town nightlife. Maybe even grab a little nookie. What the hell, the girls were certified clean by the government or they couldn't work in Boy's Town.

Maybe they could have some *fun*!

It was dangerous, of course, with the loaded van. But Cal had to be calmed down somehow. It wouldn't do to have him uptight and seething at the border crossing.

Well, the whole thing turned onto just about a total disaster. Cal launched into his fiery invective as soon as the first 'lady of the evening' approached him and playfully massaged his inner thigh.

Cal's Spanish was loud, fluent and dialectically precise enough to draw the attention of everyone else in the small bar/brothel they were in. Including the bouncers.

But first the other working girls, innocently budding feminists, surrounded the brothers and let go with a fusillade of their own.

The melee erupted from there...

Much later, as they crossed over into the States way down the border from Del Rio, Stephen swore that this was his last—absolutely last—little excursion he would go on with Cal. If he would go *anywhere* with his fucking brother again was up for grabs also. He'd had it.

They were in sorry shape.

The chagrined harlots had almost stripped them of their clothes, using their sharp painted nails to do so. Then they were turned over to the leering bouncers, who proceeded to slowly and viciously beat them senseless.

The Federales found them later, sprawled in the sagebrush outside the encircling wall that separated Boy's Town from the rest of the district. Stephen then had to use all their remaining cash—a considerable amount—to bribe their way out of a stay in the pokey.

The police had no use for them. The brothers were just gringo *maricones* in their eyes.

They were lucky to escape without a search of the van.

***

That was their last trip together.

Late that summer Julian and I began picking up the half-ton or so of pot and running it back north.

That Cal and I were little more than acquaintances when we began working for him didn't seem to matter much. He liked and trusted me, and, after meeting Julian, liked him also.

It was that simple. Getting into it.

Cal fixed us up with phony credentials certifying us as bonafide field research biologists. His connections at Stony Brook made this part relatively easy. Cal even had an office there.

The hard part would be getting back across the border and then sweating out the 2000 mile trip back to Long Island.

Cal provided us with some hand-drawn maps and a quick linguistics course in the Yaqui Indian dialect. We knew who we had to see—an Indian named Garcia Marquez would be our main man down there.

The name was heavy with meaning for me. I'd just finished reading *One Hundred Years of Solitude* and I conjured up surrealistic scenes all the way down to Huautla de Jimenez.

The first two trips went off without any trouble.

The only problem occurred when the VW van blew its number three piston two hundred miles from the Texas border. We were on our way home. It was early fall, hot enough so that the air conditioner only managed to keep the temperature around 95 degrees in the van. We really used it just to filter the dust somewhat before it came inside.

I almost had a fit when the piston blew.

But, Julian being Julian, he just dropped the engine down, disconnected the failed piston from the crankshaft, and blithely tossed it, connecting rod and all, into the desert.

We ran all the way home on three cylinders.

The engine was shot, of course, by the time we got back. But we had made it, much to the Franks' brothers surprise and delight. We were heroes to them then, even though Stephen playfully lectured us on desert driving Volkswagen vans: "You can't push the little bastards, Jonas. They can't take it. The engine overheats and blows real easy in that fucking desert. And Christ, don't—don't ever—turn on the goddamn air conditioner when the outside temperature is over eighty degrees."

We were in his big house at Cold Spring Harbor, right across the way from John Lennon's place. The van was parked in the six-car garage below us, where a couple of his boys were unloading it by dismantlement.

Stephen didn't so much as touch the stuff anymore. He didn't even smoke it. He was above all that shit.

But that was one of the real beauties of the operation. The hiding of it. The brothers had shown the Indians how to take apart the van, and then re-assemble it, only each crevice and nook was then packed tightly with their native product.

The same process was then done in reverse. They'd even taken one of the Indians north with them so as to facilitate operations here in New York.

Volkswagen would have been proud of them. It was really amazing how much grass could be packed away without a trace being seen. It made great insulation too—the trips back were always much quieter.

But eighty degrees my ass.

"Hey, it was *hot*," I told Stephen.

I was pissed he'd even said anything.

"What *good* is an air conditioner if you can't use it. Goddamn foreign abortions can't take shit..."

It was funny, me acting that way. I liked the VW. But I was speeding then, spiked up and still screaming along due to the effects of innumerable little white cross-topped tablets called Benzedrine.

Bennies.

I hadn't slept since Julian's quick-fix in the desert. I didn't want to hear any bullshit after sweating blood all the way up from Texas.

Stephen, always the cool businessman, quickly realized this wasn't the time to tell me about driving in hot weather.

He was built along the same lines as Cal, though a few years younger. They were both big boys—Stephen with a bit more flesh on him, which accented the way he held himself. His feet seemed always to be splayed wide apart, as if he was expecting to be hit into.

His aquiline nose throws the picture off though. His eyes, too. They were heavily browed over, and one always had the feeling that he must have masturbated a lot as a child. Julian and I used to laugh about it.

"We'll get you another engine, Jonas. Don't worry. A *bigger* one, one that'll work with air conditioning..." Stephen said, trying to be nice.

"Fuck you."

He still smiled, placating me. He knew what it was like. After all, it was only my second trip. I was bound to be touchy.

But I could tell then though that I'd used up all my perks with him.

But what Stephen Franks didn't know then was that I

felt guilty about it—blowing the engine—and was angry at myself for almost aborting the trip. Julian told me much later that I didn't say a word to him the entire ride back, nor let him drive. He just watched me pop bennies and curse to myself in a marathon of driving and despair. We had chugged home at less than 40 mph...

The trips were usually pretty easy though.

The brothers had outlined the entire trip stateside, much like the AAA does in their 'triptiks.' It was easy to follow and one really didn't have to think about which route to take.

They had more than a dozen different good routes that they'd developed over the years, and in combination with over two dozen 'safe' border crossings. All we had to do was follow the map and stay within the speed limit.

Which was easy the last time.

It was on the last trip, with a brand-new engine ticking away in the back of the van, that we ran into real trouble.

It was only the beginning, but waiting for Cal in Huautla de Jimenez was Nadine.

CHAPTER SEVEN

Across the dunes that stretched past the ferry terminal parking lot a few birds were flitting about in the thin-stemmed beach grass.

They (the birds) were mainly grackles, those dark-colored birds that many people mistake for blackbirds. There was also a lone robin.

Why the robin wasn't in Florida or the Carolinas by now was beyond me. Even in the sun it couldn't have been much above 25 degrees. I remembered reading in *Peterson's*—off Cal Franks's shelf—that the average robin needed 70 worms a day.

Where was she (he?) going to get any worms in this weather?

The cop was still in the diner.

The hell with it. I had to piss anyway. I'd take the chance.

I started walking over to the diner, looking meanwhile at the various license plates of the cars that almost filled the lot now. A long string of them were already in line, waiting to board the ferry.

There were cars from all over. Many Canadian, a sprinkling of mid-west states, Vermont, a Utah. I thought of a trip I made when I was eighteen, coming across the country from California, taking US 40 all the way from San Francisco to Atlantic City, where it ended. Sea to shining sea...

I had a '49 Chevy convertible then. A stick-shift with a hand throttle. It was black, and had a new white top. In good shape, too, except for the twin creases that ran the length of the car. A little momento of Easter week down in Newport Beach, south of LA.

A friend and I, drunk on beer and my first taste of something called Acapulco Gold, were trying to elude a couple of cops that for some reason didn't like my cavalier driving habits. We were winding recklessly through Balboa, the ritzy high-rent waterfront district of Newport Beach with this CHP car in pursuit when we came to a dead end.

In front of us were telephone poles set up as a barrier, each cut off about four feet high and spaced a little less than a car apart. Beyond that was a sandy vacant lot, and then the car-filled strip that formed the main drag down Balboa peninsula—it represented relative safety.

I hesitated only a moment, then proceeded to squeeze the Chevy through, leaving the perplexed patrolmen in their high-powered Dodge behind. They probably couldn't believe someone would do *that*—wreck a nice looking street machine—in car-crazy California. They didn't even try to follow us.

Anyway, I always had this yen to go straight across the country on US 40. Even before I had my license I used to study this Texaco map I carried around that covered the whole country. US 40 was the one road that went the whole way, bisecting the nation like a jagged scar.

When I left LA I drove up along the coast highway to San Francisco, crossed the Golden Gate twice for luck, then blasted across the bay bridge and on up into the Sierra Nevada. The Chevy overheated and burned a couple of valves before I hit Reno though.

This came about because the generator died.

I stopped at an auto graveyard to get another generator outside Sacramento, somewhere in the foothills—but the gen I hastily exchanged my old one for was the wrong one. This caused the fan belt to fray, and then finally break.

The Chevy boiled over while making that 8000 foot climb out of California and into Nevada. She only ran on four cylinders after that.

I ended up paying a guy just outside Salt Lake fifty bucks for the right generator.

Utah was flat at least. I could pull out the throttle, put my feet up on the seat, and just cruise along, doing maybe 35mph or so, just enjoying the desert. Loved the salt flats.

Every once in awhile I'd come across a camper truck lying on its side off the road. An old desert rat I picked up hitchhiking told me that sometimes a freak wind would come across the flats and just blow those top heavy campers right over—

***

The diner smelled like cold hamburger grease and I thought of the coffee I was probably going to drink there. I didn't see the cop, so I stupidly just pushed on into the men's room, which was a single-seat affair about three by four feet.

He was sitting on the bowl, his blue pants black shoes white boxer shorts almost under my sneakers before I realized what I was doing.

(Good morning, officer! Catch any drunk drivers lately?)

I caught a glimpse of his slack-jawed black-stubbled all-night face before I beat it out of there. He looked like he felt like I was going to feel.

Somehow I didn't feel so paranoid after that little

encounter. Cops are human too, I guess. Nothing to be afraid of, except when they got a hard on or a warrant for you.

The coffee was watery and ugly tasting as usual. It was really hot though. I could feel it burning still on my tongue.

I toyed with the idea of getting something to eat, but lit up a fresh Camel instead. At least they couldn't ruin the cigarettes.

I watched the hibernating trees across the way from the diner, their empty branches reaching into the light blue sky. They were tall old maples, planted in a perfect row by some farmer probably over a hundred years or more ago.

His fields or maybe even his house must have been beyond, the trees serving as a windbreak from the easters which ravage the North Fork every so often. Now there was a restaurant and a small marina, and beyond a state park.

The farmer's descendants probably lived in Miami Beach or Tampa now. No more of these bleak nasty winters for them.

Watching the uppermost branches I was suddenly overcome with a gut wrenching emotion. The muscles in my face bunched up as I struggled to keep it in, the tears squeezing out my clenched shut eyes. I felt like blubbering and my mouth fell stiffly open, saliva piling up and spilling over my trembling lip.

I was thinking of Jonas and the empty life I was trying so desperately to fill. It seemed so utterly impossible. Inside I was as void of life as the branches on the trees, only I felt there was no Spring for me, no budding and flowering would fill me, no sap would run and ooze out my pores. No life would ever fill me again and I would forever stand, naked as those branches, reaching into an emptiness for sustenance and finding none.

There had been such promise—now there was only the

stark realization of the true emptiness that was inside me and seemed to keep me rooted in an unyielding mire of despair and self-hate.

That I felt hate for myself then was true. I had only to look at my hands or in a mirror to confirm it. I detested my dirty clothes and hands, the broken things of my life—

I felt like a clown or a puppet in the hands of my true self: A malevolent being who took pleasure in torturing the puppet—my physical self—and forcing the puppet into one losing situation after another, wearing it down, dragging the life right out of it...

Nothing worked, nothing seemed to work, nothing – *nada, nada, nada.*

Life was an endless stream and I was just a colander, trying desperately to catch a little of it, only it continually poured out of me, leaving nothing behind.

The gnawing, wounded sensation of self-pity and disgust slowly left me. It was like walking out of a cave into the light of day. It happened once in awhile; I had no control over it. Anything could set it off.

The trees now were just as they were before, waiting for the earth to come full circle again. I held onto that thought. If things get worse, they get worse.

How much worse could they get?

Here I was, depressed almost constantly, broke, and due in court Monday morning. Plus the cops probably had my number by now. And I had to get myself up mentally to play daddy to a little boy who would be here in little less than an hour.

Wonderful—

***

I wondered where Julian was now. He had it dicked. Did the smart thing. Split.

How does it start? When is the moment that your life begins tumbling down that long slope towards the end?

I remembered one moment in my life that perhaps wasn't the beginning, but I felt for a long while that it was. I was seventeen or eighteen, maybe a little older, and came in drunk one night and had my father catch me. I stumbled along the hallway to my bedroom, my hands touching the walls for support, with my father's voice following me: "You're heading for a fall, Jonas. You're heading for a fall."

He was rightly disgusted with me, I suppose. I had quit school halfway through the spring semester, and was clamming for money, living at home.

I was miserable there, as I had been throughout my adolescence. I was broke though, with little money to strike out on my own. At the time I had a vague idea of making enough money to take off somewhere—go West, California.

I eventually did. With no money.

I wanted to be a part of the counter-culture that would— ha, ha—revitalize America. It was '64 or '65 and I was into all of it. All the folk heroes the media was hyping, the beer, the pot, psychedelics, the protests and the marches I sympathized with and ached to be a part of...

I wasn't a part of anything now. The counter-culture died with Watergate. And before that—before *that*—something died in me.

On a beach somewhere. Where a river flows out to the South China Sea. I guess maybe it was there.

Maybe that was the beginning. The end of my innocence, the end of the fantasy; the Disney movie of my life, where everything turns out *O.K.*! in the end.

Death.

I always thought of death as a *She.* Wrapped in that dark cloak, sickle slung over her back—always searching for a victim, reaching out to encircle *me* in her icy arms. Yeah.

I lost a friend then.

My *best friend.* As anyone who I tried to touch in my life, including myself, was my best friend. Dribbling his life away into the sand of that bloody beach.

Why was I thinking of *that* now?

Just the thought of it used to fill me with dread and a strange kind of nerve paralysis that made day to day living an impossible frustration. Now it was just another numbing episode in the sad story of my existence.

Jesus. I was feeling sorry for myself...

Looking out the window at the parking lot again I remembered William James's dictum that human beings only really lived when they lived at the top of their energies.

Right now I didn't feel really alive at all. My energy level was minus.

***

The cop came out of the bathroom and passed close by me as he went out the door. I had my back to him. He carried the toilet smell with him though, and it reminded me of all the stinking-dirty bathrooms, shitters, and *pissoirs* I'd ever been in.

I still had to go really bad, but the sudden thought of doing it in that toilet made me nauseous.

The whole place now was making me sick, as the open bathroom door let the smell permeate the rest of the diner. I had to get out of there; I lurched through the doorway to the parking lot.

As I quickly walked in the direction of my car I heard some commotion behind me. Someone was yelling, "Hey—hey you!"

I didn't care. I wanted to get away from that place. I quickened my steps without bothering to look back. Whatever it was didn't warrant my attention.

I headed for the clump of dunes at the end of the lot where the beach grass was high. I had to go worse now that I was moving.

Suddenly the familiar blue-and-white car pulled up abruptly in front of me with a screech of tires—so fucking dramatic—and the bathroom cop and the diner chef, if I can call him that, jumped out and accosted me.

The diner man was dressed in a dirty white apron, hatless, and had a scowl on his mustached face that would give a small child the chills.

The cop seemed pleased. "Where're ya goin', buddy?"

What—

"Goddamn bum," the diner man yelled. He reached for the newspaper I had under my arm, and I instinctively pulled away from him. Who was he calling a *bum*?

"Give me that—thief!" he cried, reaching for the paper again.

Oh, shit. I had one of his goddamned papers.

I must have inadvertently picked it up to read while I was contemplating getting something to eat in his joint.

"You're under arrest, buddy," the cop said, a thin smile spreading across his flaccid face. No one walked in on *him* in the can and got away with it.

Oh, sweet Jesus—

"Hey, man. Here, I..." I began saying that I'd pay, reaching into my pocket, fumbling with some change and crumpled bills, trying to stuff money into the diner man's hand. Scowl-face the diner man didn't want the money or the paper back now. This was too much fun. I was holding out both to him, my hands dirty and disgusting-looking, the frayed edges of my jacket cuffs flipping in the cold wind.

I did look like a bum. Right then I felt like one.

Heads were turning in our direction now. The ferry-waiters had something to watch.

"Get in the car, buddy."

Fuck me.

"Hey—can't I just pay for the paper? Christ, I didn't *steal* it! Here mister—" I tried proffering the money again, the ludicrousness and the irony of the situation hitting me like buckshot. "Take what you want."

The scowl was replaced by a hard look.

He glanced at the cop, who nodded, bless his semi-soul.

The diner man took the money, refusing the paper which I offered also now but was torn and smudged from my dirty-fingered grip.

"O.K.?" I said, looking at the cop, who was back in the car. He shot me a look that said, 'Not on your life.'

"Get in."

I walked around to the other side and got in.

The car was facing east, and I could see the ferry as it rounded Orient Point. It would be here in another ten minutes.

Great.

I was really tired. Shot. I would have liked to just crawl in the back seat and go to sleep. Let him arrest me—I was tired of playing outlaw.

A line off the back of one of Bob Dylan's albums was running through my head: i have no arguments and i never drink milk. Always liked the small *i*. It fit me.

"You got any ID?"

I pulled my wallet out and handed it to him.

He flipped through it, finding no plastic covered license but just a thick stack of cards, papers, and other garbage that I kept stuck in the money part.

Disgusted, he dumped the contents in my lap.

"Get your goddamn ID out."

I handed him my driver's license.

"This is expired."

"So? It's all you need. It's still me."

I was getting pissed off now. Scowl-face got what he wanted; he wasn't pressing it.

What was the hassle for?

"Jonas Coffey. PO Box 104, Oakdale," he read. Then looked at me, glanced at the license, then back to me.

I gave him a wide-eyed stare. The whites may be red, but the centers were still blue. I hoped.

"What sort of address is this? A post office box?"

"I move around a lot."

"It doesn't show where you *live* though. You have to have a residence."

"I told you. I move around a lot," I said, acting bored.

"Not good enough. You got anything else? Car registration?"

Oops. "No."

The next question would be: *How did you get here?*

"How did you get here, buddy?"

I could just see the rust-colored nose of the Bug-eye sticking out slightly in the line of cars ahead of us.

Zeke was taking a leak against the hubcap of the Chevy alongside. He was staring at me as he did so, and as soon as he was done he'd be over here.

I remembered I had to piss too—

"Look, ah—Officer? You done yet? I have to go to the bathroom."

"Just hold on. I'm going to have to check you out. Now, how did you get here?"

Just what I needed now. A thorough hick cop.

He reminded me of Frank Perdue, the chicken man on the tube. Same type of voice and countenance. Not as sharp, though, and had what looked like the beginning of a goiter on one side of his neck. He probably lived right here on the North Fork and never ate fish.

"How did you get here?" he asked again, voice a trifle stronger.

"I hitched."

"Huh-uh. Going on the ferry?"

Oh, God. One lie leads to another. The ferry was coming into the dock now. I could see the people piled up topside, waiting.

"Yeah."

He got on the radio then, feeding what information he had on me.

When he was done he sat back and took off his hat. "This will just take a few minutes," he said. Then: "That your dog?"

Zeke was at the door now, sniffing around and crying softly. I opened my door and patted him.

"Yep," I said.

I felt like dying then. Just close my eyes and drift off... give this *Bonaker* cop something to really deal with.

I was fucked anyway. There had to be a warrant or two hanging over me somewhere; the computerized de-humanized electronicized world was about to swallow me up again.

I knew it was too good to be true that I escaped earlier

that morning. Good things like that just don't happen to me and stay good.

I was feeling really sick.

Little Jonas would be coming off the ferry any moment now, his little arms wrapped around his mommy's neck, looking for his daddy to take him off for the weekend.

I had a dry aching feeling in the back of my throat. The pain became almost exquisite. The only way to relieve it would be to cry out, loud and long, really wail...

Saul Bellow once wrote that death was the dark backing that a mirror needs if we are to see anything. Every perception causing a certain amount of death in us, this darkening being a necessity.

Well, I'd seen enough. I wanted it over.

But how? Grab the cop's gun, which bulged enticingly out of his side holster, put it in my mouth and pull the trigger before he had a chance to do anything...

Yeah. Make the day a real horror show for everyone. The most horrible for Jonas. Little Jonas.

My son was about the same age as George Zukor's when he pulled the plug. He hung himself with some dirty twisted bed sheets in a Tampa lockup after terrorizing his ex-wife with a pistol.

He had it made at one time, too. Where'd he go wrong? Or did he never go right?

My mother told me the news about George just as we were sitting down to Thanksgiving dinner. My own marriage had just broken up. I was living on the boat then, alone and feeling crazy and suicidal.

Later that night I ran into Richie Azel in a bar and dragged him into the back where, drunk and extremely morose over George's finality and my own impending death, I proceeded to pummel the shit out of him, all the while asking, "What happened, Richie? What happened?"

Richie and George had been best friends. After Margaret, George's wife, split for Florida Richie moved in with George. They had set up a boat together to poach clams at night. This kept George busy for awhile, but then he drifted down to Tampa to hassle Margaret.

Richie said he couldn't stop him. I didn't even know George had gone down there. For all anyone knew he was still out on the bay at night stealing clams.

"Why didn't you stop him, you son of a bitch," I huffed between punches.

"I couldn't, Jonas," Richie whined, trying to ward me off.

He was stronger and bigger than me, and could have easily knocked my head off. That he didn't made me angrier.

"You fuck. Yes, you could. You could've stopped him."

We ended up drinking the rest of the night away, me crying and babbling about Whitman's preoccupation with death: "...laving me all over...death, death, death."

And telling Richie and whoever else would listen in the dirty bars we crawled in and out of about the poet's assignment for writers that democracy would fail unless its poets gave it great poems of death.

Ah—I was really full of it then.

It was an election year, the war was over, too many old friends were gone or dead, and no one would sing of them.

And no one will sing of me.

The ferry was unloading, the cars rolling off first.

I looked for Carol on the top deck. I usually could pick her and Jonas out. Carol was tall and thin, almost my height.

She had a peculiar way of standing, or carrying herself, that was somewhat unique. She always seemed to stand or walk with her knees locked, giving the impression that she could be easily knocked over, like a top heavy bowling pin. Hmmm—

Anyway, I didn't see them.

"You got any identifying marks? Any scars? Tattoos? Eh, Jonas?"

He knows he's got me by the balls now, so he's being friendly. No sense in making it easy for him. I did have a few—scars. And a tattoo. But I wasn't going to tell him about them.

The scars were the result of bad luck. The tattoo was for good. It was supposed to be a charm, a talisman.

It was in the form of a fighting cock, with four colors, on the bottom of my left foot. A sacred bird to the Vietnamese.

Ancient nautical superstition says that it will keep me from death by drowning. I got it in a little hole-in-the-wall shop off Tu Do street in Saigon. A friend took me there, insisted on it—

He used to call at odd hours of the early morning, and even wrote me a few times. His name was Paul Simpkins, was a Navy Seal back then—he metamorphosed a few more times before becoming a California biker. The last time I wrote back to him the letters were returned, marked 'addressee unknown.'

I got the scars while I was in the service too. That's where I saw Paul again—he'd become a hospital corpsman in the Long Beach Naval Hospital where I spent a few months back in '71. I had dislocated my shoulder and caught a few pieces of exploded metal in various places on my body during an attempted rescue mission on a Vietnamese beach.

I think my total time that mission was less than 24 hours. I was working for the Coast Guard, on contract from the Department of Defense as an electronics technician. A group of us had gone through Navy Underwater Demolition school for the specific purpose of destroying a couple of LORAN stations along the coast. These were used for navigational purposes, sea and air.

The mission we were on was fucked up to begin with. We did the job, but not before the NLF forces had cleaned out the stations first, making the whole operation useless, the equipment being all gone or smashed.

On the way home—back to the ship—we noticed a squad of Marines getting the shit kicked out of them below us.

We were following this river back to the sea, and the Marines were trapped on one side, the wrong side. it was almost dark, and the pilot of our helicopter, who had *zilch* combat experience or training, wanted to keep going.

Our orders were plain—blow up the stations and get out. No heroics.

Out pilot was right. We should have just got out.

We made a pass over the Jarheads, just to check out their position. We picked them up on the radio and learned that any support for them wouldn't be able to arrive before dawn.

The pilot, whose name was Wilkens, and a hayseed from Montana, was also the CO on this run, and he was caught in a classic quandary.

His main gig was search and rescue. This was the whole idea behind the peacetime Coast Guard.

But this was wartime here. And it was our *guys* down there. What do you do? Not rescue people because this was war? Follow orders?

Which orders?

We tried picking up on the ship on the radio. It was the *Glacier*, a mammoth ice-breaker that didn't belong in warm water anyway.

We couldn't get through—nothing. All we could hear were the poor bastards below us. And they were dwindling.

In our ship—the helicopter—only two of us actually seen combat before: Myself and a Navy Seal. I didn't know how he felt, but I didn't think that squad had another twenty minutes left, much less until dawn.

There were four of us—the DemoReconTeam. We did 'Blow-and-Looks,' for the DOD, part of a Studies and Observation Group. We didn't normally get into this type of shit, usually (always, let's face it) looking out only for ourselves.

We could pick up maybe a few more personnel with any degree of safety, probably—and still fly. One of the four on board was my best friend. As best a friend, I guess, as one could have in this lunatic world.

His name was Scott Shaw, distantly related—he said—to George Bernard.

He was a little younger than me. We had been through all the schools together: Electronics and cryptograph in New York, the Navy UDT in San Diego, the Ranger shit at Benning.

Scott was a member of that peculiar Irish stripe, being that his conversation was wonderfully circumspect, and any questions were answered in such a way as to leave the questioner slightly more baffled than when he began, only with an undeniable feeling that the question had been truly and faithfully answered.

This drove our instructors bananas, and left me with a fondness for Scott that transcended our friendship. I, too, was often accused of being indirect and even not particularly honest in my tortured explanations.

We both, I assumed, could trace our recalcitrance for directness to an ancient aspect of the Irish character. Scott used to say that, in being Irish, we were all lawbreakers at heart, and to 'never give them an edge.'

Sometimes I wondered who 'them' was.

He was really steeped in the literature. He could quote and paraphrase Irish writers and poets like he'd never read anything else. And he probably didn't.

He'd throw a quote out—it didn't matter where we were—obviously reciting from *some* work of literature or other, and be always ready to back it up with title and author.

He was one of those guys.

And he was really challenged. Maybe because there weren't many Irish scholars in Southeast Asia.

But he was a real one. How many times did we share a drink or some psychedelic concoction, and Scott would give this benediction, from Joyce: "I go to encounter for the millionth time the reality of experience and to forge in the smithy of my soul the uncreated conscience of my race."

He was also firm in his belief, like I was, that real freedom lay not in institutions but in opposing them. That we were both involved in the war at all was only another anomaly.

***

Time was running out for the Marines. A decision had to be made.

In true anarchist fashion Scott looked at me and made sure without another thought for 'orders' or a care for the danger. We were seated just behind Wilkens, the pilot.

In unison we cried out, *"Put it down, Wilkens!"*

We had the democratic majority anyway, and Wilkens, in response to any order, no matter where it came from, and knowing that he was ultimately responsible, did—as it seemed at the time—the right thing.

Wilkens was the only officer on board; the rest of us civilian contractors or non-coms. It was really up to him.

But in war certain decisions are always circumspect. This one was classic. We were attempting a rescue that probably wouldn't be considered by the Marine command with an H-4.

The grunt contingent was under heavy and direct fire, and was imminently in danger of being over-run. They had their backs to the river. Were in it, actually. It was too swift and deep to cross quickly.

They were dug in fairly well it looked like, and with support—say we were a heavily armed gunship, or had just a brace of .50 caliber guns—the attempt would have been warranted.

All we had, however, were a couple of .45 automatics and one M-16. We had some explosives left, but they had to be planted to do any good.

The upshot was that we were landing in the middle of an intense firefight with essentially no armed support or an adequately armored vehicle.

But we were going in—

As we hit the beach Scott was at my side, quoting, loudly, from some Irish rogue, "'No man at all can be living forever, and we must be satisfied.' Remember that one, Jonas!" And he jumped out onto the sand.

The din was incredible.

Never before or since have I ever thought that being under fire was so petrifying. All the war movies and child games of my—I used to think—violently war-like youth had never prepared me for this. The enemy fire peppered our poor bird like constant waves of buckshot, tearing holes and splintering the metal skin until I thought we'd be shredded and spread over the river behind us like confetti.

I lay flattened on the inside deck, my lips pressed against the dirty hot metal, my teeth chattering with such total fear and abandonment that they cut my lips and gums and I could taste my own blood.

I was as scared as I ever thought I could be; but, it was not to be the case. The fear was going to get worse, only I couldn't imagine it anymore. I was totally paralyzed with what filled me then.

Gone was the bravado of a scant few seconds before.

Scott and the Navy Seal were right outside the gaping opening of the helicopter, helping the remaining Marines roll in. There weren't many left; most were cut down as they left their entrenched positions.

We were only there a few seconds. Probably not more than thirty when we shakingly began to rise. Scott managed to slide the door shut as the first of the bad guys were reaching the abandoned trenches.

The fuselage echoed the fire now, as the bullets tore through the skin and rattled among us, the sickening whine and soft thudding sounds making my mouth and throat fill with bile.

I started retching up the Hershey bar and Dexedrine that I had for lunch. I had to get up on my hands and knees to do this—this action made me also more aware of our hasty cargo.

There were figures all over—many blackened and bloody, in various forms and positions. Most were wounded, a few already dead or dying.

The big bird lurched back and forth in a drunken dance, Wilkens crying back to us, "Shift that fucking weight around evenly, dammit—I can't control it like this..."

Scott maniacally moving bodies around, myself on all fours, retching like a sick whelping bitch—

Somehow I was getting better now that we were in the air again flying level. The incoming fire lessened somewhat. Random bullets *tinked*! against us, but it was nothing like before, during liftoff.

I suddenly realized we were missing Sam Barber—the Navy Seal.

"WHERE'S BARBER?" I yelled, surprised that I could still talk.

Scott looked over at me then, his thin face contorted and suddenly very weary looking, his arms full of dead meat. He looked surprised. He probably thought I had been hit, what with the bleeding from my mouth. He smiled then, his face forming in a devilish mask, accentuated by his spare goatee and the stray wisps of silver hair that curled up and out from under his cap.

Deep creases delineated his cheeks, his eyes reflecting the red night lights, and I smiled back, wanting to tell him what he looked like and how lucky I thought we were to be...

"Jonas, ya fuck. Give me a hand here."

I crawled over to him. "Where's Barber?"

"He didn't make it."

***

Somehow I helped him, and Wilkens got the pitch and yaw of the ship under control. It got suddenly quiet; rather, there was no more firing.

We must be safe, I thought then.

But the smell of burnt and dirty flesh, and the cordite flavor made me want to puke again, and quenched the idea of 'safe.'

I tried emptying myself again, but I was too dry. My throat felt like it was made of puffed wheat.

I remember now what made me take the job in the first place, going to all the schools and all, and why I was then in a shot-up, barely flying unarmed helicopter filled with the dead and dying.

I had conditioned myself to think I had what the Germans call *Todessuchtigkeit*—thirst for death. I used to take pride in thinking I was the 'live fast, die young' type. I wanted to be James Dean, John Dillinger, and Clyde Barrow rolled into one. The all-American existentialist anti-hero who could take anything that came.

And give it back in spades, *man*.

Tough. Riff in *West Side Story* was an idol of mine for years. Screw the good guy antics of Tony, or the protective, territorial imperativeness of Bernardo.

Give me Stanley Kowolski, or James Cagney in *Public Enemy*. I wanted to be *bad*.

But in that flying nest of death and gut horror I found out different. My fear increased, and I found myself reaching a point where I thought, *God – I'm so fucking scared*. I can't possibly *be* more scared.

This feeling came and went very rapidly, only it (the fear) intensified each time it came back. The groans and agonized whisperings of the wounded made it worse. I desperately didn't want to join them in their song, but was unable not to.

I cried along with them, my mouth drooling blood and saliva that I couldn't swallow.

It was almost dark, and we were following the river out to the sea. We were much too low, but with the added weight it was impossible to gain altitude.

Suddenly, along one of the last bends of the river before it spills out at its mouth, the jungle along one shore began to twinkle as if a thousand red fireflies had taken flight.

There was no sound at first, save the drone of the engine. Then we began taking another beating, the bullets zinging into us, tearing at us once again. The helicopter shuddered and shook, as if trying to shake off a deadly rider.

I could hear the firing now, a steady *tapety-tap-tap-tap*! The tiny projectiles zipping through the fuselage, finding their way into soft flesh—

My fear increased again, progressing in waves now. Wave upon wave of darkening dread, until I felt blinded by it, hoping now for the end, praying for it to be over—just *over*!

But it did not end. Some heavier artillery began bombarding us now, and from each close one we rolled tiredly, gaping holes appearing were there was metal before. My fear was almost protecting me. I was paralyzed with it and was cowering somewhere deep inside myself, not looking out, waiting to wake up.

We were losing altitude quickly. The engine quit with a personified grunt and I distinctly heard the last low whine of the blades. Then an explosion blew out the nose of the ship, leaving a dark hole where Wilkens had been.

For an instant my fear vanished. In that millisecond before we crashed I remember looking back and seeing only darkness.

We had run the gauntlet and now would meet our reward.

I suppose I was prepared to die then. God knows I wanted to at least a thousand times during that ride, just to get it the fuck over with. But as Scott Shaw used to say, invoking still another Irish blessing, "'The inevitable never happens, the unexpected always.'"

Somehow I got it together in the dark night hours after the crash. I had only a dislocated shoulder to show for it—also a few minor holes.

I made it; no one else did.

Scott had his guts torn open somehow during the impact. Wilkens was blown to bits just prior. The eight Marines we managed to 'save' probably didn't live to suffer the final ignominy.

Scott didn't die right away. We spent the last few hours together on an exposed sandbar in the middle of that stinking river, the South China Sea in full view before us.

The chopper burned to a crisp along with its human cargo.

When I say I got it together I meant that I managed to drag myself and Scott out of the wreck. He was dying but coherent, and I probably would have dragged him out anyway.

"I guess we didn't make it, Scotty," I said, crying, trying to hold his wound together with my fingers. "I'm sorry, man."

He was really a mess. Something had grabbed him in the groin and ripped upwards to his rib cage.

We ended up lying on our sides in the damp sand, my one useless arm underneath his body, somewhat supporting him, my other arm wrapped around his lower guts.

We were positioned like lovers on a warm summer night, trying to garner what little warmth there was left in our bodies.

"Sorry, man..."

"Ah, Jonas," he said, his reedy voice still alive with a lilt. "Is it not written that 'They came forth to battle, but they always fell?'"

Like I said, no one made it. But I did.

The Coast Guard wanted to charge me with something. They wanted somebody to blame it on. After all, they did lose a helicopter and an officer.

I was a real fuck-up from then on. Ran away from the nut ward in the VA hospital a few times, usually stealing a government vehicle to do so. Scarfing drugs was another trick. Anything to cause trouble. I'm not proud of it.

The last time I split I was hitchhiking across country and hooked up with a grass runner in New Mexico. We crossed the border near Las Cruces.

He was another crazy bastard. Red-haired crew cut; dyed purple Army field jacket with a Captain Crunch decal and his name, spelled *Thom*, on the other pocket, stenciled in with candy-cane red and white stripes; drove a cowboy pickup truck and carried a big .45 Army Colt revolver.

It was interesting that he had a gun like that. Almost an antique. Packed away in my father's house, two thousand miles and a million light years away, was another just like it. A legacy from my grandfather.

Thom was small-time and didn't care.

He'd come out of the army with a strong taste for heroin. Kicked it on his own. In the summers he was a river rat, running trips down the Colorado through the Grand Canyon, dodging the rocks in a big rubber raft and hooting at the hell-bent-for-water as the tourists screamed.

In the desert one night we tripped on some orange barrel acid I was carrying.

We lay on our backs, practicing falling into the sky. It was May, the sun moving from the constellation Aries into Taurus, the night sky bright with planets. Near morning Mars, Uranus, and Neptune hung up in the blackness like bright balls. They made an eerie string, gods of the under- and over-world joined by war.

Thom was despondent in the desert morning chill for awhile, then he'd be ecstatic. We were waiting for someone to deliver, so I imagined he was just anxious. The acid brought it out in him, I guess.

He had his big gun out, aiming at the planets I'd pointed out to him, and talking endlessly about touching the stars. He hadn't talked much before, but he didn't have to.

Now he babbled on and on about exploring the rings of Saturn and getting high on the gasses of Uranus, riding up there on a bullet. Then he'd be crying about being pinned down in the desert, unable to ever reach them.

I wish I'd gotten to know him better—

Just before dawn, the coldest part of the night when the desert creatures finally sleep and the coyote ceases crying, Thom, my Captain Crunch cowboy who I'll never know, stuck the cold metal barrel of his revolver down his throat and pulled the trigger.

I lay there, right alongside him, for a long time after, until I could no longer stand the sun.

The next thing I remember after that is turning a corner in Los Angeles and checking into the Resthaven Psychiatric Hospital. I was there a few weeks before they found out I really had no money and sent me back to the VA hospital in Long Beach.

CHAPTER EIGHT

The ferry was docked; cars were rolling off.

I hoped they weren't on board—

Zeke was pressing his head into my lap, his whole body practically in the seat with me.

I had to relieve myself really bad now.

"Look, officer," I began, trying to sound courteous. "I really have to take a leak. Why don't we go over to the diner to finish this?"

"Just another minute."

He had a smile on his face that could have frozen vodka. He'd probably get off on me wetting my pants. He liked busting weirdoes like me.

What would someone else do in a situation like this? Piss on the seat? On him? Hunter Thompson's Brown Buffalo, Raoul Duke came to mind: "When the going gets weird, the weird turn pro."

Yeah. Maybe I should just freak out.

I was almost there anyway. We were the center of attention as it was. I could see me now in court, with Carol's lawyer reading off all my disgusting habits and escapades for the judge, and having the judge's gavel come down three times and him—the judge—saying, in an echoing, God-like voice, "Ye shall never again look upon, touch, or otherwise see your son, Jonas Coffey, again, by the order of this court."

And then the bailiff would lead me out, wrapped in chains.

I'll hold on a little longer...then turn pro.

A few walkers were coming off the ferry now. I couldn't see Carol and Jonas yet.

They were usually right up front. Maybe they weren't going to be there, thank God.

An old couple stumbled by, the woman clucking to her husband, her hands clutched in front of her. She looked at me, then said something to him.

They stopped.

"Ohh, the poor dog. What happened?" the old woman said. "Did he get run over?"

What??

They came a little closer, both of them looking concerned. Then I noticed that Zeke was lying across my lap in a grotesque twisted position, as if he *had* been run over.

The cop, writing on a pad, just shot them a glance and went back to his report.

"He'll be O.K.," I said, rubbing Zeke's ears.

This caused him to groan in the almost obscene way he does whenever I do that. It's an action that's guaranteed to elicit sympathy from anyone.

"But he *sounds* like he's in pain," the old woman said.

"You should get him to a vet immediately," her husband put in.

"I know," I said sadly, innocently. "But..." I nodded my head towards the cop.

"Ohh, that's terrible!"

Zeke was groaning louder now, twisting his head deeper into my crotch as I massaged his big black ears. Labrador Retrievers are notorious for this type of act, and Zeke was no exception.

Zeke's body did look terrible.

His hind feet were off the ground now and twitched uncontrollably. I pulled him up more on top of me. No sense in letting him go now.

The old woman talked to her old man. "John, why don't we bring the van over here? We can put the poor dog in the back and get him over to Dr. Decker's..."

Animal lovers. Good. There was hope yet.

The old woman looked like Ruth Gordon, right down to her pixie-like mannerisms. I was hoping she'd turn into my fairy godmother.

The cop was noticing now.

He leaned over and said, "Anything I can help you folks with?" He was nice to them. Probably reminded him of his parents, if he ever had any.

"Officer," the old woman said. "This young man's dog is in pain. My husband and I can take him to a veterinarian. A *good* veterinarian. In our car. Couldn't you fill out the accident report later?"

Without even looking at him I could tell he was a bit perplexed. I didn't turn my head. I didn't dare yet. I just kept rubbing those black ears.

Zeke responded beautifully. Good ole Zeke.

Her husband was dispatched to get the car, and the old woman made clucking and cooing noises at Zeke.

"Your dog was run over?" the cop asked me in a low voice, though he didn't keep the sarcasm out. This did not go past my new benefactress.

"Officer, this dog is in *pain*. I don't know how you can sit there and ignore his crying..."

"'Mam," he began. "I wasn't aware..."

"You must be deaf or heartless not to heed this poor broken animal. Was it *you* who hit him?"

Beautiful. She's a regular bleeding heart. Probably *hates* cops.

Her husband pulled up in a brand new van.

On the side was lettered *St Francis Home for Abused Animals*.

He got out and stumbled slowly over to us. Both of them moved real slow.

Zeke was in ecstasy now, howling away in my arms.

A crowd had drawn around us. They were mainly walkers from the ferry. Whoever had witnessed the altercation earlier, with the diner man, had left.

I scanned the crowd for Carol and Jonas while at the same time trying to look innocent and afraid for my dog. I was just a kid on the road, my only companion an old black dog, and now look what's happened...

"What happened?" people were asking, as others filled in with, "The cop ran over his dog," and pointed at me, amid 'oohs! and aahs!' Things were looking up—

Meanwhile, the old man was getting a stretcher out of the van. A stretcher yet! His wife was holding the door of the police car open and another man was cradling Zeke's lower half as he yowled away.

I didn't dare let go of him. He was enjoying the attention as much as I was.

Then I saw Carol.

She was holding Jonas on the outer edge of the crowd. When she caught my eye she shook her head in a knowing, disgusted way. She was onto our act; that was for sure.

I just hoped she'd remain cool enough to hang back for a bit. I know she'd like nothing better than to see me in the can again.

They had Zeke on the stretcher now, and I had to

relinquish his head. He was still twisted though, and really looked broken.

The cop lay a heavy hand on my shoulder as I started moving out of the car.

"I don't know what's going on, Coffey, and I don't really care," he told me in a menacing voice, low enough so the old woman wouldn't hear him this time. "I'm letting you go, but don't let me catch your crummy ass around here again."

He threw my license into my lap.

Crummy ass, huh. Nice.

As soon as I got out he pulled away and I helped the old man load Zeke into the van. Zeke lay there, very content, tongue lolling, his brown eyes shining.

The faker!

But he'd saved my crummy ass...

The crowd dwindled away and Carol sauntered over, Jonas happy on her hip.

"So what's all this shit, Jonas?" she demanded. "That fucking dog isn't hurt and you know it. What happened, the cop find you with a joint up your nose and you pulled the 'old sick dog' routine?"

Jesus, she could be irritating.

"Carol, come on," I said, reaching for her, trying to steer her away from the van.

She rudely shrugged me off, then thrust little Jonas into my arms.

"Give me the money," she said.

"Wait a minute, will you, for Christ's sake—" I was trying to juggle Jonas and get my wallet out.

But she grabbed the wallet out of my hand before I had it out of my hip pocket. "I'll get it. I gotta make the ferry back."

I looked over towards the ferry. It was full with cars now and was ready to cast off.

Time really flies when you're having fun.

Carol got fifty out and handed back my wallet.

She was pissed off about something. "No shenanigans, Mr. Coffey. I don't want the baby mixed up in any dope deals or any other shit or you'll never see him again. You hear me?"

"All right, Carol. Don't worry about it."

"Yeah, don't worry about it, he says. Just keep out of jail with *my* son."

But she was suddenly smiling now, her eyes misty, as she always was just before leaving me with Jonas. I never could understand her. All hell and commotion one second and softly sentimental the next.

She hugged Jonas, saying, "Goodbye baby, mommy loves you..." And then she was off, running for the boat in her stiff-legged way.

Zeke was standing in the van now, scratching himself with one hind leg like he always does. He stretched out his wet nose to sniff little Jonas.

The old woman and her husband were dumfounded.

"Come on, Zeke, you old bastard," I called to him.

He jumped out of the van and started dancing around us like a big puppy, clawing me and licking Jonas, who laughed his baby laugh.

I didn't know what to say to the old woman and her husband, so I just mumbled, "Thanks...he's all right now...I guess."

I didn't know whether I was laughing or crying. I felt like both, and Jonas asked me, "Why are you crying, Daddy?" as I put him into the car.

Zeke always managed to bridge moments like this by

either jumping up on me or scrambling by in some way, always making a real pain in the ass of himself, which he did now—thank God—clawing by Jonas to get in next to him.

Jonas laughingly punched him in the back, exactly the way I always did, yelling, *"Get back there, Zeke-ee!"*

I really loved that dog.

I still had to go to the bathroom, bad, but we were home-free once again and I got in and started the Bug-eye up.

It was a long way home.

CHAPTER NINE

Later that night Julian called.

I had just gotten out of the shower, my first in a week it seemed. I always cleaned up my act when the boy was around. Somehow I felt like more of a father then.

The call was collect, of course. Person to person, from Ft. Lauderdale.

"Hey, ya fuck," Julian began in his usual prefacing manner.

I was fumbling around in the ice box for a beer, wondering how many this call would take. The usual number was two and a half.

I dug out a Schimdts that had lain on its side behind an un-eaten container of scungilli salad for a least a month, the label beginning to slide off as I unscrewed the cap.

"Hey, you son of a bitch," I saluted back. "When are we leaving for St Lucia?"

It was a standard with us. Pick a place one of us hasn't been, and let's go there! But I had planned to meet him somewhere this winter. An island trip was just what I needed.

"St Lucia? Fuck that. Listen, I got a boat to move and I'm gonna need..." The rest of his words came out garbled.

"What? Ju, I can't make you out!" I shouted stupidly.

A boat to move? What the hell was he talking about now? We used to move quite a few—in the old days. Sail 'em south in the fall and north in the spring. Or wherever in between.

Got to see a bit of the Caribbean that way—the Virgins, St Maarten, Antigua. Did a lot up and down the east coast and the Bahamas, too.

Wasn't much money in it, but it was fun. Except now Julian had his own boat. Maybe he needed the bucks. Who didn't? It was always something. I just hoped that it wasn't a dope deal.

I cursed the phone company and hung on while squawks and squeaks and what sounded like wire halyards banging against a hollow mast came out of the receiver.

Julian came back on. "...yeah. Meet us in No Name Bay on the fifth...it's called the...funny name, huh? Sounds Jewish..." More squawks—like a flock of geese caught in a net.

It was blowing outside. A winter northeaster, maybe forty knots or so, and cold.

The little fuck was probably sweating down there, any breeze a welcome relief, and I was up here freezing my ass off, the floor so cold I had to do a dance to keep my toes from getting numb.

Screeeech! Whang! Whang! Squaaaccck – eck!

"...it's a plastic pig, but so what? Regular American Standard."

Julian liked to evoke toilet bowl manufacturers when discussing fiberglass boats. It was still a lousy connection.

"What? Julian, I can't..."

"Hey, this connection sucks. And I lost that credit card number. Bring it with you, O.K.? We'll need it down there."

"*Where?*"

"I told ya. In...pick up and deliver..."

Squickkk! Whang! Whang! Whang!

The noise was ridiculous.

"Can you call back, Ju? Jesus, I can't hear a fucking thing."

"...the *Melchoir*, in No Name..."

Christ, I wasn't getting any of this straight. Why couldn't he learn to write?

"...hit St John, then...gotta be good..."

I got another bottle out.

With the lack of communication on this could only be a one-and-a-half beer call. But you never know. Julian was still on the line.

Then suddenly—

"...see ya then, Jonas. Oh, bring some ups, O.K.? I gotta get off, this fucking noise is too much. What do ya got going up there, a hurricane? I'm sweating my balls off down here. No wind for days, like that summer in Key West, remember? Really weird for this time of year."

The last came through clear as a bell. I jumped on it.

"Hey, go over it all again. Where? No Name Bay? The *what? Melchoir?*" I yelled at him, sweaty balls or no—

He sounded really distant now, almost as if he was fading away. But the connection was clear. I could hear background noises.

"Maybe you ought to take the Rambler, Jonas. Leave that red thing of yours at home. There's a lot of heat around here..."

The noise came back. *Squeeeek! Bong, bong, bong, bong, bong, bong—*

"...fucking nazis everywhere—tell me where to get off, who the hell does he think he is, anyway? *Who needs his shit?*"

It sounded almost like he was arguing with someone else who was standing there with him. Julian sounded strangely agitated all of a sudden, as if just talking was a strain. But maybe it was just due to the connection—goddamn phone could drive you nuts.

Julian was rattling on, like he *was* arguing with himself. Suddenly he became clearer: "We're right near Rebozo's place, Nixon's old buddy. You can't miss it…watch out for the gestapo, Jonas. Gotta go, see you on the…" *Whang! Whang! Clack!*

He was gone. Another cryptic conversation.

I felt really cold. My head was in the refrigerator and I was standing in a puddle of water. I had been so intent listening the whole time I had the reefer door open and was staring at four bottles of cold sweating Schimdts and some rotting lettuce.

I shut the door and hung up the phone.

The bottle in my hand was empty. I dumped that and got out another beer. Well, I got away cheap with that call.

I leaned against the wall awhile and tried to remember if there were any stray Camels left in any shirt pockets that I hadn't looked in yet. I forgot to buy any on a regular basis, and always ran out when it was really inconvenient to get more.

Jonas was asleep in the bedroom, so I couldn't run out. It was late anyway—fuck it. I'll look through a few clothes piles.

I always thought better when I did some mindless task anyway. And I had something to think about now.

No Name Bay—Key Biscayne. That's where the compound was, Nixon's compound, or what had been his. And the fifth, if Julian meant December, was less than two weeks away.

The *Melchoir* must be a fairly new fiberglass boat. The kind that's made more for partying than sailing, very beamy, with high topsides. And an interior similar to a Winnabago motor home, hence Julian calling it a 'plastic pig' and 'American Standard'—terms he lavished on any vessel that wasn't wood or traditionally designed. But that's what was out there today.

Phone calls. I always had problems with them. Somehow that means of communication was inadequate for me. I never got messages straight or was able to think effectively while on-the-phone.

Salesmen loved me. I could never say no. I was a sucker for newspaper subscriptions and free insurance estimates. Arguments I lost. My patience disappeared and I got easily tongue-tied and frustrated. Any conversation even remotely emotional was a disaster—

Talking with Carol was the worst. I always got bad news over the phone. She'd call, prefacing her remarks with 'Yeah,' like it was hello or how are you. She usually ended with a 'Yeah' too, if not just a *click!*

"Hello?" I'd answer.

"Yeah—and when're you paying the health insurance? The last six times I went they gave me a hard time."

"Hello, Carol. I paid it."

"Yeah. Bullshit. They won't take me, *or your son*, anymore until they get *paid.*"

"Look, is he sick?"

"Sick? He's had that cut on his hand and the doctor wants to see him again but *he can't*, because his friggin' father, who's *supposed* to pay the doctor bills, doesn't want to."

"I sent them a check..."

"Yeah—well, you take your son there. I don't have to put up with this shit."

"Carol, look, I..."

"Don't hand me that crap. I know you're not broke. Yeah, you got plenty of money for dope, and your *little friends!*"

That usually did it. I got laid on the average of twice a year, even when I was married. I usually started losing it when she started in on *that*—"I'm paying the fucking bills, Carol. *You* walked out. *You left me.* I paid the goddamn health insurance."

We were on a family plan at one of those community health centers. It cost $117.51 a month, which I usually didn't have. They had just switched over to quarterly payments, a mistake for me, since every three months there was even a bigger nut to pay. It just made it easier to fall behind.

"*You didn't pay shit!* I was there, with *your* son, and if it wasn't for Medicaid I couldn't even do that. So I'm taking him to *any* doctor within walking distance. You'll get the bill."

"Wait a minute...look, call the health center first. Don't just go there withou..."

"I *can't* just go there. I don't have a car, remember?"

"Well, how did you get there before? Jesus, Carol."

"It's none of your business how I get *anywhere*, with or without *our* son. *You* take him to the health center. Take some *responsibility* for him, he's *your* child, too."

"Christ."

"What's the matter? Isn't that one of your favorite words? *Responsibility?* Yeah, and you plan to keep on seeing him you better start payin', buddy, or just forget about it...*Yeah!*" *Click!*

Conversations like that would really make my day. They usually came in the morning, early, about the time Jonas would get her up. I was never ready for them.

CHAPTER TEN

My weekends with little Jonas were happily haphazard. He'd putter about the house, playing with forgotten toys and making a mess of things. The place was a wreck anyway, except on the odd day when I gave the neighborhood cleaning lady, Yvette, twenty bucks and she'd straighten things up.

I usually had her in before Jonas would arrive. She had a good system, somehow getting the place all together, dishes washed and clothes put away, beds made and tub scrubbed in less than an hour and a half.

It was *so* worth it.

If she wasn't so fat and set in her ways I think I would have married her. She could probably cook, too. I doubt she would have left her husband for me though. He was bigger than she was, and he would cringe if she so much as raised her pudgy hand. He'd sit outside the house, waiting for her to be done, making the springs sag even more in their middle-aged Pontiac.

That fall Jonas and I stayed inside mostly. I was always a little hyper at first, unused to having him about. I was afraid to let him out of my sight. But after a couple of hours we got along really well. We'd get on the same wave-length, or, rather, I go on his, and we'd play for hours in some simple game like rolling a ball up and down the hallway, or making pyramids with books and then knocking them down.

I really liked it. It was like *T'ai chi*—using one's opponent's own strength to defeat him. My opponent was my other self, the angry lunatic of impetuousness and frustration. Jonas would exhaust me, and I was glad for that. His pure laughter was therapeutic to hear, and my soul devoured it.

Jonas and I never had problems; he only cried when he accidentally banged himself, and then only for a minute. I'd cuddle him then until he stopped, then tickle him until the simple laughing joy gushed out again.

We spent some real happy times together. The only bad part was taking him back to the ferry. We never talked on the drive to Orient Point; we both knew the fun was over for now.

His goodbye kiss, with his mother standing there, all bubbly-looking for him and daggers for me, always felt distant and cold, mature, as if he was never going to have anything to do with me again.

Like I betrayed him. Just dumped him.

I wonder how he really feels? Does he flit from moment to moment, like Zeke does? And when he's left by me, does he really feel betrayed?

I usually picked up a six-pack at the deli in East Marion for the trip home Sunday night. Most of it was gone by the time I hit the expressway, the empty bottles clinking in the space behind me, each *clink!* another tick on my time-fuse.

I drove like a maniac going home after dropping Jonas off. I didn't care. I felt betrayed too.

This weekend was going pretty well. My mother wanted to see Jonas so we went over there Sunday morning. It had warmed up some, and the two of them took her golf clubs out in the backyard and she tried teaching Jonas how to hit the ball.

She had bought him a real club of his own, and the old man etched his name on it. It was the smallest real golf club I'd ever seen, and Jonas kept trying to swing it like a bat. He could hit the ball though.

The old man and I watched from the glassed-in patio. He put me through the usual interrogation.

"How're things between you and Carol, Jonas?" he began slowly.

He didn't like broken families, having come from one. I know it hurt him just to see me and think about it. I didn't like thinking about it either, much less dissecting it constantly.

Our conversations usually did so.

"The same," I answered.

"Any idea as to what you're going to do?" he'd then ask.

Same questions, same answers.

I felt like saying, "The same," again, but I didn't want to piss him off. We still had the afternoon and dinner to get through.

"What I'm going to do..." I said it slowly, annoyance creeping in there. God, I didn't want to get angry. "I don't know, Dad."

That was no good either. I didn't want to look at him. He was fumbling around his shirt pockets, looking for a smoke, which he didn't have.

The next question would be—

"Give me one of your *cigarettes*, will you?"

I gave him a Camel. He searched a little further for matches, then I gave him my lit butt. The whole act was almost a game with us.

The sun broke through and Jonas was out there catching golf balls that my mother hit gently to him. He was laughing, having a good time.

They were on the little putting green that my mother tended faithfully in a corner of the yard. Her hair was blown in front of her face, and she looked years younger in her thinness. I wished then that I could catch this moment, photograph it with my brain, hold it always in a secret place so I could take it out and cherish it at will.

A lump of emotion rose in me and I felt my eyes swelling. My lashes were getting wet. A little voice inside of me was calling, "Mommy, mommy, mommy..."

"Are you going to keep clamming this winter?" my father asked, his voice steady and reserved, puffing on the cigarette and tucking his shirt in, which was already tucked in, but which was something he always did when he was expecting an *answer* from me.

"I don't know."

I said it again.

Damn it. I was going to ruin the day no matter what. Stupid bastard. I added quickly, "Julian called last night. He's got a boat to move to the island. He wants me along. It's all set," I lied, "so I guess I'll probably go."

"Oh, really?"

He was happy now. I was talking *definite plans.*

"I have to meet Julian in Miami on the fifth. Probably drive down...he doesn't have a car there, you know."

"What kind of boat? Is he leaving his there? What's he going to do with it?"

The old man was hot now. He really liked to talk plans. Especially boat trips. He was a sailor, had a big boat. He was into it. So was I—I even had a Coast Guard license to carry passengers. Not that I ever used it.

"Ahh..." What am I going to say now?

"That girl still with him? She was a knockout, but I think she lost a few end nuts along the way."

That was the consensus on Nadine, who—now—was Julian's old lady.

"I don't know. He didn't mention her but I guess she'll be along," I said. Strange I didn't think to ask him, but last night's conversation was difficult as it was.

My father didn't like many of my friends. Burn-outs and weirdoes, he called them. Julian was O.K., though. He was the most eccentric of the lot, but harmless, I guess, to the old man. And he was a sailor.

When Julian was building his boat, or, rather, finishing it off, the old man would go down to the yard and the two of them would kick ideas and techniques for doing various things. Julian would even come around to borrow tools from him, then spend an hour or so just shooting the shit.

A lot of the old man's thinking seemed to appear in the finished boat. But that was how a work of art was arrived at, using techniques and knowledge based on earlier trials to create something beautiful. And *Ishtar*—Julian's boat—was beautiful, right down to her teak decks and varnished mahogany interior. I was jealous; I should have been building a boat instead of feeling sorry for myself.

Finally my mother dragged Jonas in and we went upstairs to eat. Somehow I always dreaded meals there once I was on my own. What cross-examinations I managed to sidestep earlier were usually intensified once I was sitting down and unable to turn away or otherwise politely escape.

At the table I would avoid discussion altogether, and used to look up to the shelf near the fireplace where some of the little reed boats I made as a kid were still displayed, or, probably, just forgotten there.

They were weird little craft. I'd taken bulrush reeds from the marsh that stretched beyond the backyard, tied them in rolled bundles, and then fashioned the bundles into boats.

I was very young when I did this, for I don't really remember making them now. I always, for as long back as I could remember, looked at them with a sense of *deja vu*. People always commented on them, telling my father that I could work with Thor Heyadahl next time he did a raft trip, or in a survival school somewhere.

That I didn't build boats out of blocks of solid wood like other children was hurtful to him I think. But one time my mother told me that, of all the boats he'd ever seen or been on—and he'd been a sailor all his life—my father would say that mine, the simple reed boats, were the most beautiful.

As my life became more and more complicated once I moved out of my parent's house, and my life didn't seem to be 'going anywhere,' everything I did was questionable. What I did for money was always an interesting enough topic to precipitate any number of heated arguments.

The old man didn't consider digging clams a way to make a living. It wasn't just an *unsuitable* form of employment; to him it wasn't employment at all, no matter how much money I made.

This was before he knew anything about my running grass or any or the other illicit deals I was in on, though he may have guessed. My father was a career military man, a soldier. Though he may have moved about quite a bit, from base to base, my mother and I stayed put, just waiting for him. He had set ideas about nearly everything.

I remember one time arguing with my mother about him during a particular rough period I went through as a teenager. The old man was all for signing me up the moment I turned seventeen. It was too early for the real shooting war in 'Nam yet; the arguing just beginning.

I used to enjoy going around the house when my father was home, reciting that poem of Sanberg's with the line, 'somebody will give a war, and nobody will come.'

It used to make him berserk.

After one particularly pithy exchange, which ended with the old man storming out, my mother stuck up for him. I was really amazed at that.

She ended up telling me how difficult it was for a career soldier to be nearing retirement. I didn't understand what she was talking about. I must have been all of fifteen, maybe.

"Just remember this," she told me then. "The military mind is ill at ease in the absence of enemies."

But that was the old man.

I always managed to leave that house, after no matter how long a time, with an acute sense of loss. As if I'd left something behind that I could never find again; something irreplaceable.

As I left there that Sunday with Jonas I had that sense again. I used to blame my father for it, but this time I knew that there was more to it than that. It was as if the pieces of my life that my father represented were breaking off behind me and drifting off, up into space, or just out into it—like the jettisoned pieces of a rocket headed for the great void.

CHAPTER ELEVEN

Two and a half weeks later I was standing in the lobby of the Royal Biscayne Hotel with Nadine.

I had arrived in Miami the day before, after a regular hellride in Julian's 'car.'

Besides three flats (one a vicious blowout that sent a speed limit sign and a *Slow Men Working* contraption, complete with blinking yellow lights, to the scrap pile), I also spent precious hours in a couple of lockups for speeding.

The car was a mechanic's nightmare and a death-trap to anyone doing over 40 mph in it or in the immediate vicinity. It was a 1967 Rambler one-time station wagon that Julian had 'converted' into a pickup truck.

The alleged vehicle looked like it had been attacked with a chain saw and bound up with bailing wire and silver duct tape. The brakes were a case in point. They had once been hydraulically operated, like a normal car. But there'd been a problem with them, so Julian had 'fixed' them. Now the only stopping device was the emergency brake. It did, however, work the front brakes, too.

The thing could move though. Just outside of Norfolk I made a wrong turn and was doubling back after heading towards Virginia Beach. I was purposely staying off the big interstates. The speedometer didn't work, of course, and it was late, maybe two in the morning, so I was letting it roll—and clocked by a local Mountie doing 74. Luckily there was a magistrate 'on duty,' so I paid the $100 fine and got out of there after only an hour or so.

The second time, and you'd think I would have really watched it by now, was just north of Charleston on Highway 17. I had stopped in McClellanville to visit an old buddy. On the way to his place I picked up a six-pack and got into it before I got there. He wasn't home, but I was into the beer now so I kept going towards Charleston, cruising along nicely, doing a steady clip, figuring to visit one of Carol's cousins for the night.

Highway 17 runs right through the Francis Marion National Forest and is a pretty straight run. Francis Marion was known as the Swamp Fox back during the Revolutionary War. The British had a hell of a time finding him and his men because they'd fight and then just disappear back into the swamp. Probably the white world's first guerrilla fighters.

I was ruminating on all this, getting drunk, when I passed a car going the opposite direction. It was too dark to make it out, but I had a suspicion and watched in the rearview as it turned around and came back right behind me.

I was tipsy and I knew it. I stiffened up and held onto the wheel like I had *rigor mortis*. Sure enough, the red flasher came on so I slowed down and then pulled over. He didn't even need his siren.

I quickly got out of the car since the last beer had fallen over when I stopped and tried to hide it and I felt the smell would give me away. Luckily I had a pack of Clorets for just such an emergency; I chewed on four or five as I tried standing tall.

I bullshitted him up and down, dragging out every name I knew in the area, and I knew a few. Quack, quack, quack.

No good.

In South Carolina, when they stop you, and you're from out of state, you're busted. We left the Rambler there and I left in handcuffs. Christ.

At the station I had the customary phone call. There was no magistrate 'on duty' here, so I couldn't buy my way out. I call Carol's cousin, Billy,

Billy had really helped me out once before. I didn't want to hit on him again; I owed him too much. I always felt funny about things like that. I had planned to see him under better circumstances, but now here I was.

The phone rang for a long time and I hoped he wasn't playing a gig somewhere. Billy was lead singer and guitarist with his own band. He was also a full-time grass dealer. He was a regular long-haired country boy and whenever I heard those lyrics, 'I get stoned in the mornin' an' drunk in the afternoon,' I think of Billy.

He was home.

"Billy?"

"Yo!"

"This is Jonas...Jonas Coffey." There was some noise in the background like elephants stampeding down Echo Canyon. Phones...

"Say what?"

"Jonas," I yelled. "Jonas Coffey...I'm *busted*, man."

The cops were getting a kick out of this. Here was this wise-ass Yankee who talked like a native son but can't even get bailed out...har, har.

Billy caught on real quick.

That word 'busted' cuts across a lot of static. He came right down, pulling up in a stripped late model Ford that at one time would have been pinned as a moonshiner's rig but now was perfect for moving fairly large quantities of grass while blending into the countryside.

I spent a couple of days with Billy, mainly reminiscing family-wise and listening to the new songs he'd written. He was pretty good.

He also did some deals. The day or so I rode around with him, he never made a deal for less than twenty-five pounds, and I never saw the dope. He told me that Charleston now is a doper's paradise. There are probably as many dope dealers per capita there as there are in New York or Tampa, making the area wide open for entrepreneurs.

I had to get out of there. Billy made it too easy to stay, and I'd almost made South Carolina a permanent residence once before by playing dope games.

I paid another fine and left. It was the third of December and the next day I was in Key Biscayne, making inquiries about Julian.

After visiting a couple of marinas I found out about No Name Bay. After one look at my scruffy appearance the marina operators pegged me as an itinerant doper looking to score. No Name was an anchorage used by night sailors.

One marina had a post office, though, with a kindly looking arthritic old lady as proprietor. She wore gloves like Adam Trask's mother in the film version of *East of Eden*.

This place was just like the small PO at Bahia Mar in Ft Lauderdale. Very convenient for leaving messages or forwarding mail. Business was usually pretty lax in these small outposts so the postmaster or mistress was usually glad to oblige someone's wishes. However bizarre—

"Hi, I'm off the *Cannabis Courier*, right down the way? Could you give a message to someone for me?"

"Sure."

"Tell him to meet me at the number four flasher, midnight, on the eighteenth."

"Tell who?"

"Don't worry, you'll know."

"Okeydokee..."

Somehow messages got through and parties united. For government employees, the postal clerks in these out of the way places were pretty good. They were usually either semi-retired or young, and possibly evidenced that peculiar attitude known to employers as 'showing little initiative' and being 'inefficient.' They were also almost always courteous and kind, and especially willing to help—attitudes that never seem to gel right with government institutions. No wonder they weren't in the mainstream.

I was about to ask the kindly postmistress about *Ishtar* when a tall character, looking like a swashbuckler right out of *Captain Blood*, came into the tiny PO vestibule. He had such a big handlebar mustache that I felt like asking him if it was real.

He eyed me, like maybe I should do something. I didn't know what, so I asked the old lady about *Ishtar, sotto voce.*

She said she didn't know anything, but our whispered conversation (ever notice how people really dig getting secretive if you lower your voice?) seemed to pique Captain Blood's interest. I swung my head quickly in his direction and he turned away, pretending to study the new stamp issue posters on the wall.

This character was a real one, all right. All the way down to the death's head tattoo on his back and the pooka bead bracelet on his wrist. He was shirtless, of course, with the sort of body that'd look right either on a chopped Harley zooming along California One, or at the wheel of a seventy foot schooner sailing full bore up through the Windward Passage with a load of Jamaican in the hold.

I stepped away from the window, wondering what to do now, when Captain Blood squared off in front of me. I was looking down at the floor and noticed his dirty feet first. His body seemed to be rocking back and forth on them, like he was ready for battle.

I quickly looked up into his eyes; if there was going to be trouble I'd see it right there. The eyes were black, the black of a deep water canal at midnight—and there were *things* in there. I could almost feel them. It was like looking into twin caves where you knew monsters lurked.

"You lookin' for a berth?" he asked.

Something about his voice stuck me as funny. I couldn't quite place it. "Ah...not really," I told him. "No. But I am looking for a boat called the *Ishtar.*"

"Don't know her. But I need a crew. Week at the most. Pay for your passage home, plus a hundred bucks."

Christ, if he didn't sound like some sort of pirate right out of Stevenson, or even Jack London. He could have been Pete LaMaire, off the *Dazzler.* All he needed was a Frenchy accent.

That was it! The accent—the voice. He sounded like Yosemite Sam. A hundred bucks, huh?

"Tell me more..."

"Can't. Not now. Leaving right away. Gotta be off...make Tortola in five days..." he rattled on.

He'd never make it. The Virgins were at least a full week away. I followed him out of the post office.

"Come on," he said. "You look salty enough. Ever sail a big 'un like *that* before?" He stretched an arm out, indicating the end of the pier in front of us.

Big 'un was right. She was seventy foot if an inch. A little the worse for wear, but still beautiful. It'd take all the strength he and I could muster to sail that old girl: She had running backstays and a real widow-maker of a bowsprit; a main stick that would punch holes in the ionosphere and a boom that hung over the ass end far enough to haul a lifeboat up and let it swing free. She was narrow and mean, and probably set enough sail to blanket a pair of twelve meters.

But if anything could make Tortola in five days, she could. I wondered aloud what happened to her regular crew.

"Busted," he told me. "Got drunk and disorderly in the hotel bar last night, wrecked a few tables and chairs, then played squeeze 'em with the waitress. We were just stoppin' for some water and diesel. Come around from Mobile the last week. Hit some bitchy weather roundin' Key West. The boys wanted to see land again..."

One handle of his 'stash jumped up and down as he talked. With his voice and tattoo all he needed was a three-corner hat and the jolly roger flying from the masthead to be Long John Silver.

Hell, why not go with him? Sure, it'd be dangerous. He was a lunatic, obviously. But look at that boat!

I looked around a little, shifting from foot to foot, thinking it over and for the first time since I got down there soaked up a little atmosphere: It was a bright day, the bad weather having cleared off (if I wanted to believe Captain Blood), the remnants scudding away on the horizon. A pelican splashed into the clear water in front of us and a few dolphins gamboled up the channel leading out of the bay.

This was picture-postcard Florida at its best. And a scant week ago I was freezing my ass off in New York, depressed and miserable.

It was impossible to feel that way here. I was suddenly

really glad that I came down, whatever happened. The possibilities seemed endless, as if I couldn't make a wrong move. I felt a slight surge of power within me, like my thermostat had been cranked up.

I was ready for anything, and I thought of that line from *Julius Caesar*: "There is a tide in the affairs of men, which, taken at the flood, leads on to fortune—"

Ah, Brutus. Yeah. What happened to him? I also remembered that promise I'd made to myself concerning chances taken when one (me) need not take them. Especially in dealings of dope, which this chance reeked of.

I couldn't tell whether or not my tide was flooding anyway. If anything, it had been ebbing for quite some time and showed little chance of turning. But all I really had to do *here* was just let myself be towed along and maybe something would...

"Oh, sir!"

My vision of playing dope pirate on the bounding main was broken by the reedy voice of the ancient postmistress who was fluttering down the dock towards us, arms akimbo, a piece of pink paper clutched in one arthritic hand.

"Are you Jonas Coffey, by any chance?" she called from fifty feet away.

For some reason I didn't acknowledge her right away. We were the only people out there right then, and though I'm naturally shy there was no good reason to ignore the poor woman. I think I just felt betrayed somehow, like John Dillinger with his lady in red. Paranoia runs deep when you're having evil thoughts.

Besides, I was already to let myself be swept away by the bandit standing there at my side, who now seemed to be taking even more of an interest in me. He had one eye shut and was regarding me sternly with the other, squinting like old Long John himself with another victim in sight. Or maybe he was already having second thoughts about me—in certain circles my name might arouse considerable anger.

I didn't hesitate long. Sighing, I waved at the woman and started towards her, leaving my companion still in cycloptic study.

Seeing me coming, she trilled out, "Here's a note for you, from someone named Nadine!"

I quickened my steps. Contact at last! I snatched the pink missal out of her frail claw. It read:

Dear Jonas,
Julian had to leave suddenly but will
be back on the sixth. If you have the car
meet me at the Royal Biscayne Hotel. If not,
wait here for Julian to return on the *Melchoir.*
Yours in Jesus,
Nadine
P.S. Someone will probably be here to meet you.
His name is Randy.

Aha! No wonder I didn't have any luck before. *Ishtar* was not the vessel to ask for. I should have inquired after the *Melchoir.* Strange name. But all right, now what?

I asked the aging old bird what the date was, ascertained it was still the fifth of December, and then thanked her profusely. She turned around and kind of rickety-rocked back into the building. Poor old woman. Reminded me of Feather, an old Labrador I once had with the same problem. Once the joints go, that's that. No more volleyball.

Captain Blood was right alongside me. "Find your people?"

"Yeah, I think so. Look, thanks for the offer, man, but…"

At the end of the dock now the schooner was moving. I was looking over her supposed skipper's shoulder as she quickly pulled out into the channel with what looked like a full crew. There were a couple of guys forward coiling dock lines, a striking blonde perched on the taffrail, and a long-haired brunette at the wheel who looked to be very much in charge.

I was suddenly very pissed off.

"Your boat's leaving, chum," I put tersely.

He turned around and regarded his loss calmly, a smile growing under the handlebars. "Oh, well. Easy come, easy go. Had you going there for a minute, though, didn't I?"

Who likes balloons broken, especially fanciful ones? Yeah, he had me going all right. A real con artist. I'd have to watch myself. Somehow Julian seemed to collect characters about him like lamps do moths on hot summer evenings. Trouble was that the mosquitoes and flies came too.

I gave him a pretty stern look. I don't like being conned like that—I was too easy, too gullible. Instances like this just made me more aware of it, embarrassingly so. I was constantly so caught up in my dream world that I had difficulty telling where reality began and where it trailed off. Guys like him made me aware of how hazy things actually were for me.

"*You* must be Randy," I said venomously.

"At your service," he minced, dropping all at once the Western twang.

I didn't know where we were going, but right now I knew that I didn't want my dick pulled the whole voyage. I was too tired.

The schooner Randy allegedly had been the captain of

was disappearing around the bend of the channel. I looked after her longingly. Especially after the two shipmates aft, their contrasting hair, blonde and sable brown, blowing in the breeze that flowed past the bent palms lining the north side of the channel.

I could just make out the name on the voluptuously shaped transom as she passed out of sight: *Running Wild.*

What a beautiful name. It conjured up all sorts of images for me, many including the two girls on board. And there they go!

And here I am.

I turned to find Randy looking at me with a big grin on his face. I was still annoyed.

"This one of Julian's little jokes? Really funny," I fumed. "I don't need this shit."

"Hey, man," Randy said, his voice so different now I had trouble thinking he was the same person I was just talking to. "Man, just take it light. Ju-ju said you were O.K. Just wanted to check you out. He said you were a *dreamer.*"

Each word now he spoke in a distinct manner, with what seemed to be an urban Black accent. So Julian said I was a dreamer, huh? But I still didn't know what this guy's act was. He could be anyone.

"Where is Julian, anyway/"

I then remembered the *communique* I had read moments before. I crumpled it in my hand. Suddenly things were going differently than I had planned. Here I was, playing some asshole game with some character out of a third-rate pirate movie.

I looked him over again, trying to notice anything different about him besides his speech. He looked the same, but inside I could feel the change, as if my inner projectionist had maybe switched reels from color to black and white and the change was just catching up to me or I to it.

If nothing else, the film was dubbed.

It was a switch I'd noticed before in my life, when things somehow cease being *real*, and I proceed in almost un-thinking fashion, watching myself in my own movie, laughing at the fuck-ups and feeling glad that it wasn't *me* doing those stupid things...

"All right, wise guy," I said. "Where do we go now, and to see who?" I could check *him* out too.

"Oh, come on, brother. Let's be friends. Nadine is waiting on us."

"Really? Where?"

"The Royal Biscayne."

Maybe he'd read the message over my shoulder. Still, he'd used the familiar *Ju-ju* for Julian. Nadine did that too. Maybe they were in cahoots to drive me nuts. Randy's accent now had switched to a dignified Bostonian *patois*.

"I trust that settles your questions about me, Jonas. I may call you Jonas?"

All I could do was shake my head and say, "What *is* this shit? Who *are* you?"

He laughed. But it was a Yosemite Sam laugh—"Har har har. Just keeping in practice, Jim...Jonas."

I half expected him to slap his knee or me on the back. If he touched me I think I would have punched him. He was a fucking lunatic, all right. Interesting, maybe, but a lunatic.

He made me feel as if someone had loosened a few screws that held the top of my head down.

It was still early in the day, and there wasn't a cloud to be seen anywhere. But the air was fresh and salty-tasting, with a touch of dampness that reminded me of Nantucket or Block

Island. Strange that the air should feel that way here—we were too close to the mainland and the air had a distinct North Atlantic tang to it. The feeling was more of an inner thing, though, as if I had brought it with me, or it followed me here and was just arriving. Strange. I wondered how much it had to do with Randy.

I asked him a few more questions and he filled me in somewhat. The *Melchoir* belonged to a corporation made up of three fat cats who were constantly in danger of getting thin. They were commodities brokers who, always having an eye out for an easy buck, or saving one, wanted to have their yachting and play with it too, the boat making an excellent tax shelter.

Julian had convinced them that he was a top notch captain and would sail the boat for chartering purposes with us as crew.

This was according to Randy.

It didn't sound like Julian to me. I had known him long enough to know that he wouldn't be content sailing someone else's boat for long. That's why he built *Ishtar*—he could sail charters on her if he wished to.

And what did he need Randy for? Nadine was nimble enough on deck. Julian had nothing but praise for her abilities there. But maybe the *Melchoir*—

Aw, shit. What was I getting all excited about? Probably the deal was very different than what Randy knew. It probably *was* some kind of dope deal. Julian just told Randy some sort of bullshit to keep him quiet.

Maybe the *Melchoir* was a beast to sail. Sometimes you can't have enough crew.

But Randy?

From what I could make of him, sitting there alongside me, rambling on about Nadine, the *Melchoir*, California, Florida, etc., all in a Manhattan accent now, he was a street freak.

His costume was simple enough. Threadbare jeans and a beret, both articles patched here and there colorfully. He could be a California biker or a Puerto Rican gang member from the west side.

But earlier he'd impressed me with his salty demeanor. He was confusing to look at. Even worse to listen to. He seemed a conglomeration of every type of freak I'd ever come across. An Everyman of Hipdom. And I already knew him as a natural con man. He gave me the impression that whatever he didn't know he would fake or otherwise lie about.

Where does Julian find them, anyway?

I asked Randy about the Royal Biscayne. I understood it to be a pretty posh place, and wondered why we were meeting Nadine there.

"The owners have a suite there, my boy," Randy said, doing W.C. Fields now. "Top notch. Yaas—these folks are really top notch."

He winked then, and somehow a ray of bright and intense sunlight must have reflected off the surface of his open eye, for all I saw as I looked at him was a blinding light that for an instant seemed to go out, leaving a dark hole which appeared to be endless, the edges of the hole rimmed with fire, then the blinding light came on again, the intenseness of it painful to experience.

I turned away quickly, my eyes back on the road. We were driving along by then, the landscape changed somehow as if suddenly dusted with a layer of cosmic debris.

I had the sensation of *deja vu*, but not remembering where or why sent a chill right through me.

CHAPTER TWELVE

The driveway leading up to the entrance of the Royal Biscayne Hotel is circular and paved with millions of tiny pink shells.

We rolled up in Julian's death-trap and stopped in front of the polished marble steps that lead into the lobby. Flamingoes balanced serenely in the small pond the driveway encircled, and rows of sweet-smelling and magnificently colorful flowers added to the rich ambiance of the place. I could smell hibiscus and jasmine. It felt good just sitting there. Even the air tasted lush and expensive.

A distinguished looking man immediately appeared at my window. He was wearing a morning coat.

"May we help you, sir?" he said politely. He reminded me of Boris Karloff.

There were a few other cars parked along the driveway in front of the steps also, so I began to get out.

"No, we're just meeting someone inside," I told him. He looked to some kind of majordomo.

"You *cannot* park...here," the man said, still polite, though there was an edge to his voice.

"Oh? We'll just be a minute."

I then realized that he was concerned about the *car.* The thing was really an eyesore, and the hotel manager, or whoever was in charge of this guy and all the other houseboys, valets, etc. would have this one's ass if we left it here.

"Oh...O.K., then. Where do we park it?"

I think he didn't want me to leave it anywhere on or near the property but was too polite to tell me so. Or maybe he was scared. I could see him looking questioningly at the holes in the hood that Julian had made with a pick-ax.

The Rambler was the type of vehicle that you wouldn't want to get out of your own car if you got in a fender-bender with it, for fear of who—or what—may be behind the wheel.

But I was out of the 'car' by now and Randy followed suit.

Seeing Randy, the man in the morning coat turned a slightly darker shade and said to him, "Sir, I do believe that *you* are not permitted back on this property."

He said the word 'you' like he was speaking about a six-month-old piece of meat he'd just found rotting away on the back shelf of the refrigerator. Randy shot me a what-me-worry look and climbed back into the passenger side.

Jesus. Why'd I always have to get stuck with the scumbags? I tried a smile on the man, but he had no use for me now. Whatever Randy had done was enough to sour the day for me anyway.

On the steps now four more houseboys stood straight in line. They looked pretty big for boys, and I sure didn't want to argue with them. I decided to call Nadine from a pay phone.

"Jonas Coffey!"

I was halfway into the car. Nadine was standing in the lobby entrance, hands on her hips, wearing what looked like a *dirndl*—the type of colorful dress native peasant girls wear in Dracula movies—and suddenly commanding our collective attention.

She was magnificent, of course. The Royal Biscayne lobby is quite a backdrop. Lesser men than myself could command armies from those steps. But a *dirndl?* In *Florida?*

What manic phase was she into now?

The goonish houseboys looked sheepish and slightly silly now, as did their majordomo, so I mounted the steps, disregarding them as I passed. Nadine was a magnet.

"Hello, Nadine."

She looked great, even in that outfit. For some reason, probably nothing more than sex, I was immensely attracted to Nadine. She had deep-blue faraway eyes that seemed to mirror my desires, so I usually had difficulty looking at her. I didn't want to blink. I just wanted her to drink me in somehow. There were times that this infatuation was embarrassing— from the beginning she was Julian's girl. Julian was her man. I was...friend.

I often wondered 'why not me?' She'd met us both at the same time in the desert there, near Huautla de Jimenez. The circumstances were a bit strange, of course. She had been living in wait for Calvin Franks, with something like torture and mutilation in mind. Julian and I were just there to pick up another load of grass. And I was already prejudiced against her, having listened to a summer full of stories about her from her ex.

But I wasn't prepared.

No, I wasn't prepared at all. Crazy or not, Nadine had a way about her that kept men tripping over their tongues. She was beautiful in that innocent sense of dirty-faced children and the con-man's knowing wink. One was so intrigued with her that you didn't want to go to bed with her as much as just wanting to be there when she awoke.

She had a child's look and a woman's movements that attacked you first in the guts. You were in love before your libido knew it. She was a pervert's fantasy and a young man's wet dream. She commanded both the old man's sigh and the matron's secret wish.

She was a tease and a flirt, but you could never accuse her; Nadine was so in her very being. She was as mystifying as she was crazy and as crazy as she was beautiful.

She had that cascade of blond straw hair, hollow cheeks split by an aquiline nose she could have pecked you with it was so sharp, and a big-joint accented body that seemed to move like a toy doll, jerkily, without flow, but each movement somehow sending tremors through me. I noticed the same effect in other men also, the passage of her body causing visible palpitations and sighs of desire. She was too much for me to handle in my lonelys.

That Julian won Nadine was a mystery to me. Two opposite poles could not be more apart than Cal and Julian when it came to tastes aesthetic or concrete.

But then Julian did not want to own Nadine. He just accepted her. But then it was surprising that Nadine, coming from such an academic ken, would fall for someone who thought the written word was a poor excuse for trees to be made into paper instead of boats. And she more than fell for him, she *listened* to him. She accepted him like their being together was predestined.

Julian had Nadine give up her better world through chemistry trip and focus in on the immediate. The immediate became *Ishtar.* Nadine helped Julian build her from scratch. She learned how to sand, paint, measure and cut; she drilled and screwed, glued and clamped. Then Julian taught her how to sail.

The amazing thing was that through it all Julian held his famous temper and Nadine did as she was told. It was amazing to watch: Two former monsters getting along, absorbed in each other and the boat. I wasn't in touch that often during that time, but when I did see them I couldn't help noticing how eerie it seemed. Julian, normally reticent, was more so. But he was incredibly content, which was almost against his nature.

Whatever effect Nadine had on him it seemed for the better, and from what Cal Franks told me about his former wife, she had radically changed also.

Right at the beginning of their affair Julian had wanted to get out of the dope business at the first chance. With Nadine now, he didn't need it anymore. Of course, I wanted to stay on—I pushed for it, right up until the end. The rats and the captain always go down with the ship. The owners clean up on the insurance.

***

"Didn't you ever really wonder about it," Nadine asked. "I mean, the cosmic implications of our all being together?"

We were up in the suite, talking over 'old times.' A half killed bottle of wine sat on the window ledge next to me. Moist warm air, pregnant with tension, eased in over the sill and dumped into the room, bringing with it the heavy aroma of the Florida night.

"You mean about the bust?" I said. "Or everything else in my...life?" I was a little loaded. Drunk, rather. Randy was passed out on the floor.

Nadine laughed. I laughed. We'd known each other for years now but never had had a private conversation. Like Saroyan once said, "There was an awful lot to say, and no language to say it in."

Save one.

I thought about trying to fuck her. That's all it would have been. It was communication at its basest level—grunt to grunt. I was almost drunk enough to try it. But the thought of her rejecting me was too much to handle.

Besides, she was Julian's 'girl' and I wasn't sure I could get it up anymore for a hustle-tussle breathe-hard with *that* hanging over my brain.

Anyway, the last 'sex experience' I'd suffered through was a night long embarrassment. God, what a pain in the ass sex was! It always managed to fuck—ha, ha—things up. The varied connotations of that word remind me of the ditty that goes, 'Why do you think they call it *dope?*'

Nadine started pulling off her costume. It was an involved act, what with the built-in corset and all those petticoats. This was going to take awhile, so I stared out into the night.

Something seemed to be brewing out there and somehow I knew I'd be brewed along with it. The prospect was a little unnerving. I decided to be straightforward and ask Nadine what's what.

"So, what's what, Nadine?" I didn't turn around. No sense in being aroused any further.

"What, the dress? It's just a dress—"

"Ah, come on, Nadine. You look like something out of an old Lon Chaney movie. They don't wear those things in Translyvania anymore. Besides, this is Florida. Miami, for Christ's sake."

I turned around. It was safe. She'd either wriggled quickly into cut-off shorts and a tee-shirt or she had them on underneath the 'dress.'

Soren Kierkegaard's face was on the tee-shirt. Nadine looked incredible. Maybe it wasn't so safe.

"It's native dress. For me, anyway. I am a Hutterite, you know. And besides, like you said, this is Miami," she said benignly.

I didn't know what was going on, besides the part about her being a Hutterite. Cal had filled me in on that part of Nadine's life and prejudice aside, I didn't get the connection. That she was lu-lu occurred to me. She'd done so many chemicals that she was lucky her eyeballs weren't in backwards.

"Somehow, Nadine, I fail to see what Mister J. Hutter has to do with Miami. I thought your sect were simple folk. Living out in the wilds of Canada in communes and that sort of thing. And didn't you renounce all that when you became a scientist?"

She didn't answer me right away, and I suddenly thought better of that approach. Nadine had left the simple life of the Hutterite commune and then did a one-eighty and turned on, tuned in, and started to proselytize. The fact that she was with Julian showed that she had abandoned the soapbox for awhile. Or had she?

"Where is Julian, anyway?" I asked her, seeking a degree of normalcy. I kind of needed it now. It was late and I didn't want to get in a heavy theological/scientific argument, especially since I was here on 'vacation.' But Nadine's eyes were suddenly aglow. I'd lit a fire somewhere.

"Glad you asked that, Jonas," she said positively.

Suddenly I had the feeling I was in *for it*, instead of in *on it*.

"What do you know about *scientific creationism?*"

***

Until the sky began to lighten Nadine pursued me with all there was to know about creationism. The creationists were having a big hoo-doo at the downtown convention center, and were footing the bill for Nadine's suite at the hotel—notwithstanding what Randy had told me, but I had trouble believing anything he had said. But why Nadine? She was a guest speaker. And it seemed that she had put as much energy into creationism as she had into psychedelic drugs.

Nadine was an expert on the bible, thanks to her Hutterite beginnings. The garb, of course, was the idea of the convention big-wigs. She was into it, though, and took pains to look the part, though simple the dirndl is not. I wasn't too sure they wore them around the commune, either, but who am I to quibble?

It was a shame really that I didn't get more out of her spiel. I was exhausted, but played willing audience with her as lecturer. Hell, I'd done it enough with her ex-husband. She had the same obnoxiousness but was somehow charming also.

She went through it all, from Genesis to the Scopes trial to the specter of godless communism. That the evidence wasn't very convincing didn't lie with Nadine. She presented it in a very positive way.

Much of it was shameless, however, even to a layman like myself. I mean, those fossilized dinosaur tracks and human footprints, supposedly made at the same time, that were found in Texas have been proven to be false. Even I read the papers once in awhile.

But no matter, Nadine was adamant. Her scientific background plus her Hutterite origins made her a natural for the creationists. She didn't have to do any further research. Nadine had had it all.

We watched the sun rise while sharing the windowsill. Nadine was obviously happy. All her scientific training and her early life had before seemed to be always at odds with each other. Now she was fulfilled. She had a purpose. And if that purpose was diametrically opposed to clear thought and scientific method, so what?

Now, at least, it all seemed to fit. Great gaps filled in and unexplainable phenomena taken care of. Creationism was a panacea for a knowledge-weary world. No problem, mon. God said it, I believe it, and that settles it.

For the life of me, I was jealous. That's what I wanted—
not to be another knee-jerker, but to be fulfilled, like Nadine.
Have a purpose...meaning in my life. Make it simple.

Somehow, though, it was too simple.

I wondered what Julian's attitude was towards this whole
act. I couldn't help reminding myself what he'd said over the
phone, something about *nazis*...

We were four stories high, there in the Royal Biscayne.
Our bare feet dangled over the sill. We were talking easily
now, the menace of Charles Darwin and Stephen Jay Gould
forgotten. Out on the vast lawn some groundskeepers were
playing with the water sprinklers.

I felt good; it was like an early morning out of my
childhood. Nadine being my sister, and, like siblings do, we
were talking over the day's mischief. Early morning risers were
leaving the hotel entrance just below us. Maybe we'd get some
balloons, fill them with water—

I turned and peeked back into the room. The lights we
had forgotten to turn off blazed away, making the room seem
festive. The décor was fifties art deco, done with a furtive
starkness, as if the Royal wanted to be opulent but didn't have
the guts. Randy was curled up near the bathroom door now,
looking like someone's shaggy dog. I'd almost forgotten him.

"What's his act?" I asked, jerking my head towards the
inert body.

Even asleep he seemed to be telling a lie. He'd crashed
much too quickly much too long ago to still be unconscious.
Almost as if he did so just to listen in on our conversation.
We'd spent the day and a night in the room together. I slept
some of the day when Nadine had to go out, but I thought
Randy had also.

When the three of us were together that evening Randy

didn't say much at all. He just seemed to watch the interaction between Nadine and me, like he was studying us, and before that became too apparent—I was shooting him questioning looks, like 'What the fuck are you looking at, anyway, buddy?'—he lay down and went to sleep.

"Randy?" Nadine answered, her blue eyes clear and beautiful in the morning light, an innocence in them that couldn't possibly be denied. "He's just someone we picked up along the way."

"We?"

"Julian and me." She looked at me quizzically. "Look, he may be a little off the wall, but who isn't these days. We needed crew for an island trip and he was available."

"Doesn't he have a home?"

"Maybe. I don't know. He seems to know his way around, though. He's been really helpful lately, in a lot of ways. My people at the convention think he's pretty nice," she said, then added, "There's something special about him, don't you think?"

I noticed the 'my people' for the umpteenth time. And 'special?' Randy?

"He seems to irritate people, it seems to me—including the headwaiter here in the lobby."

"Oh, him. He doesn't like us—we creationists. He's probably a communist."

Of course. A nice simple answer.

"But why the bullshit? He really led me on for awhile down at the marina, something about owning a big schooner, and needing crew—did I want to sign on, excetera, excetera." I told her the story.

Nadine laughed. It was a nice laugh, pretty enough, on her, but I felt the point of it.

"What's so hilarious?" I asked her, plainly annoyed. "The guy is a weirdo, I tell you. He keeps switching accents...Christ, I think if he was on the phone he could pass for anybody—or any type. Hey, I know that I'm easy, but for awhile there I was about up to here—" I indicated a spot over my head.

She was still laughing. "Oh, Jonas. Jonas, Jonas, Jonas. You always *were* easy."

She didn't make me feel any better. "He also told me that this suite is rented by some fat cats who own the *Melchoir*," I added testily.

Nadine blinked, her eyebrows—pale as the moon—stretched high. But then she yawned. "Yep, that's right. They're creationists too. Wow, am I tired."

She smiled, her narrow lips pulled back, revealing the edges of her ivory teeth. I felt a sudden chill, as if maybe she'd take a bite out of me.

"Life's a bitch, isn't it, Jonas? Just when you think you got all the answers, *Wham!* I know, 'cause it happened to me."

I was tired too. Damn tired. I could feel a couple of days growth under my chin whenever I put my head down—something I seemed to be doing a lot right now involuntarily.

I was nodding, and if I nodded enough I'd end up ruining the carpet that ran up the marble steps sixty feet or so below us.

I wanted to ask Nadine if she thought that she had all the answers now that God was on her side. Somehow I couldn't get it out. The proper words kept slipping away. I just kept staring blearily at the blue blue water that stretched out beyond the lawns and gardens of the hotel and the white white sands of the ocean beach.

CHAPTER THIRTEEN

The *Melchoir* was a fine vessel.

She was fifty-one feet long with a seventeen foot beam, made of fiberglass with the interior finished by Winnebago, and made to 'sleep' many. Yes—she was wide and dry and high, as they say, with about enough sail area to propel (maybe) a twenty-two foot daysailer. But then you needed the mast anyway to hold the radar and various antennas up, including one for the 30 in. color TV.

She was a beast, the epitome of what's happened to sailing yachts when big corporations began building them.

The *Melchoir* had all the grace of a Hudson River barge I once saw that was aground off Staten Island. Some bums had moved on board—it was there for quite awhile—and had painted on the side, in big white letters, 'OUR YACHT.'

We met Julian on board at the marina. I said hello to him, grinning and shaking my head, but drew little response. I knew that he despised these boats. He even shook my hand—surprising for him.

Well, a buck was a buck. I guessed he was going to play this gig to the hilt. If he didn't mind sailing on the *Melchoir*, I wouldn't either.

We spent the day provisioning and I didn't get much of a chance to talk with Julian alone. Either Randy or Nadine was right there, and it wasn't until we shoved off and were into the Gulf Stream that we had a moment together. The whole trip had been pretty sketchy until now and I was anxious to learn what I could.

The night was dark, with little visibility. The sky had been clear leaving Miami, but the weather over the Stream always tended to follow its own head.

It was slightly overcast now, but showed signs of clearing again. The air tasted kind of dusty—another strange phenonomen for this area. It reminded me of sailing off Los Angeles when the Santa Ana wind blows, bringing desert sand with it out to sea.

We'd set watches, and Nadine and Randy had gone below, though they'd stayed on deck long enough to make me think I was being 'watched.'

"This is some *baby*, Ju," I said, trying to open a conversation. I had the feeling I'd better try pretty hard. "And she even sails, besides packing a dozen or so people in her."

I was amazed at her size. She was almost gutted below, with a quarter of the berths most vessels of her size tuck in. Almost as if she was made to carry cargo...and maybe she was. I had been making comments similar to my last one all day, with little response save a 'Right' or 'Yeah, it is, isn't it?'

I could tell that Nadine had talked to him—or somebody had. The night before I had spilled my guts out about being on the straight and narrow, what with Nadine's bible talk and all. I was hoping I wouldn't have to spell things out for Julian. He was acting more distant than usual, and it was embarrassing for me. I used to be the hell-raiser. Always the one to yell 'GO FOR IT!' at the slightest indication of a 'deal.' I never wanted to be a stick-in-the-mud.

Julian had a habit of chewing on something when he was thinking or nervous or both. He looked like he was chewing gum, but more than likely he was jawing the end of a pencil or a piece of electrical wire. And sometimes he chewed on paper.

He was doing it now, and I began having the feeling, which had been back there all along, that this trip would be more than I bargained for—if I had bargained for anything, and I hadn't. I always just took what was coming.

After his last non-response I watched the sails for awhile, then blurted out the question I'd been meaning to ask since Miami.

"How'd you get this gig, anyhow? I don't mean to pry, but I kind of got to…things are a little fucked up here, it seems to me, and I'm trying to keep my head straight, as it were," I asked, wishing I wasn't so impetuous.

Julian was never good at hiding anything; he had the opposite of a poker face and the deceptive ability of a three year old. He now stared straight ahead, which brought his sight in line with the companionway hatch cover.

"It's business, Jonas. We're doing a favor, but still business. It's a good run, easy pickings."

Favors? Business? "What the hell for?" I said. "Do you really need it?"

"Did we ever?" Julian cut back quickly. I knew too well what he was referring to. "I don't know where your head's at now, Jonas. Nadine said you want to go straight—whatever the hell *that* means. But sometimes it ain't that easy. The world can't just stop spinnin' because you're tired of the direction it's turning in. Now we gotta do what we gotta do. No sense in throwing away easy money—I need it as much as you. Living on a boat can get to be expensive, ya know."

I knew. I knew too much. Promises, promises. What good were they if you couldn't keep them? The point of 'Did we ever?' rankled me. Julian held a grudge, I felt, and now I owed him.

"What's the deal?" I asked, slipping back into my old

scamming self. It was amazing how quickly one gets back into old habits. Hell, Julian asked me along because he needed me. Can't ask much more of a friend.

"You want to be *in* now? Or you just saying so to be 'polite?' I can drop you off in Puerto Rico, you know."

"Fuck you, Julian."

He laughed. "I'll just say this: There's more than meets the eye here."

"Look, I just can't handle the bullshit anymore. I'm burned out. No matter what I do fucks up. Even when I try to be a good boy something happens to make *that* impossible. Either I'm scamming, trying to be slick, then fall on my face, or else I try and do the right thing and then I get it worse."

"Yeah. Good intentions..."

I finished it for him. "Mean sloppy shit!"

We both laughed at that one. I was feeling better now. Like old times again.

"Why dontcha get us a couple of beers, Jonas. We'll see what we can see here," Julian said, keeping his eyes on the sails.

I went below and dug out some beer. Maybe things'll be all right. Being with Julian again felt good at least. I had a purpose again.

I suddenly thought of little Jonas, probably fast asleep, fifteen hundred miles north. I missed him. I remembered the trip we'd taken, a simple delivery from Tampa to Boca Raton when Jonas wasn't quite a year old.

We had two weeks for the job. The boat was brand new, a forty foot ketch. I'd phoned Carol and had her and the boy meet us in Key West. The owner was a sort of friend, so he didn't mind who we had on board, so long as the boat was in Boca on a certain date.

We decided to spend a few days, maybe a week, cruising around Bimini and Cat Cay. It was February and hell up north with record low temperatures and plenty of snow. So Carol went for it, even though we were about over with us as a couple. I guess I was still trying to hang on the family idea.

The trip turned out to be a disaster, of course. 'Good intentions...'

Jonas got really sick the first night out. He was burning up with a fever and puking. Carol was seasick. It was blowing, howling rather, that night—but we kept all sails up. We wanted to make Bimini by the next evening, and, besides, Julian and I were having a ball.

I broke my big toe fooling around on the foredeck with another jib—a smaller one, in deference to Carol's complaint that I was purposely trying to scare her. The toe didn't hurt right away, but the thought of it sobered me up somewhat.

Below decks was a shambles. Everything was tossed over; there was broken glass and food and other crap all mixed together. I hadn't been below since we'd left Key West. Now I was annoyed, first at myself, for being stupid enough to break my toe, then at Carol for 'causing' Jonas to be sick.

It was all her fault, of course.

Only then, standing knee-deep in the garbage, bent over the boy's sweaty body, did I realize how sick little Jonas really was. I went topside and told Julian. We changed course. Bimini was out of the question now.

We put in through Alligator Reef and made it up to Key Largo by dawn. This was the end of the trip for Carol. We had to hitch a ride to the hospital for the boy. He had a serious ear infection.

The last I saw of them for some time after that was getting on the bus for Miami. I remember standing there, barefoot in the gravel, my big toe blown up like a red balloon—watching them get on the bus, and then the bus leaving, riding out of sight down the highway.

After that episode Carol always referred to me as the 'big sailor' to the boy. As in, 'Your father, the big sailor.' Yeah.

***

I came up out of the cabin and handed Julian his beer. "Thanks," he said.

Now I didn't feel like talking. I had to take a leak so I went aft and hung on the back stay with my beer in one hand while leaning over the transom.

The night was dark, and the boat was slipping right along. This part of the Gulf Stream had a lot of phosphorous plankton in the water and our wake streamed behind us like a comet's tail.

I was depressed—again. The feeling seemed to come and go so quickly. I rationalized it, thinking it was because I was thinking about the boy. But I still felt like just slipping off the stern and following that phosphorescent wake right back to…as far as I could get.

Be so easy.

I thought about Frost's 'Death is a quiet step into a sweet clean midnight.'

"Hey, Jonas?" It was Julian

"What?"

"Take it for a sec, will ya? I gotta piss too."

He was suddenly right alongside me, his hand up on the stay, just touching mine, over it almost, like he wasn't going to let me go. I felt better, and left to grab the wheel.

She had a bit of a weather helm and was almost up into the wind. When Julian finished I offered him the wheel again.

"Here you go," I said.

"Nah. You keep it awhile. I'll stand some of your watch later. We gotta talk, anyway. There's a few things I gotta show you." He went below.

I felt a lot better after drinking the beer. Just one'll do it sometimes. And the sky up ahead seemed to be clearing— either that or we were getting out of the Gulf Stream.

Julian came back up with some charts and two more beers. We spent the rest of the watch going over the 'deal.'

Thanks to Nadine's friends it seemed like a piece of cake. They always did.

All we had to do was get the boat to St John where we would rendezvous with another boat, pick someone up off it, and then sail somewhere else. Where and with whom were unknowns at this point. The deal seemed a little strange, and I told Julian so.

"Jonas. Look, I don't know these guys. I only do the sailing. We got nothing more to do with it than that. We put in, pick this guy up, and then rendezvous with..."

"I thought it was the other way around?"

He stared at me a moment, then said, "Right, Jonas. Right. Right you are."

O.K. So I was going to be left out in the cold on this one. Maybe I should get off in Puerto Rico. But I hadn't been to the Virgin Islands in a long time, and that's where we were supposedly going.

I was being bamboozled by an old buddy, and the feeling wasn't easy to get used to. Fuck it, I was a big boy. Julian must have his reasons. I wasn't going to ask before, but I was now.

"Why is Randy here?"

He answered me quick on that one. "He's the only one who knows what the other boat looks like."

Oh.

"Jonas, I don't *know* anymore than that. The deal is a package. I don't know the whys or the wherefores or any of it besides what I've told you."

Right. Maybe I'd better change the subject. "If you don't mind my asking—"

"What?" Julian replied. "Who the hell *are* these people?"

That wasn't it, but why not? "Yeah. I thought they were big-time scientific creationist types. Fair weather scientists and would-be preachers..." I was going to say 'like Nadine,' but dropped it. "Southern bible-belt folk who had an ax to grind, or use for that matter. Somehow I get the feeling that this whole movement—Nadine's 'people,' as she says—is mainly fueled by the conservative backlash to the raucous Sixties, if I may coin a phrase."

"You may be right, Jonas. But they're businessmen just the same. They gotta keep the meat on the table just like us common folk."

So maybe this *was* just another dope deal. Probably cocaine, since that seemed to be the contraband of preference these days. Probably Julian was under pressure from Randy to keep me in the dark right up until the end. 'Muggling was always a strange business. Sometimes it was a hell of a lot better not to know too much.

"Just business, huh?"

"Yeah. The way I see it creationism is just another business. Or better yet, another money laundry. God knows there are enough of those around now. For all we know this whole deal is just another tax dodge. The fat cats who engineered this caper may just be in it for the swindle—changing dollars to Swiss francs to German marks to whatever—and then back to dollars again. Maybe even gold. And they have to do it all on the sly."

"You don't think that it's dope, then?" I said, having the feeling he was placating me.

"Does it make any difference? When the bucks are high enough it doesn't really matter, does it?"

Yes, it did. But I was tired of saying so. Especially to myself. But I'd learned one thing—this definitely was not the old Julian of the 'Go for it' days. He was thinking now, and making speeches like I used to. He seemed angry too, but not at me; something more was afoot.

"I don't mean to get personal," I said. "But I guess it's time that I did. What's with you and Nadine now?" I wanted to know for a number of reasons—one of them was that this seemed to be more her deal than anyone else's, and I felt that I was being left out for some reason that seemed unexplainable.

"What do ya mean, what's *with* us?" Julian answered testily.

I was getting too personal. But it was too late to back off. "Hey, Ju—I know she's a bit of a flake, and so do you. She's intelligent, though, maybe too intelligent for...any of this."

"For *what?*"

Oh, shit. This was way too personal. I could see the whole thing: Nadine talking theology and scientific theory with various over-educated assholes while Julian chewed on his napkin. "I wasn't talking about you and her. I mean this whole deal—the anti-evolution crowd. I mean, Nadine is a scientist, at least she was, just like Cal, and just..."

Julian suddenly went below. More like he bolted. I don't think he ever really liked Cal Franks. But maybe there was more to it than that. For a fleeting moment I thought that Nadine had gotten to him.

Nah...but maybe.

She was a weirdo, that was for sure. She'd taken to Julian

right away. And she'd hung out, just waiting for him to show her what to do on the boat. They'd built *Ishtar* together. She did calm him down. I suppose that was an accomplishment. And she did bail us out after the bust.

That was something I owed her too.

The bust. I really didn't want to think about it. But there it was, coming back to haunt me. It was another knot on my incredible string of fuck-ups. But, like the man says, 'If you want to play, you got to pay.' That it was all my fault was the bad part. And just when I thought we were being so cool.

CHAPTER FOURTEEN

To those in the 'movement'—anti-war, peace, or whatever—of the last few decades getting arrested was an accomplishment. It meant that you paid your dues. But drug busts don't count. You ended up on the same undesirable list, but somehow it was easier talking about getting popped at an anti-nuke demonstration.

Mexico.

That's where we met Nadine, Julian and I.

She'd ambushed us outside Huautla de Jimenez using stage lights, firecrackers, and German swearwords. I knew who she was right away. Who else would be out in the desert the middle of the night ambushing a VW van?

We had just settled down for the night when she *blitzkrieged* us.

Somewhere she'd gotten hold of a bunch of M-80 firecrackers and some Fresnel spotlights, and had been waiting two months for Cal to return. No one told her that Cal wasn't returning anymore—it was just me and Ju-boy.

We'd gotten there about eleven that night, after pushing on after dark, which was no mean feat in that desert. The roads were never meant to be traveled by anything that had less than four hooves.

We were asleep. At least I was.

The side door was suddenly yanked open and the M-80s started going off—I thought I was having a nightmare.

Then, because of the lights, which lit us up like a tent show, I thought we were being busted by the Federales.

I was scared either way. Julian had the presence of mind at least to get out of the van at the first explosion. I was stuck in my sleeping bag like a kitten in a paper sack.

Nadine saw Julian split. She then figured that Cal must be alone inside so she began haranguing him in German, much of which I'm sure even *she* didn't understand.

It was then that I realized what was going on. I had almost been expecting some kind of craziness. Cal had mentioned just before we left this last time that he wasn't paying support to Nadine anymore. "That'll piss the Nazi bitch off," he chortled.

Ha, ha. He wasn't in the line of fire.

I finally stumbled out of the van and into the glaring lights. Her voice trailed off—she'd been using a powered megaphone.

"Nadine?" I said shakily, squinting into her rented spotlights.

It was quite an introduction.

Afterwards it took some doing to convince her that she really didn't need Cal Franks anymore. Julian did most of that. I was smitten with her too—but that's how the mop flops. I mooned a bit, and they both put up with me nicely. Like new lovers do when they have to put up with *someone* during the first tempestuous days of a new relationship.

We loaded up as usual. The process took about two full working days, what with the dismantling, packing, and subsequent reassembly. But two full working days up north can easily be two weeks in the central highlands of Mexico, providing plenty of time for Nadine and Julian to get to know each other fairly well. They frolic'd about like adolescent goats, playing tricks on each other, and me—almost as if they were both feeling guilty about leaving me out of the heavy breathing stuff.

It would be silly to say I wasn't jealous. Hell, Nadine turned me on. But I thought I handled it all right. Maybe, though, I could have thought things out a bit more. Sometimes it is so easy to look back and try to see at just what point you made the fatal error. Where did I go wrong? I shouldn't have been so cocky, that's for sure. Maybe if Nadine hadn't been there...

More conjecture. Anyway—

We finished loading and headed for the border. We crossed at Matamoros this time, just to get back in the states quicker. Nadine was with us.

Once we were all clear I called Cal. This was customary. The trip was cake from here, a three day jaunt back to Long Island, and the brothers needed time to set up deals.

I was in a booth at a truck stop about halfway to Galveston. I remember the call pretty clearly, for it was one of those moments where I should've zigged instead of zagged— probably just should have kept my mouth shut.

I always called Cal at his Stony Brook office. There wasn't anything suspicious about this, just the field research niggers checking in. It took awhile to get through, and I thought about what Cal would say if I told him that Nadine was with us. I wasn't planning to. But thinking about it now, he maybe knew. Cal couldn't have planned a better way to get back at her. Nothing did happen to Nadine, though. Sometimes things work out that way.

I finally got him on the phone. Of course, the conversation had to be coded. We had contingency plans and such, in case of emergencies and/or fuck-ups. Up until now, though, everything had been cut and dried as far as legal hassles went.

"Cal? This is Jo."

"Jonas. Good to hear from you," Cal answered evenly.

"Just checking in," I said. "Be home in about three weeks."
I always said weeks for days, just in case.

"Huh-uh..."

"Got plenty of *data* for you this time. How's by you?"

"Hmmm..."

Cal was usually more talkative than this. I was watching
the traffic go by on Highway 77 and almost didn't hear his
next words, which came very quickly.

"Not good, Jonas," Cal said. "Not good at all. Your data
will have to be rechecked. Let me have your number there and
I'll get back to you."

Like a dolt, I just kept up my end of the conversation.
"Great, Cal. I'll see you then," I stupidly said, and then almost
hung up. A couple of seconds cranked by. *"What?"*

"Gimmee the number there, Jo. This is serious, and do it
in code," he said quicker than before.

Hoo boy.

I read him the digits, advancing each integer. Then I
started sweating.

I could see Julian and Nadine making goo-goo eyes at
each other in the VW. Cal wouldn't say it was serious unless
it was. He never fucked around on the phone. I knew that he
was going to call back from a booth in another building and it
would take awhile. I was getting more paranoid by the second.
I hated waiting.

I began looking for unmarked police cars, and immediately
spotted three or four likely looking vehicles right there in the
parking lot. Jesus—were they onto us? Where were they? Had
we been followed from the border? I could already feel the
cuffs being slapped on my virgin wrists...

Cal called back. "Jonas, we got trouble. Stephen's being tailed and we think his phone has been tapped. You can't bring that shit back here."

"What?"

"Don't come back with it."

"What are we supposed to do? The shit's built right into the damn thing. What happened, anyway?"

"I told you. Stephen's being set up…I think."

"Why? Somebody else get popped?"

There was a pause on the line. I remember staring directly into the finger holes on the dial where someone had scraped out the numbers. Cal then said slowly, "One of the mechanics."

So that was it. One of the little gnomes who could take a VW apart blindfolded was on the wrong side now.

"So they know," I sighed.

Two thousand miles away Cal sighed also. "Looks that way. Sorry, Jonas. Ditch it, if you can."

So the jig was up. There were three mechanics now, and all of them had been down to Huautla de Jimenez to train the people there. It was just a matter of time.

"How long ago did this happen?"

"A week ago."

"But we're over the border…"

"I know that," he said.

"Then *why* weren't we stopped there?"

"Who knows, Jonas. Maybe the little bastard didn't spill all the beans. Either way, get rid of it. There's too much at risk."

I was thinking pretty quickly now. Maybe, just maybe, we were O.K. If the DEA boys hadn't stopped us at Brownsville, just inside the Texas line, maybe we were clear.

I said to Cal, "You mean you want us to dump everything? Including the van?"

"Yes, damn it! Are you and your pal going to take it apart? Just leave it—or junk it. That'd be the best bet. Have it crushed. Make it extinct, like the mastodon and *Barbourfelis*."

"What's that?"

"What? *Barbourfelis?* A sabertooth tiger that lived about seven million years ago..."

Why'd he always have to do that? Whenever Cal was upset at all he dropped little known facts on me like crumbs—and I always took the bait. But I thought I knew why now. He was thinking of the last time he was in the van. What'd he touch? What pieces of plastic or metal held his immortal finger prints?

We couldn't really just abandon the van. We were fucked if the cops found it and knew what it was. We'd have to hide out forever.

Cal was right. It'd have to disappear or...

"Look, Cal," I said. I had an idea. "If we got this far maybe we could go a little further. I mean, it won't be easy just to ditch this thing. It's too new. And they'll check the airports and places if we leave it there."

"*What* are you saying?"

"I know a safe place."

"For what?"

"To get rid of the van and the grass."

"*Where?*"

The fuck. Now he was interested.

CHAPTER FIFTEEN

I had an idea all right.

There was almost a thousand pounds of Mexican grass stashed away just under the VW's epidermis. At, say, a wholesale price of $100 per pound we were talking a hundred grand. Even at fifty a pound we'd make out. And Cal wanted to shitcan the whole thing. That was fine with him. He and his brother already made their pile.

Now I wanted to make mine.

"What do you got in your alleged mind, Jonas?" Cal said slowly, his conniving voice melting in my ear.

"Maybe I can move it," I said. "But I don't know...either way it looks like *you* lose this load."

I could almost feel him fidgeting.

"Just dump it, Jonas," Cal finally said. "Don't fuck around. Drive it all off a bridge somewhere, into a swamp. Come on, there's got to be plenty of places down there."

Fuck him. He just couldn't stand the idea of someone else making out.

"You want us just to dump it? They'll probably get us anyway," I said, trying to sound depressed. "O.K., Cal. Will do. We'll get rid of it."

"Good, Jo. Good man."

I didn't say anything right away. I was a 'good man' now.

"Cal?"

"Yes, Jonas?"

"It's been nice…"

"Jonas, don't worry about a thing. If you get busted we're behind you all the way."

Cal sounded so sincere it was almost enough to make me vomit.

He went on. "But don't worry. You'll pull through. *Just get rid of the van.* Don't try and fuck around. Get rid of it today. Remember, it's everybody's ass if you're captured, pal, so…"

He was really making me sick. Cal and his brother had their asses covered so well you couldn't get at them with a neutron bomb. The van was registered in a phony name, but in my handwriting. And they were covered really well up north now, I was sure. Nothing was going to happen to them as long as we didn't make it home with the bacon.

The mechanic could talk all he wanted to, but the brothers Franks had to be in possession, and it didn't look like that was going to happen. Besides, they probably already paid him off—or maybe not. Those Franks were cheap bastards.

It didn't matter though. If we were busted in New York the authorities might want to make a big case out of it and try to drag the Franks in more. But down here we were definitely on our own. The federal drug enforcement boys or the locals would try us where they caught us. And Yankee college kids (we were a little old for that category, but we were still affiliated with Stony Brook) with a half ton of smoke was good press. Somebody could even make a name for themselves.

All this ran through my paranoid head as I hung up the phone. Cal was still rattling on about how he'd take care of us. Ha, ha. We were fucked, all right.

But not quite yet. I had plans.

I got back to the VW all hot and excited. Maybe it was just a reaction to the incredible paranoia I was dealing with, but I was cooking.

I filled in the two lovebirds on the events as they stood. Then I outlined my plan.

The way I saw it, all we had to do was make it to Charleston, South Carolina, and Carol's cousin Billy—good ole Billy Books—would take the grass off our hands. He was the only one I knew who could handle that much weight all at once. And then the money was all ours. Fuck the Franks boys. They were cashing in early, or rather, they weren't cashing in at all.

We were.

I was so excited at the prospect of making a hundred thousand dollars that I almost didn't hear Julian when he asked the fateful question: *"Do we really need it, Jonas?"*

I remember then laughing out loud, right into his face, and then just burbled on with my plan: We'd Earl Shieb the van; Nadine would drive (they wouldn't be looking for a woman); steal license plates for each state we passed through (I already had my eyes peeled for plates right there in the parking lot that looked easy to remove); maybe drive only at night...

But I remember Julian's look now.

Baby-faced Julian. I bulldozed him. Telling him we were better off doing it my way.

I kept up a running stream of bullshit right through the South—Nadine doing the day driving—until I was so exhausted (I'd eaten all the speed I had in a paranoid frenzy before we even got out of Texas) that just twenty miles from Billy's place on the outskirts of Charleston, just before dawn, I sideswiped a farm truck on one of the interstate detours.

I had been trying to pass him and didn't make it. There was no one else on the road. He was just going too slow for me and I cut in too soon. The impact wasn't much, but it tore off the right rear corner panel and with it about 50 pounds of weed.

We both stopped, which was probably the wisest thing to do. I gave thought at the time to just keep going—fuck 'em. Charleston and safety was just twenty miles away. But, in retrospect, stopping let Nadine, who was asleep in the back of the van, escape capture later on since she had the presence of mind to lay low right after the crash.

The good 'ole boy who was driving the farm truck—an ancient Ford flatbed—was inordinately interested in the 'insulation' that was spread all over the dark highway. It wasn't quite dawn yet and I rattled on a blue streak about the qualities of European sound-dampening methods while Julian pried the Ford's fender out.

At the time I didn't know what to do about the grass spread all over the highway for a hundred feet or so. I couldn't very well try to pick it up, not with the farmer busting my stones about Yankee drivers, foreign cars, and what the fender would cost him—plus why 'Thet foreen piece of shet' needed 'insulation' anyway.

Julian finally straightened out the fender to the farmer's satisfaction.

Morning had broken, fully light now, and I was shitting bricks. I gave the farmer a hundred dollars, effuse apologies, and we split, leaving him shuffling around the 'insulation' still spread over the blacktop with one manure-covered shoe.

We stopped at an unopened gas station about ten miles further on and I got out to call Billy from a phone booth there. Nadine went to the Lil' General store next door to get me a coffee and Julian stayed in the van.

And that's how we were when they got us.

Nadine watched it all over the salesgirl's shoulder as she waited for her to ring up my coffee and some M&Ms for Julian. They took us away pretty quickly. I never did get through to Billy.

Nadine then asked the girl, who wore pigtails and a bright, down-home expression, when the next bus left for Charleston.

CHAPTER SIXTEEN

The legal hassle that ensued took all the money I had and most of Julian's. We spent the next year or so slogging our way through the South Carolina legal system.

We were nailed, so it was really just a series of pay-offs and extensions—maneuvers that our hot-shot lawyer guaranteed would eventually keep us off the chain gang. The money was well spent, I suppose. We never did have to do time on a prison road crew. We did, however, spend an interesting week in the Charleston County lockup.

They treated us like big-time dope smugglers. I guess we were. We made the national news and were mildly infamous for a few days. The press had a ball with the van before the sheriff's department cut it up with acetylene torches.

That was an event in itself. Estimates of the dope encased therein ranged from two hundred thousand to over a half million dollars. The reporters even arranged to interview Clyde Oakley, the farmer whose truck I'd hit, with the poor VW van being carved into scrap metal in the background.

We watched the whole show from New York, on illegal R&R since we weren't supposed to leave the state. Ole Clyde there was wearing those same shit-encrusted shoes he had on the morning he'd gone to the highway patrol with a handful of our marijuana and then fingered us.

Of course, we'd been disowned by Calvin and Stephen

Franks. Hell, we had a lot of balls trying to score with *their* pot. If we'd just dumped the whole thing into a swamp somewhere in Texas, like Cal told me to, everything would have been hunky-dory.

Billy saved our ass with the good dope lawyer he kept on retainer. Splansky, his name was, and he was pretty straight with us right down the line. Especially after he found out that we really didn't have the big bucks everybody thought we did. I give him credit for not shit-canning us when we couldn't come up with the fifty big ones for the quick fix he'd arranged before the first pre-trial hearing. We weren't in Billy's league even and I hastened to straighten things out. It took all we had anyway for the slow fix.

Splansky was O.K., though. He spoke in that soft Carolina low-country drawl, and was fond of saying, "Boys, it ain't the meat, it's the motion." Then he'd laugh, his shirt-busting belly heaving up and down like a small boat in a rough sea. He was a real one.

In the meantime, to show we were 'nice boys,' we had to get jobs. I ended up on a shrimper out of McClellanville and Julian worked in a couple of Charleston boatyards as a carpenter. Nadine helped out with his legal expenses.

I was *persona non grata* for awhile, even though Splansky, who was about the best there was, was my man through Billy.

It took awhile, but we were finally cut loose. I ended up with failing to report an accident, a misdemeanor, and Julian paid a fine for littering.

But justice has its price. I was flat on my ass financially, with no prospects save fishing. Julian at least had Nadine. She'd stuck by him, and almost a year to the day after we got busted the two of them laid the keel for *Ishtar* right there in Charleston.

We were all friends again by then and the laying of the keel was an occasion, as it is whenever a vessel begins being built. Everybody was there: Billy, his girlfriend Suzy, Splansky, Bob Bishop (with whom I'd worked on the McClellanville shrimper), Nadine and Julian, of course, and a few others who had become either friends or were narcs watching Billy and us. We could never figure out just who some of the hanger's on folk really were.

Our last court appearance was scheduled for the following Monday, so the party was two-fold. Afterwards, Billy and I, with Suzy, made the after-hours pub rounds. It wasn't really kosher for us to be seen together, but what the hell, I was leaving in a few days and we wanted to say goodbye properly. Besides, I'd swore off the dope racket.

I tried thanking Billy, but there wasn't much I could do for him. He had money, a good looking woman, and no worries—save the usual.

"Jonas, don't fret over it. Someday I'll need you," Billy told me then.

All I could come up with were some tired clichés about how I really owed him, etc. He gave me some advice, punctuated with a few stiff pokes with a stiffer finger—

"Just watch your ass with the people around you. Your friends there—" He shook his head. "That Nadine is a regular space cadet. I know you got the hots for her." How'd he know? Was it that obvious? "But Julian's a good old boy. I like him. Just steer clear of those Jew brothers—remember Jesus on Golgotha."

Billy said the last like it was some kind of benediction, even made me finish my drink as he did his. Then he added, "These Semites have to be watched. Look what they're doing to us with the oil now. The bastards—your bastards, Jonas—should've taken care of you. I would've."

"You did," I told him.

"Yeah, but you're family," Billy said. And he was then. Carol and I had tentatively decided to 'try it' again. Why, I don't know. Low points are never good places to renew relationships. "What I mean is that when you're the *Man*," Billy went on, "I mean the guy with the purse. You take care of your people. And you do this no matter *what* they do—you follow me? Even if you gotta *kill 'em!*"

I got what Billy was getting at. In the dope game, the only thing that matters is the money. He made it explicit that we were lucky that we weren't part of someone's compost heap somewhere.

"It don't pay to fuck around, Jonas," Billy growled, his voice fitting right in with the smoky late-night-early-morning gangster joint we were in. I felt then as out of place as a nun in a topless bar. Even Suzy looked sinister, her decadent-green polished nails tapping a final tattoo on the hard-resin bartop. "You wake up one day with shit in your pillowcase and cement for a blanket."

***

Billy was always one for proper parting words. I wondered about him and what he could make of *this* deal. St John was still a long way off. I had plenty of time to think about it. At least this wasn't my set-up. If we fell on our ass again I couldn't be blamed. I was just going along for the ride.

Stupid fuck. I should bail out when I get the chance. But I wouldn't. I'll just keep playing the game until there was no more game to play.

Julian came back up long enough to tell me that it was now my watch. Somehow I had the feeling he didn't like me anymore—like right after the time we got captured. I felt like asking him about it, but let it go. He wasn't the old Julian anymore. The time was once when we'd bullshit right through both our watches, talking and drinking like the next moment we'd be swallowed up in the void.

I always played the schemer and Julian the strategist, engineering over the rough spots of my dreams. We'd once made many a night come alive that way, the burning light of our visions occluding even the dawn.

The last time we'd been together was the drunken night last summer when we'd ended up stuck in the sand off Dune Road with the Bug-eye. That was a night. We'd begun by plotting to destroy somehow the Gold Dragon, preferably with the Franks brothers inside. It didn't work out, of course. We ended up being buddies again with those connivers. We'd gone in their new place gunning for bear and wound up playing the nice guys.

Julian and I never were the tough guys we would've liked to be. Besides, the bouncers were big. We should've had Nadine with us. She wouldn't have let us get talked down by Stephen Franks, who sweet-talked and buttered us up like the prize turkeys we were. All the satisfaction we got was the way both brothers kept a phalanx of their rubes close by the whole time we were there.

Stephen and Cal knew that we were still angry at getting the cold shoulder when we got busted. But nearly three years had gone by, and that was enough time to soften anyone up. And Cal and I had been sharing the same shrink, only I wasn't going to bed with her. But the brothers were still scared—which was good, even though it wasn't their fault. It was mine.

***

The sky cleared off as dawn came nearer. The gibbous moon hung just below Castor and Pollux, in the constellation Gemini. Mars was leading Saturn and Jupiter in a slow race, and I was glad I wasn't asleep. It was a night for dreams, maybe nightmares—and I was suddenly very tired.

I thought about Scott Shaw. The sky was clear that night, the night I lost him.

The sky over Indochina—in all the Southern Ocean—was so different from the one above me now. I tried to picture it, but I couldn't. I just could not remember it, not a single detail.

The Southern Hemisphere of the world is so vastly different—even the stars. No wonder things were so fucked up for us there.

There was no hold on reality. Like the last line from that movie, where Jack Nicholson's partner tells him, "It's Chinatown, Frank. Chinatown."

The inscrutable, enigmatic East. Chinatown.

I felt like I was there again, on that stinking bloody dirty beach—shuddering, shaking, blindingly afraid—all the symptoms of an exotic physical illness or a serious mental one.

I felt very alone. I must have slept, for someone had put a blanket over me and I didn't remember it. And I had dreamed, or I thought I had.

I suddenly remembered the dream I'd had that morning out at Orient Point, waiting for the ferry. It was as though it happened in the last few seconds and not weeks ago—maybe I'd dreamed it again. If I had, right now I felt as if there was something added to the dream—something more was said by the tiny figure in the desert—whatever it had to do with I didn't know.

Dead ahead the horizon was a flamingo pink band. The wind had dropped to almost nothing, and the mainsail was going *harumphh!* with each swell. I was feeling damp.

There was movement below. I rose and peeked down into the cabin. A pretty pair of legs were braced in the galley area.

Nadine.

I called down to her. "Hey! Morning, glory—"

She came more into view. Her hair framed her delicate face, and the longer strands swung to and fro with each roll of the *Melchoir.* Nadine was beautiful in the morning. I was terribly jealous. And horny.

"*Bon matin,*" she called up cheerily. "Would you like some coffee?"

That's not all I would like. "Yes," I said. "If you'll bring it up I'll have some with you."

The sun was cresting the horizon and the air had that peculiar morning smell that held such portentous moment. And the boat was suddenly totally becalmed.

The day was ours, now. Mine and Nadine's. At least the next few minutes were. I fantasized Nadine and I being alone on the boat, the atmosphere just right for a naked romp on deck, perhaps a swim before the wind picked up again, and then, the sweet salt water dripping languidly down her supple back, we lay together on the after deck, our bodies tenderly touching...

"Here we go, Jonas," Nadine said in her husky voice, handing me a steaming cup. The cup was very hot on my finger tips.

Nadine sat down with her back against the cabin trunk. She didn't have a cup.

"Thanks," I told her.

"Hey, I'm the hostess, right?" she said, laughing. "How'd you like that blanket? Keep the chill off?"

The blanket. So it was her.

"Yeah. Right, thanks," I said, pulling a corner of it away

from my chin. "When did you come out with it? Was I asleep? I think I was—"

"If you were asleep, Jonas, you were very close to waking. You were thrashing around out here like mad—trying to get away or to something."

"What was I doing?" I felt embarrassed, caught in my childish nightmares. I kept my eyes on her pretty feet.

"It looked like you were crawling."

"Did I say anything?" I asked quickly, looking up at her now.

Nadine looked back at me, her eyes steady on mine. There was something in her look, something strange, and, to me, uncomprehending. It was as if she were trying to figure out who I was, as though we had just come across each other. I felt pierced. There was a power in her gaze I'd never dealt with. I wasn't horny anymore.

"Do you know *why* you are named *Jonas?*" Nadine asked then, as if we were somewhere else, and the question was significant beyond normal comprehension.

That was too much for me. I laughed, and the spell was broken, if there had been a spell. But I felt a little twinge, an almost painful shudder, as if a raw spot on my psyche had been rubbed. And for a second I felt the dream again.

"Yeah. I'm Jonah the Jinx," I told her. "Toss me overboard and I will..."

A sudden gust of wind hit the sails, and the *Melchoir*, as heavy as she was, lay over on her beam ends, her mast almost horizontal, the spreaders and boom in the water.

I had all I could do to hang on.

The blanket that had been covering me blew off to starboard and spray from the now furiously churning sea stung my face as it came aboard. Water was pouring into the cockpit and the side deck was totally under.

I let go of the main sheet and bent forward to untie the jenny trim, struggling with it until it suddenly ripped loose from the cleat, the line disappearing overboard. For a few seconds the boat lay there, as though letting go of the sheets was useless.

Finally she started coming back up, fighting the wind all the way. The noise was incredible; the crazed seas coming on board sounded like artillery fire as they hit the decks and cabin trunk. I thought the boat would be pounded to pieces, each wave punching her, shaking her—sending terrific shocks through the hull that I felt in my balls.

I'd never experienced anything like it before. I was awe-struck, and didn't know whether to shout for help or try and get below before I was swept overboard.

Then I noticed that Nadine was gone.

"Nadine!" I screamed. *"Nay – deeeeen!"*

The motion of the boat made moving difficult. I clutched onto the wheel and looked about. The day, which moments before had shown every promise of being utterly clear and beautiful, had turned into a black nightmarish murk which surrounded the boat in a hellish fury.

Ahead of us, where the horizon had been, was an ugly yellowish gray cloud; streaks of purplish red seemed to move about in it like heat lightning in a mid-summer's night sky. Behind and to either side hung the blackest of blacks, as if the sea itself had disappeared and we were in a sort of cosmic space, falling sternwards into a timeless abyss...

A fear shot through me like I'd never felt before. This wasn't real: I couldn't bear to lose someone else. But Nadine was gone and the *Melchoir* seemed to be sliding into Hell itself.

The companionway leading to the main cabin was wide

open and water from the ocean poured in from the cockpit. The drains should have taken care of the water, but it was impossible under this onslaught. I had to get the cabin sealed off or we'd sink.

Where the hell was everybody? Julian and Randy should have been up here by now. We had to come about and search for Nadine.

I reached the companionway hatch and struggled to slide it back. Down below I saw at least three feet of water sloshing around. On a boat this size that was almost enough to sink her. Maybe we were already doomed...

I yelled below, but my voice kept being drowned out by the thundering seas which broke over the *Melchoir* with regularity now, like storm waves on a rocky beach, relentless and unending. Maybe they were hurt down there, tossed against a bulkhead and knocked unconscious, or with broken limbs—

What to do?

I couldn't douse the sails alone. It'd be suicide to go out of the cockpit without a safety harness and where were those, anyway? Earlier they had been hung just inside the hatch, where I like to see them. I remembered seeing them there. But they were gone now.

Securing the companionway doors and hatch I realized that I'd have to make it on my own. I had to get us about somehow. Nadine wouldn't last long in this rough water.

I began thinking how I'd drop the sails alone when that sick-looking yellowish spot ahead, that I'd perceived was the rising sun (wrong!), began to pulsate and expand at the same time. The reddish streaks were pumping through it like blood in a cancerous heart. It looked alive. Malignant.

The storm seemed to increase in its violence, the wind

suddenly ripping the sails apart, as if with a giant claw. White-toothed combers swept us from stem to stem, each one colder than the last as they broke over me. I shuddered again and again, my teeth chattering such that I had to make an effort to keep my tongue from being chomped to bits. I was cold, so very cold now, and around me only blackness.

I hung my head in misery and with a shock realized that I was naked.

My skin was a dull white in the murkiness and I felt thousands of goose bumps form a thick hide over my body. I had to get something on. Some sort of material was lying in a pile at my feet; probably clogging the cockpit drains, I thought.

I struggled into the stuff. The material was very coarse and uncomfortable, but there was nothing else. Then I knew what it was.

The material was burlap. The same type of bag material we used to sell clams in. I was wearing a burlap sack. Across my chest I could read 'State of Maine Potatoes.' It didn't matter much now. There was nothing left to do but pray.

Something fluttered by my head, and I ducked, thinking it was the rig coming down about my ears. I did not feel anything, so I looked up, and a white bird, a dove it seemed, was holding its own in the still howling wind just above me. The bird had its little head cocked as it just seemed to soar there, its wings hardly moving, and its eyes, or eye, seemed to be studying me with great interest. There was something familiar about the bird. The eyes...there were flecks of gold...

***

Nadine was gently brushing the hair out of my face with her fingers. Beyond her I could see the bright light of day pouring through the companionway, the polished brightwork gleaming out in the cockpit beyond that.

The *Melchoir* wasn't moving; rather, she moved differently. We were in port somewhere, at anchor.

"Greetings, traveler," Nadine whispered.

I looked at her, and felt suddenly foolish. "I'd like to ask what happened, but..."

"Don't worry. You'll live. You seemed more exhausted than anything else. No fever. Your body temperature was very low, matter of fact."

I was lying on one of the saloon berths in the main cabin. Nadine was leaning over me. The sun was out, and the world seemed at relative peace.

I was calm. I had been dreaming, that's all.

"Where's Julian? Randy?"

"They're ashore," Nadine answered.

Christ. I realized that I fucked up things again. "I'm sorry, Nadine. I really picked a great time to sick out on you guys."

I tried to get up, but suddenly felt very, very weak. I tried to lay back down, but first Nadine put her arms under me and held me up while she propped a pillow behind.

It was exceedingly pleasant having her close. Guilt pangs were coursing through me, however—

"Thanks," I said. "I'll get out of here in a little bit. I'll just get back in the car...well, it is your car, isn't it? Well, anyway, I'll just hitch a ride to the bus station or something and..."

"What are you talking about?" Nadine suddenly asked. "You are *not* going anywhere."

"Ah, come on. I'm just going to screw this deal up, too. I've already put you behind at least three or four days by getting sick."

"But we are not behind, Jonas," Nadine replied quickly. "Where do you think we are?"

I blinked. "Aren't we back in Miami?"

She laughed then, a good old Nadine laugh. "Miami? Oh, God, Jonas—"

She reached behind me again and helped me sit up. "Come on," she said, and then we were standing.

I stood looking out one of the cabin ports. A couple of gigantic white cruise ships were tied up at a pier a hundred yards away. The West Indies dock. There were dozens of small yachts at anchor all around us. The scene was instantly recognizable. We were in the harbor at Charlotte Amalie, St Thomas.

I sniffed the air. Sweet smelling, filled with peculiar island aromas, but there was another smell present also, a dream-smell.

I was dumfounded.

"How?" I began saying, but I must have collapsed, because the next thing I knew I was on my back and Julian was standing over me, grinning like a Cheshire cat.

"Ready to go back to work?" he asked, a glint in his eye. He was chewing on something too.

I felt all right, but inwardly, deep within, something wasn't quite right. It was as if I sat on top of something alive and growing—something that was both within me and without me, and that by the slightest move, whether right or wrong, on my part, this something would awaken.

Very un-nerving, to say the least. But I was at a loss to explain it. I'd just have to be cool.

"How're you doing, Ju?" I said. I started getting up, but immediately thought better of it. This time I was determined to stay conscious. No sudden movements. I lay back down.

"I'm fine, but how are you? Think you can stand?" Julian said, sympathetically this time. "Here, let me."

"Jesus, I'm *all right*," I said, noticing the sudden irritation in my own voice. I didn't mean to be cross, so I accepted Julian's hand and came to a sitting position on the settee, my feet on the cabin sole.

But I still wasn't ready for this yet. Not until I found out what was happening to me. But at least not I had my feet on the floor.

"All right. All right. Now. What happened?"

"You've been coasting the last few days, Jonas. Don't know why; Nadine's been watching you like a hawk, and you've been O.K. I mean, no vital signs taking a dive, or anything like that."

Julian said all this rather matter of factly. I watched him as he talked, and he really didn't know how to lie. But he was different somehow. He wasn't the old Julian. I put it down to maturity this time.

"But *what* happened? All I remember is this crazy dream and then—it seemed like seconds ago—I woke up, with Nadine here, and we're in St Thomas."

"We stopped there for awhile," Julian said, "and Nadine did say you got up for a bit—but you've been babbling on and off for days now."

"But where are we now?" I almost shouted.

I noticed Julian just looked at me blankly. I half expected a I'd-better-humor-him stare or a retort for my outburst, but Julian showed no outward signs at all.

I sighed. "What happened to me, Ju? Did I just pass out—O.D. on life? Catch malaria or something?"

Someone began coming down the companionway. "We're off St John," the someone said. "And you *don't* have malaria."

It was Randy.

He was dressed funny. The Randy I knew dressed like a

strung out California biker. But here he was, long hair and all, wearing a pair of dark trousers and a simple white shirt. I mean he had *trousers* on, like out of a Sears catalog.

He looked very clean and preacher-like. Eerie. Before he'd just been part of the movie.

I wondered aloud on the change. "What're you all dressed up for? Goin' to meetin'?"

Randy stood quietly by the galley stove, his hands crossed in front of him. The cabin lights were reflected in his eyes. There was something—something familiar—in his look.

I took a step towards him, almost embarrassed by the utter silence and complacency with which he stood there, and then I saw it. That which was familiar.

The light from the lamps was reflecting off tiny specks in his eyes. Flecks of gold.

CHAPTER SEVENTEEN

We were walking up a steep incline. It was very dark, and only the white of Randy's shirt in front of me kept me going in the right direction on the twisting path we were on. Julian was just behind me.

Up until now I'd been skeptical about this whole operation. I didn't know much to start with, and now I felt I was losing touch with that. I was never one much for prophecy, or paying attention to my dream life—though that part of my makeup was extensive, the dreaming. And costly. But something was happening within me where I distinctly began to feel that I had a major part in the script.

I glanced back down the steep hill we were climbing now and then. The anchor light on the *Melchoir* glowed softly in the warm night. There seemed to be no other boats in the little cove we had anchored in.

I had no real complaints. There aren't too many more pleasant places on earth than St John. Julian and I had sailed most of this part of the Caribbean in one boat or another. I remembered this bay in particular, where the boat was. A small island lies within the bay, shaped like a half eaten watermelon rind—called, of course, Watermelon Cay—makes it unmistakable. Its white crescent shaped beach gives it away.

I once took a boatload of vacationing female schoolteachers there for a weekend, not knowing anywhere else to go with them. It was my first time in the Virgins then.

I was handling the charter for a friend of a friend, somebody who'd had a small fracas with the custom boys in Cruz Bay, on the other side of St John. Seems he neglected to declare a few items or something and was detained. He had, however, a regular charter captain gig with one of the charter outfits and they needed a 'body.' Preferably one that could handle a fifty foot ketch and was licensed. Anyway, he asked Julian to take over for him, but Julian didn't have a license then and I did.

So there I was, thrown into the breach. I picked the charter up and sailed them around St John until we came to Watermelon Cay. It looked perfect, so I decided to drop the hook—and had one of the better weekends of my life. Especially after those schoolteachers realized that there wasn't anyone around to give a damn if they sunbathed *au natural.*

But that was back in the good old days, when I did things just for pleasure. Now I wasn't sure why I did anything.

The path we were on got worse the higher we went. I wondered if Nadine would be wherever we were going. I wanted to talk to her—especially about where that dream began and where it ended—if it was a dream.

Things were certainly dreamlike now. The heavy growth we were going through may have been a trail, but it had been little used. And no one was talking.

We paused for a minute. I guess Randy was as much as a lowlander as Julian and me. He sounded winded, but he remained erect while Julian and I sat down. We faced north. Slightly to the right the lights of the British island of Tortola winked in the velvet darkness.

Tortola was just across a narrow body of water, called the Narrows, from St John. Jost Van Dyke was further north in the distance.

Pleasant it was, just sitting there, soaking in the warm night. I was totally rested. I felt like I'd just stepped off the plane from Kennedy, leaving the winter behind. And I had left the winter behind, only I'd just lost a week somehow, sailing here on a fat plastic pig of a boat. Strange.

I could see the *Melchoir* far below us, gently sleeping on her tether. She wasn't that bad of a boat, of its sort. I didn't have much of a chance to really sail her though.

I suddenly remembered I didn't even know what day it was. We'd been underway for maybe twenty-four hours when I'd cashed in. It took at least a week of heavy sailing to get here. I thought about asking Julian, but he was being very quiet.

No one, in fact, seemed to be busting out with conversation. But then people usually aren't that talkative after an extended sea voyage, especially on a small boat. It tends to make one introspective and slightly withdrawn. Experienced sailors seem to hold things in well. They have to; in tight quarters tempers are easily upset and emotions can run high unless something is done to control them. This control usually carries over beyond the voyage, hence reticence in speaking even while on terra firma.

I had no problem here. And it suddenly occurred to me that maybe I ought to see a doctor or somebody. And not just Dr. Nadine Griffiths-Franks. She may have pronounced me fit, but I wasn't in the habit of knocking off a hundred and sixty hours or so of shut-eye. Who knows, maybe I was narcoleptic. I could add that to my list of accomplishments.

I wonder how that would look on a resume—a single line with just *Narcoleptic* on it. Maybe it would even get me a job somewhere, as a mattress tester, or a pillow tryer. Or maybe someone would think I was some sort of narcotics agent. There we go. Jonas the Narc—

God, I was really getting carried away. Must be the altitude. We were up at least two hundred feet. But the air here was nice, and I felt that I could sit here all night.

I remembered that I was going to ask Julian something—right, *what was going on and what am I doing here*: "Beautiful night, huh?" I began, not quite the way I expected. Sometimes things just came out. "Reminds me of the first night we were here, remember? We left the boat in St Thomas, came across on the ferry to Cruz Bay, and then you hooked me up with that boat full of schoolteachers."

I sighed then, and all my questions seemed to drift off into the air. I was content. What the hell did I care how or why I got here. Something inside of me, though, wanted to be a prick about it.

"That ended up being a really 'bare' boat, didn't it?" Julian snickered.

"Yeah," I mused. What'd I want to ruin things for? But I had to know—"Hey, what's..."

Randy hadn't spoken a word, that I could remember, since I 'got up.' But now he said quickly, "Come on, we'd better be going on. They're waiting."

We continued climbing. Julian did tell me about meeting someone named Taylor on St John. He was some sort of connection for us. I was torn between demanding more information and just letting it flow—what the hell, I hadn't felt this rested in years. So what if I can't understand what happened to me.

Besides, conversation was impossible while we were climbing, and Randy, who had turned into some sort of leader now, seemed to want as little communication as possible between Julian and myself. Everytime we bantered even a bit, Randy cut in with further exhortations.

We came onto a section of the hillside that had been cleared off. I saw a rough road of sorts leading further up, and then we suddenly came upon a couple of vehicles parked one in front of the other. They were both four-wheel drives and set up high. The road out must be a little more than a two-goat path.

Then we came to the house.

It was partly built right into the hillside, with a deck providing a spectacular view. Mounted on one corner of the deck platform was one of those large Celestron telescopes—the type you could read the serial numbers off low flying satellites with.

The rest of the house seemed to match the view from the deck. Incredible. Sheets of glass, each one easily eight by twelve feet, made up the whole north side. The roof looked peaked in a funny way, thought I supposed it was to catch the southern view also—we were almost on the crest of the mountain. It was too dark to really see how the house was constructed, but it seemed to be cantilevered right over the steep hillside we'd come up.

We mounted the deck, and Randy slid open a glass door to the house. He waited for us. He could wait—I wanted to see. That telescope looked really intriguing. I started over towards it and then heard Nadine's voice.

"Rand, Julian—good. Everyone is ready," she said, her voice huskier than ever. "Jonas?"

I had my back to her and was drinking in the sight of nearly all the Virgin Islands. The night was so clear I felt I could just step over the railing and land in Tortola. The lights at West End seemed so close that I felt I could touch them.

"Jonas?" she called again.

Christ. And I had my hands on the telescope. "I'm right here, Nadine," I answered.

"You can play with that later," she said. "Come on in."

That last sounded like a command. Well, maybe now I'd find out the score. I wasn't sure I wanted to.

Inside, the place seemed more immense. We walked through expansive rooms and hallways, all with a view, and with many levels. I was amazed how much space continued to appear.

I heard many voices now, as though there was a cocktail party in progress. I followed Nadine up still another flight of stairs—spiraled—until we came to another whole level. Here the house was similar to the north side, only now it was higher and the fabulous viewing deck stretched to the south.

There was a party going on.

Off to one side was a bar set-up, complete with uniformed native, and a lookalike was going around with a hors d'ourves tray. Nadine led me by the hand past some well-tanned contented looking people, who all seemed to have stepped out of a Gucci ad.

We came to a group surrounding another one of those telescopes. They had it trained on something in the northwest. The barrel pointed up beyond the corner of the house. I wanted a peek, too. But first I had to talk with Nadine.

"Nadine," I said, trying to be polite. "I gotta talk to you—"

"In a minute, Jonas," she purred. "But first I want you to see the—uh, *Doctor*—Devin."

I was suddenly face to face with a bearded gent the size of a Frigidaire, who resembled either a biblical artist's conception of St John the Baptist or Farley Mowat. His beard was enough to make a vain hermit jealous. It flowed down from his granite-like features to somewhere around the middle of his rib cage, as un-cut and wind-blown and as wild as Spanish moss hanging from an ancient cypress. White-looking, but with flecks and spots and stains of the original black, the beard's only rival the eagle's nest which began a good six inches above the night-black brows.

A *patriarch* if I ever saw one. He would have intimidated Moses.

"Doctor—" I began, sticking out my hand.

The giant grabbed my hand with both of his as if they were paws, and pressed them together, my open hand in the middle like a slice of bony roast beef in a thick sandwich. He then raised his arms and my own followed until he had my right extremity and both of his at his eye level.

"*This is the hand which shall guide our ship,*" he bellowed out, his voice a practiced orator's thunder. His eyes were looking over my head to the crowd on the deck. He paused, and behind me was absolute silence.

"It is the hand of Jonas—the *Jonah*—sent by the Almighty to Nineveh to convince the heathen to renounce their evil ways. And now," he began speaking quieter. "He shall be more than our Lord's herald and harbinger. This time he shall bring proof of the Almighty's very existence to the heathen in the heart of their dark hearts. For in the midst of the wilderness, in the voluminous pit of man's sin, the Son will be born again—to rise and to lead his children to everlasting peace."

The giant's eyes, which for a moment there were almost red with an inner fire as he spoke, now were cold and gray, and he dropped my hand like it was dead meat. He turned on his heel and walked through the crowd, which parted like the Red Sea, into the house.

Everyone went back to what they were doing.

I stood there like an ass and looked around, staring back at the few who eyed me a little longer than usual.

Nadine was still at my side. "What the hell was *that?*" I asked incredulously.

"That was the man we call the *Devin*," she said matter of factly.

I was out of breath, and could feel my ticker pounding away. "I know, I met him," I told her. "Or rather, he met me." But he seemed to already *know* me.

She had turned away, and was leading me onward again.

I pulled her back. "Look, Nadine, I don't mind doing a deal. But the shenanigans have to be explained. I can't work in the dark anymore."

"Dr. Taylor, Jonas Coffey," Nadine said, introducing me to a pleasant enough looking person. We shook hands—nothing strange happening this time—and then she quickly introduced me to a half dozen or so more people, all of whom seemed to have a 'Doctor' in front of their names. Everyone was nice and smiling and there were no more dramatic moments.

As soon as the routine formalities were over they went back to clustering around the big telescope. Dr. Taylor, though, stayed with Nadine and me.

"Now that we've taken care of all *that*," he said, gesturing towards the people I'd just met. "And the theatrics," he added, smiling at me knowingly. "We can talk."

I liked him already.

Dr. Taylor must have been in his early fifties, or so he looked, but gave the impression of being younger. He had a baby face—more precisely a baby head, for his head was strikingly large, with a high broad forehead and soft benevolent features, and was perched atop a relatively thin neck, which in turn opens out onto a solid, almost hefty frame. His hair was thinning on top and graying to the sides, but he looked in good shape. Liked he downed a fistful of vitamins and jogged a ritual five miles every morning.

He had a few words with Nadine that I didn't catch. I was trying to see, if possible, where or at what the telescope was aimed. There was that new comet or star that had been making the news lately and maybe that was the focus of interest here.

Besides, I had to *do* something to get my equilibrium back after meeting with the *Devin*, or whatever. I was fidgety. Nadine left. Taylor said a few words to the group and turned back to me.

"Let's go inside," he said.

I followed him off the deck and into the house. People watched us go as though I was the proverbial lamb. A few, I felt, seemed to look askance at my passing—as if they wanted to forget I was ever there, regarding me as something not quite worthwhile.

We ended up in an office-like room set at one end of the house. There were hideous masks lining the walls and other artifacts from some tribal culture. A plaque underneath one identified the piece as pre-Columbian.

A large picture window faced due east towards Virgin Gorda. The view, of course, was superb. The house could have been hung from a hot air balloon and the look out no less beautiful.

"So what do you think so far, Jonas Coffey?" Dr. Taylor asked.

"I'd like to live here," I answered. And meant it.

"Oh, the view," he said innocently. "People are always entranced by it. I had this house built with that view in mind. I wanted to be able to see all around me. As a boy I was fascinated by pirates, you see."

He watched me, seeming to judge my interest.

"That's what originally drew me to the Caribbean. The

173

incredible historical adventure of it. I wanted to *be* a pirate. A freebooter, a buccaneer. To live that free and easy life, doing what I damned pleased..."

He stopped talking for a moment, just watched me with one eyebrow raised. Then he said, "That touch base with you?"

"What?" I said. He got me there. He touched base all right. I was right along with him, even a little ahead. "Yeah. Yeah, I know what you mean, Doc."

We both stared out that big window. Away to the southeast, beyond the horizon, were the Lesser Antilles: St Martin, Guadeloupe, Dominica, Martinique, St Lucia, St Vincent, Granada—stretching right down to the fabulously rich coast of South America. A pirate's dream world right out of Stevenson and Defoe. And still a sailor's paradise.

"However," he harumphed, as if such thoughts were the forbidden fruit of the intellect, "we're not here to play pirate."

This surprised me. Bullshit, I wanted to say. You want us to handle some goods for you without legal sanction. If that wasn't playing pirate, or 'freebooting,' I had no conception of the terms.

My thoughts must have been on my face, as usual, because he gave me a quizzical look. Then he sighed.

"You really don't know what is going on, do you?" he said, finally.

Aha. So now he was going to 'level' with me. Big shots always act this way. First, spit out little bits of information at a time so the peons don't get smart too quick. Then, let the dummies who are doing the really dangerous work think they really know what is going on.

Keep 'em happy! Make 'em think they're 'in' with the 'in crowd.' Tell 'em it's dangerous—they can get hurt. Sure, it'll be rough, but the rewards will be high. If, and a big IF, they follow instructions and don't—repeat DON'T—ever do anything different than planned.

I thought I was going to get that speech now. The set-up speech. The one which enables the boss later to say to his partners, 'He's O.K. I laid down the law. If anything happens, we're covered. Don't worry, it'll be *his* ass, not ours.'

Instead, Taylor began talking about Haley's Comet.

"I saw you itching to get a look through that eyepiece out there," he began. "You know, everybody thinks that for the last few years we've been watching for Haley's. And we have..."

He seemed to peer out the window a little harder, as if it would blaze by any second now. "It'll be by again in '86. Everybody will see it then. Most observatories today, however, are hot to make the first sighting. You just met an expert on planets and comets outside on the deck a few minutes ago. Dr. Morowitz, from Kitt's Peak observatory in Tucson. And there's also Dr. Chaney from Mount Palomar." He paused to look at me, then went on.

I felt like I was an audience again for Calvin Franks. I must have an easy-looking look.

"I'm an astronomer by inclination myself," he said, "though my primary field is anthropology. You might say that I'd be more interested in Johann Palitzsch, the German farmer who sighted Haley's comet on Christmas Day back in 1758 than in the comet itself. But to tell you the truth, Jonas, that's not really what we're looking at out on the deck. No, no. Haley's is much too dim for that little scope out there. Right now the comet is only at 24th magnitude. Something like sixteen times fainter than the dimmest stars and galaxies you could see with that little Celestron scope. No, we're looking at something else. Something relatively new. Something that hasn't been in the sky for two thousand years."

Someone came into the room, and Dr. Taylor turned around. "Ah, Dr. Leigh," he said.

I recognized Leigh as one of the people I'd met earlier. He seemed a straight forward type. Even looked like a scientist, if that was what these people really were. I had my doubts, though for no other reason than a hard feeling I had just below my sternum.

Leigh was totally bald, with a kind of sloppy overall look to the rest of him. Like he got his head shaved for convenience. His face was interesting also—with a strangely benign smile that edged on the lunatic.

"Dr. Leigh, Jonas, has recently returned from the mideast. He's brought back some rather interesting documents he's, ah, located there." Taylor spoke with a somewhat different tone now.

Leigh smiled at me. "I would say they're quite important. Scrolls of this magnitude…"

Suddenly both of them became rigid. They appeared to stare over my shoulder, behind me. I had the hard rock feeling in my gut increase somewhat. I turned around slowly, my eyes not leaving Taylor and Leigh—whatever it was, I felt I wouldn't like it.

Standing there now, his figure filling the doorway, was Randy.

"Important. You would say it was important, wouldn't you—*Doctor*—Leigh?"

His tone was baiting, and Randy seemed very much in charge all of a sudden. He'd led us up here—where was Julian, anyway?—and now he seemed to have these two characters under his multi-talented thumb.

I was lost. But at least I thought I knew Randy. He was a con man. Nothing was going to change that for me.

176

Leigh didn't seem to like being baited.

"I assure you, Dr. Rand, the scrolls are genuine. And, if you notice, everything else is right on schedule," he said definitely, nodding at Dr. Taylor, who in turn smiled in my direction.

I began to get the drift. Maybe it wasn't dope. Artifacts, ancient scrolls that had to be smuggled into the states for a secret buyer. The fact that the room we were in was filled with pre-Columbian art, worth a fortune in the right hands, strengthened this idea. Definitely a brisk market in this type of thing, especially if you knew your stuff.

I smiled back at Taylor. Something like this could be fun. Like an old Bogart movie. And it wouldn't conflict with my vow to play the game straight. That is, no *dope*—this was different. This was history.

I looked at Randy, expecting a big grin on his puss, too. He was scowling, though.

"So everything is set stateside, then," he said. "And I suppose there are no other observatories in the world that will question our findings? Or other archaeologists?"

"That is why we have—" Taylor cleared his throat, then went on, "a contingency plan."

"Yes, I'm aware of that," Randy said. "The only one who is not so far is the pigeon."

"That," Taylor said uneasily, avoiding my glance, "is Dr. Griffiths department."

Taylor and Leigh were obviously not comfortable with Randy's candor. I wasn't either. I had a feeling who the pigeon was. But why they were—or Randy was—so blatant about it I didn't know.

Randy sat on the large desk casually and picked up a small stone or clay figure that I'd noticed earlier. It looked female, with a very buxom shape. "You really shouldn't leave something like this lying around, Doctor. It's almost proof of the theft."

Taylor was livid.

He spluttered, "I wouldn't call it a *theft*, Dr. Rand. If Begin hadn't given the Chief Rabbinate jurisdiction over Israel's archaeological sites this did not have to happen this way. But perhaps even you can realize that things are working out better like this. At least now *we* are in control."

"Of what? Do you really think that you are in 'control' of anything?" Randy snorted. "Maybe you ought to read some of your own literature."

Just then a couple of imposing figures appeared in the doorway. I hadn't seen them before, but I knew their ilk—big and hard-looking—protective types. I was sure that they did not have titles in front of their names.

"Yes, Klaus?" Taylor said.

The blond one answered in a guttural voice that evoked an image of jack-boots and rabbit punches. He said something in a language that sounded German, and in a deep, hard manner that fit him. His partner, swarthy but not any softer, stared at me with dark eyes that turned down at the corners. I wondered what it would take to make him laugh.

Taylor turned back to Randy. "We shall see, Doctor. We shall see," he added angrily.

With that, both Taylor and Leigh left the room, followed by the goons.

There was obviously some friction at the top here. But I'd seen enough cop shows and endured a few interrogations myself to have a suspicion that maybe it was planned this way. It'd be right in line with Randy's style. But even if it wasn't, I didn't want to get involved in internal bickerings. At the moment, though, I was curious about something else. The heavy stuff could wait.

"What is this thing, Randy?" I asked.

He looked at me like we were old buddies. He was a strange son of a bitch, all right. "This? This thing," he said, hefting the figurine like he was weighing it, "is a statue of the goddess *Astartes*. She was a fertility goddess."

"Like *Ishtar?*"

"Yes. Like *Ishtar*." He smiled. "Only Ishtar was a bit earlier. Sumerian, matter of fact. Astartes was worshipped by the ancient Hebrews."

"The Jews? I thought they didn't do that sort of thing."

"What sort of thing?"

"You know. Graven images and all that," I said.

"You mean the Commandment. Yes. Yes, but they did. Shiloh and his men found evidence of that. And it fits—my how it fits! You see, that's why—one of the reasons, anyway—the *Netorei Karta* and other ultra Orthodox Jews are against the dig. The whole thing is a national scandal over there right now. They're saying that by discovering the tombs of David and the kings of Judah archaeologists would be desecrating a medieval Jewish cemetery. Such bullshit!"

Randy was excited now. I'd never have thought he could get this way. Maybe another show for me.

"That may be true, though," he said. "Maybe they *would* be digging through graves. But the importance of it all! What they are hiding is the crux of the matter. But it almost doesn't matter now. Leigh found something there which will change history."

"Who *is* Leigh? You sounded like you were making fun of him before," I asked. This was getting interesting.

"He's not really a doctor, I can tell you that. He doesn't

have a pee-aitch-dee. Either do I, for that matter. All these characters have made up titles—some are real, of course, or else not one would have listened to them so far. Leigh is little more than a professional grave robber."

This was turning into true confessions. It worried me that Randy was telling me all this. I might as well just play along, but I felt something stirring inside me.

"Then who are the rest of them?" I said. "And that *Devin* guy?"

"They're the creationist people. The big bucks behind the movement. And right now they're on the verge of the most momentous event since..." He stopped then, as if he couldn't find the words. Very much out of character for Randy, or maybe very much *in* character.

"Since what?"

"Since the last time," he said pensively.

"The *last* time?" I said slowly. An uncontrollable feeling, one like water on the verge of boiling, starting to grow inside me—

"It's the *Second Coming*, Jonas."

CHAPTER EIGHTEEN

The Second Coming.

At first I wanted to say that I didn't know what Randy was talking about. I mean, I was practically an atheist. I didn't go to church, and Faith was my Aunt Roberta's middle name—as in Roberta Faith Coffey. But, like most people in the Western world, I knew something about the bible. It was great literature. Suspect, to be sure, and inaccurate, but as stirring in places as it was boring in others. Practically everyone I knew in my early life had a name chosen from that book, mine included. And I had continued the tradition with my own son, giving him my name.

But the *parousia*—the Second Coming of Christ. That was an event mentioned many times throughout the New Testament. According to St Paul, it could not take place until an apocalypse occurred and the Antichrist appeared. The *parousia* would be preceded by a great religious revolt. A great apostasy. And the advent of the man of sin, as Paul puts it, who'll be characterized by great impiety and pride. Antichrist.

By the aid of Satan, Antichrist will perform fake miracles, and man will be led to adopt sinful practices and erroneous doctrines…

All this ran through my head as I sat there silently. It was strange how it all came back with such a flourish. All the Sunday school stories, the seemingly endless and pointless discussions in confirmation classes, and the...despairing, endless battles with the old man, my father: "You're heading for a fall, Jonas. It won't come today or tomorrow, but it will come. You will be damned..."

***

"Bullshit!" I suddenly cried.

I had been sitting on the corner of the desk, but now I jumped off and circled the room. What exactly was so upsetting I didn't really know, but I wasn't so interested in the whole project anymore. I paced angrily, a rage erupting within me.

Randy put out a hand, silently, to either calm me or stop me. I slapped his hand viciously away as I came by him.

"And *who* the fuck are *you*, anyway?" I screamed at him. "You're just some kind of con artist—you bullshit everybody. I don't know what these other poor bastards believe, but I *know* that I don't believe *you!*"

I was getting loud, and my voice seemed to echo in that room. And each echo seemed to give me some sort of power. I felt it; it made me stronger. And louder.

"All my life, you sanctimonious lying son of a bitch, I've had to put up with your kind of filth. You play the easy game, make life out to be a cut and dried ecstatic experience that is played by some kind of rules. Rules that only you know, that you change as soon as someone—like me—gets too close to the bacon. Too close to the heart, the meat, the gold. And then you snatch it away: 'Not yet, my son.' You say, 'You're not ready.' Well, *damn you!* I don't believe it! I don't believe you! You understand?"

And now I was screeching directly in his face. My body felt huge and all powerful. The room seemed suddenly to have shrunk, and Randy just as puny and as fragile as the clay figurine he still held in his hand.

I seized it.

"Astartes. A goddess, you say? Well, follow your goddess—follow your god."

I raised the statue over my head. Randy's eyes followed it, and I took immediate and intense pleasure in seeing a look of fear come into them.

I looked down on him from what appeared to be a great height, though I could see every detail on his thin strained face. His skin was parchment white, and flecks of my spittle hang on his chin and high cheekbones like frozen drops of dew. The drops seemed to gain color as I looked. They were red now, the color of blood...

I let the statue fly. It crashed through the picture window and into the darkness beyond.

"Follow your graven image straight to *Hell*, you bastard..."

A sudden rush of hot night air engulfed me, and I was on the ledge, pieces of glass crunching under my feet. I felt a touch, like from a single beat of a great wing, and then I leaped into the black before me.

***

I was in a huge outdoor amphitheater.

Above me the sky was filled with stars. I lay back in the comfortable seat I was in and thought about how clear the sky was tonight.

Everything was in its place. The constellations were all perfectly defined. There was the Big Dipper right in the middle. I always found that first—then followed the pointer stars, Merak and Dubhe, to Polaris.

Now I had my directions set. I checked out the Big

Dipper's handle: Alioth, Mizar, and Alkaid, three stars which, if followed right along the curve they formed, would lead you directly to Arcturus, in Bootes. I then looked for the constellations along the ecliptic, the ones making up the Zodiac.

There was Spica, in Virgo, right on the eastern horizon. Then came those bright stars Denobola and Regulus in Leo. I could even make out Cancer. And there was Gemini, right smack dab overhead, with Castor and Pollux shining so brightly.

There was Orion, just off the path, in the southeast. There was his belt, and the stars Betelgeuse and Bellatrix, each making a shoulder. The belt lined up with Sirius, the dog star, more to the south. It struck me then that it must be quite early in the morning, the way the stars were situated now. Just before dawn...

Suddenly the sky above changed, and the crescent moon was moving very swiftly along the ecliptic. A voice, which had been going on before it seemed, now got louder, or more distinct: "...and Venus is the only bright evening planet in December, visible low in the west-southwest shortly after sundown..."

I looked over there, and there it was.

"This hasn't been a good evening cycle for the planet, however, since it is too far south and its position relative to the sun at setting keeps it low in the sky. The view of Venus improves in late December, as its position to the sun's east brings it to..."

I must be a planetarium somewhere. But where?

The voice went on: "...the northerly curving part of the ecliptic. The early crescent moon passes above Venus on the night of the 28th, as shown here..."

And there it was, the slim crescent crowding the bright spot of Venus right over the horizon. They even threw in some water and island masses, with a slight glow behind, to make it realistic. Nice touch.

"...at about six to six-thirty P.M."

The sky changed again, and the voice went on.

"On December tenth, Mercury, in superior conjunction, enters the evening sky..."

I decided to leave. The show was interesting, but I had enough.

I found myself in a hallway with many double doors opening to different lecture halls. A sign outside one stated simply: The Solar System—A Lecture by William James.

I put my ear to the small space between the doors and heard a greatly refined voice ask if there were any questions. The lecture must be over, so I hesitated. I fidgeted a moment, then decided to go in.

The hall was packed.

A smoky haze hung in the air, and I could smell stale booze and cheap dope. The main aisles were littered with bits of paper and other garbage, and there was a man asleep or passed out under a pile of newspapers just inside the door.

The crowd was alive, though, and a party atmosphere prevailed. A bottle crashed on the stage front and a roll of toilet paper sailed through the air. Somebody four or five rows down suddenly turned and puked in the aisle. It was like being at the Rocky Horror Picture Show.

There, coming down off the stage, was the great philosopher himself. As he reached the floor a determined looking bag-lady approached him.

"Mr. James, we don't live on a ball rotating around the sun," she said. "We live on a crust of earth on the back of a giant turtle."

The great man stared at her for a moment, then obviously decided to be gentle. "If your theory is correct, madam, what does this turtle stand on?"

"The first turtle stands on the back of a second, far larger turtle, of course."

"But what does this second turtle stand on?"

The old woman crowed triumphantly. "It's no use, Mr. James. It's turtles all the way down!"

The audience cheered her. James stepped back and had to duck an empty Schimdts beer bottle. The crowd hooted at him. He dropped some of his notes, but before he could pick them up off the filthy floor a frizzy haired person in KISS makeup—an ultra bizarre form of rock star regalia—dropped their leather shorts and started urinating on the scattered papers. The mob roared as the bag-lady now emptied what seemed to be twin bags of garbage and old clothes over the great pragmatist's head.

I backed away hurriedly, and was soon out in the empty hallway again. I wandered along, too timid now to venture into any more lecture halls.

Outside every set of doors was a sign stating what was going on inside. Some of the signs were printed in foreign languages. I could make out some of the meaning if the language was one of the Romantics. I began to be intrigued again. I ventured closer to the doors.

I came upon one which stated: *La grande Rafle du Vel d'Hiv.*

The Big Roundup of somewhere. Maybe it was a French rodeo, like the Calgary Stampede I'd gone to once in Canada. Underneath was a date—Juillet 16, 1942.

That clinched it for me. July 16, 1942 was my birthday. I was still intimidated from my experience earlier, but the coincidence in dates was too strong a lure. I pressed myself against the doors.

From inside I could hear some sort of hub-bub that seemed slightly off-kilter. It wasn't the normal crowd noise, which I was attuned to hearing now, since behind each set of doors I came close enough to I could hear some sort of audience reaction to whatever event was taking place inside.

But behind these doors something seemed amiss; there was a moaning type of murmur, which swelled intermittently, and then broke up into what sounded like singular voices. I listened for awhile, trying to guess what was going on.

A few times I heard a mechanical clatter, followed by a few outright cries. There were other cries also, but not of the same type. These came in another language than French, which I guessed was German.

These cries sounded like orders; only orders given by someone who was not wholly familiar with the language. I finally simply could not contain my curiosity any longer; I pushed open the door and stepped inside.

I was in a huge sport arena. In the center were race tracks set up for bicycles. And there were bicyclists racing. Only on the tracks also, competing, so it seemed, with the racers, were people. They looked to be from all walks of life: women, children, old and young men, rich, poor, *bourgeois*...

They were all trying vainly to avoid being run down by the bicycle racers.

The tracks were really packed and the people seemed to have no where else to go. There were men with submachine guns stationed along the bleachers who menaced the poor souls on the edge of the crowd.

It was a lot quieter than I would have expected for such an absurd event, especially a Gaullic one. The people were all

French, that was unmistakable. Their accent was Parisian. The difference in articulation and voice quality between the speech patterns of Paris citizens and the rest of the inhabitants of France was as striking as that of a Brooklyner and a citizen of, say, Montana.

The mechanical noise I'd heard from the hallway was when one of the racers collided with one of the multitude swarming over the tracks. It was mainly the women with children in arms and the older men who were knocked down. The cyclist who hit them would merely pick up his momentarily halted machine and continue. And while this was happening every few seconds now (sometimes several collisions would take place simultaneously), the men along the side with the submachine guns kept herding new participants into the arena.

Directing things, it seemed, were two figures seated side by side on a trapeze which swung back and fro high above the surprisingly docile crowed below. They were crying out, or shouting, rather, in German. A distinctly non-classical German, too. It was more slang—similar to that used by the young *Instandbesetzer* and *Gastarbeiter* of modern Berlin—the young people and workers, all non-German, who flock to that divided city looking for excitement.

Then I recognized one of the men on the trapeze: It was Field Marshall Petain, complete in his Vichy France uniform. That explained the similarity in dates, I guessed.

A man was moving towards me from the side of the arena. He had a submachine gun like the others there. He was also wearing a black beret and dark clothes, similar, I noticed, to the others also.

He came up to me and demanded, "Votre papier!"

I pulled out my wallet and showed him my driver's license, the Florida one with my picture on it. I didn't want to end up in the arena like the rest because of mistaken or inadequate identification.

The man studied my license for a minute and thrust it back at me. I happened to glance at my picture on the license before I put it away. In it, I was wearing a black beret also.

He stood alongside me.

We resumed watching the goings on below us. I imagine he thought that I was O.K. He smelled like garlic, and I could sense the oily feeling of the weapon he carried. The oily feeling seemed to emanate from the man himself after awhile.

I asked him who the other man was on the trapeze with Petain. He eyed me coldly for a moment, as if I was supposed to know. I gave him what I thought was a pretty good Parisian shrug—shoulders hunched, eyes squinted, mouth turned down, head tilted just so, arms akimbo and hands flat out...

I did it so well I felt that I'd be stuck in that position.

He laughed. Frenchmen are always good for a joke. He answered triumphantly, "La grande homme de lettres—Paul Claudel!"

He slapped me on the back like a comrade. He was very proud of his heroes, and his exuberance spilled over on me. He grabbed me and I was bussed on each cheek, French style. As he did so, his gun, which swung from his shoulder on a dark leather strap, hit me in the groin several times. It was acutely painful and I backed away from him. He wouldn't let me go, however, keeping one arm tight around my shoulders.

We faced the inner arena again and I began to feel suffocated. A stench rose from the massed herd below on the bicycle tracks. But somehow it didn't seem as bad as the now over-powering rotten egg and rotten meat smell that came from the creature clutching me.

I struggled slightly, but in vain. He had me.

With his free arm he gestured to the poor souls below us. Poor souls that I now felt I would rather be with. He muttered a phrase over and over again, while shaking his head from side to side, indicating the whole stadium: "On se debrouille...on se debrouille...on se debrouille..."

We'll see it through.

I felt disgusted and dirty. I'd just about given up hope of escaping when a train whistle shrieked. Some doors were thrown open below and the guards started hustling the people off the racing tracks and out the doors. Beyond then I could see billows of steam, and I could hear the hiss of powerful freight engines.

The whistle sounded again, this time almost impatiently. The train didn't seem to want to wait for its cargo.

Suddenly a man in the crowd below bolted. He scrambled over the heads of his fellow captives and made right for us. Some of the people in the crowd cried, "Arret! Arret!"

They obviously knew what was going to happen.

A few of the guards cried, "Halt!" and pointed their weapons at him, but hesitated to fire.

The man came closer, crawling then bounding over the bleacher seats, his face a sardonic mask, hideous in its stark-white thinness.

I was afraid. The man looked like an angel from Hell, coming up out of the pit to claim another victim. I trembled, and almost involuntarily huddled closer to my own captor, who seemed to feel my fear. He patted my shoulder, as if to say, "It's all right. I'll protect you from this fiend."

I wanted to chew my nails, I was so worried. But when I brought my fingers up to my face I saw that they were very dirty. They were covered with dried blood and excrement. Under the fingernails was black almost halfway to the cuticles, and the nails themselves were very long and hard, as if I used them for digging.

The fiend was moving closer now. He must have been weak. But still coming closer. I could see him a little clearer in the garish lights that hung along the ceiling in places. His garment seemed much too small for him, but he was lost in it anyway—his arms and legs were very thin. Skeleton-like. He was frightening to look at.

I asked my former captor, but now my guardian, why the fiend looked so thin. He replied that all the fiends had not enough to eat ever since they—indicating himself and the others with weapons—had stopped the fiends from stealing, and then eating, little children.

That was enough for me. I turned and demanded the weapon. A true comrade now, he handed it over with a smile. He seemed pleased to accommodate me. He stepped back and started to sing in a warm baritone. I expected "La Marseilles," but instead he sang Maurice Chevalier's "Paris sera toujours Paris."

It was somehow very appropriate.

The fiend and I were almost eye to eye now. I was surprised he had made it this far so quickly. A moment ago he'd been way down there.

His sardonic grin suddenly disappeared, and in its place was a calm look of acceptance. I felt my own mouth widen, and my lips stretching into any ugly smile which bared all of my teeth. It was painful, and I couldn't get rid of it—like having my jaw locked in the dentist's chair.

And this was his fault, the poor trembling creature before me.

He was on his knees praying.

I ordered him to get up, my voice guttural and ugly

sounding, as if I was choking on something. He spread his arms out, still on his knees, and hung his head.

I fired at the large gold star on his chest.

He flipped backwards, and began a slow descent, end over end, back down to the center of the arena, looking like a big slinky going down a long empty stairway.

Gunsmoke hung in the air.

The smell was pleasantly memorable. I was suddenly transported, reminded of the Saturday mornings I used to spend with my father, plinking away at bottles and things with the .22 he'd given me. The sky was always blue and clear then, and there was never any wind. The smoke from the gun would hang there in layers, like cigarette smoke at a cocktail party.

I loved the spent gunpowder smell. I would always sniff the spent cartridges on the way home, and sometimes long after, just to keep those memories alive. They were the only happy times I ever had with the old man.

Later, when I was much older, I would go down to Vic's Shooting Range to fire the Colt .45 revolver that my grandfather left me. The gun had been his service revolver while he'd been in the calvary. He'd chased Pancho Villa with General Pershing into Mexico with it.

My grandfather really didn't leave it to me, though. I liked to think he would have. My father gave me the gun the day after my grandfather's funeral.

We were clearing out his effects from the little house he'd spent his last years in, and I stumbled on it. I must have been sixteen or so, and it had been some time since the old man had taken me shooting. I guess I was trying to recapture something between us when I asked my father that day if we could shoot the big revolver sometime.

"You go ahead and shoot it, Jonas," my father told me, somewhat derisively. "If you think you can..."

He was annoyed at me for some reason or other at the time. That's why he challenged me like that. But he seemed always to be annoyed with me.

I took the gun anyway, and practiced with it at Vic's. I liked the smell there.

I even went to Vic's and shot once after I quit working for the government. Actually, the Department of Defense didn't renew my contract after the Coast Guard helicopter fiasco that time just south of the DMZ, and I had freaked out. I couldn't blame them, though I still wanted the work.

I remember there being a lot of cops there then. Or I thought they were cops—they looked like it to me. They all looked soft and had mustaches, most of them overweight, and they handled guns uneasily, like a woman would mechanic's tools.

I got all set up and squeezed off one round.

The acrid smell of the freshly burned powder seemed to slam me in the face. Funny how it didn't affect me when I first came in that night. The same smell permeated Vic's.

But now I was nauseous. I dropped my grandfather's revolver, tore off the ear protectors and ran outside where I vomited profusely. I never went back.

***

The smoke from the firing of the oily machine gun hung in the air, then began to build and swirl like quick-moving thunderheads in a mid-summer sky.

Far, far below lay the arena. The man I'd shot I could not see, but the bicycle racers were still speeding around and around the track.

They were alone now. The rest of the stadium was empty.

***

"So. What do you think, huh?"

I was standing on a street corner in the little town of Babylon where I grew up. Scott Shaw was with me.

"So. Come on, Jonas. We be getting something to eat, or what?" Scott said.

He had on a rain slicker and pants, and was wearing rubber boots, the type local clammers always wore. They were distinctive looking boots. Made in Norway, chocolate-colored, and fleece-lined.

I used to love those boots. To a local adolescent they stood for all the romanticism of working on the water. I remember how thrilled I was the first time I bought a pair.

The novelty wore off after a number of years, though. The boots no longer impressed me. They were very comfortable, especially for walking around in, but the quality seemed to degenerate as the boots went up in price.

The manufacturer made some changes in them. The first thing was the bottom tread pattern. The newer boots had the bottom put on in Taiwan, and with a different tread pattern. Somehow the boots with the Taiwanese bottoms never lasted very long. I never go more than a year out of them.

We were standing just outside Jimmy's Dinette. Jimmy's was a homey little place right in the middle of town. He had a breakfast special for $1.03. Jimmy was Greek.

The way our shadows were falling on the sidewalk told me that it was early morning. That was the time of day I usually went to Jimmy's. Looking down, I noticed I was wearing black tie shoes, like I had when working for the military.

We started to go inside. "What are you doing here, Scott?" I asked him as I held the door open. I didn't remember him ever being in Babylon before.

"Oh, I was here before the war, Jonas. Always looking out

for you, you know," he answered, speaking in that sing-song lilt.

I loved hearing him talk. I was suddenly overcome with a desire to listen to him for the rest of my life. We sat down, and I started blathering on about how he should settle down here in Babylon, work with me on my clamboat, and just talk to me.

Jimmy came over to get our order. He folded his arms on the counter, a dishrag in one hand like he always had, and listened to me go on. Jimmy looked so melancholy. So did Scott, but he smiled at me with that bright Irish gleam in his eye, and the thinning hairs on his head glistened as if they were touched with a silvery mist.

"But you don't *have* a clamboat anymore, Jonas," Scott said when I stopped. "You don't fish for fish."

I looked down at my shoes. I wasn't dressed for it, that was for sure. I told Scott this. He just shook his head.

It was very quiet in the diner. I could hear a clock ticking—very slowly, it seemed. Outside, across the street, there was a bank building. I knew it to be Manufacturers Hanover Trust. But the lettering, which was chiseled in stone across the front of the building, looked different somehow. From where I usually sat in the diner I could always look out and see those letters very plainly. Now they said something else.

I was hesitant to leave Scott, but I had to see what those letters smelled out now. I started to get off my stool, but Jimmy said, "Jonas, wait—your pack."

I turned around and Jimmy slid a pack of Camels towards me. I always bought a pack there just before I left every morning. He had them cheap. Sixty cents or something. I picked up the pack, staring at it.

"I'm coming back, Jimmy—" I started to explain, but

the picture of the camel on the pack held my attention. I was drawn into it, and, suddenly, for the life of me I couldn't remember where the camel was, or what he was standing on.

"What do camels stand on, Jimmy?" I asked him. I felt foolish—like I was telling a joke at a serious moment.

"Sand—" Jimmy said.

I turned to Scott. He was sipping from a cup of coffee, like before, but now he was dressed in dark commando fatigues. He had on those paratrooper jump boots we always wore when we were going on a mission.

"Sand—" Scott said.

I turned away quickly. At the end of the counter, where it makes a sharp turn near the door, two men were seated, facing me. They had on dark suits, hats, and sunglasses. I recognized them as Ackroyd and Belushi—the Blues Brothers, from the movie.

"Sand—" they said in unison.

"Sand," I repeated after them. It was almost funny now. I felt good.

I got off the stool and stood for a moment, but the floor felt strange. I looked down, and my feet were buried in a loose golden sand. It was very warm sand, and I was barefoot now, and I took pleasure in lifting my heels in and out of it, one at a time, as if I was marching.

I was laughing, and my hair shook around me. My hair was suddenly very long again, as it had been before I went into the army. I touched it. The long hair seemed to give me some sort of invincibility. Whatever was going to happen now I was ready for.

I turned around, still marching in time in the sand, and said to Scott, "So what's our mission this time—to kill Gentiles?" I had wanted to say, 'to kill Jews;' it just came out wrong. But Scott was gone.

The diner was gone.

I was alone on a rough desert. It was familiar somehow. I started walking.

By the angle of the sun it was getting late in the day. I was heading east, and had a purpose—a mission—though I knew not what it was.

CHAPTER NINETEEN

I woke up in a little room without glass in the windows. That was the first thing I noticed. The trade wind breeze came right through and was riffling the pages of a book that was on a makeshift table in the middle of the room.

I was in a hut, actually. Just a one-room dwelling. The place was very simple—no door or windows, just the openings. The only furnishing was the bed I was on and the table. And there was a rickety-looking chair. But not much else.

The floor was made of rough-cut boards, as was the rest of the hut, including the furniture. It was an old West Indian style house.

The table appeared makeshift because it looked like it was made from a packing crate. But upon closer inspection I see that it was just constructed roughly. Substantial enough. The legs and supports were lashed with seine twine, and appeared very tight. The chair probably belied its strength also, for it was put together in the same manner.

The wind was blowing pretty hard, as it usually did in the late afternoon in the tropics. Beyond the door opening I could see water. The hut must be on a clean beach somewhere, or just set back in the trees off one. The sand pretty and enticing from where I lay. It'd be nice to walk there now, barefoot—the heat of the day chased away by the cooling trades.

The pages of the book on the table flipped faster. They were very thin pages, and they'd be ripped if I didn't do something. I got up to close the book.

As I did so, I wondered if I was dreaming again.

I know that I was dreaming—I could recall all of it like it just really happened. But it couldn't have. So I must have been dreaming.

I picked the book up. Recognizing what it was, I snorted, "Of course—of course, of course!" Like in the Barnes and Noble bookstore ad.

It was a bible.

Some of the onion-skin pages were all curled up like hair rollers on someone's head. I began to straighten them out, keeping a couple of fingers on the place where the book was open to when I picked it up.

I was pretty sure I wasn't dreaming now. I was too cocky and cynical. I was being used somehow. This last touch was too much—the empty room, the open bible.

I laughed out loud.

"Fuck 'em," I said. "Fuck you, you bastards!" I angrily yelled out the doorway.

I remembered the events of the night before. The argument, or rather my explosion with Randy. The statue through the window, leaping out...

I pulled the chair close to the table and sat in it. I had the bible in front of me, my fingers still stuck in place, but the book closed. I was almost out of breath. I sat there, trying to calm myself.

Zeke came to mind.

I wonder what he's doing now? Is he O.K.? I pictured him lying by the fireplace in my parent's house. His eyes were open slightly, and he was sighing. His tail started to thump, and a slight tremor ran through his body. He lifted his head a little bit and sniffed, as if he was trying to recognize something. His eyes had that cataract-dullness to them.

Zeke was old now. Older in his own lifespan than I was. I didn't want him to die.

There was a poem I read once in a magazine, and then read over again, and again. I *knew* the poem and I wrote it down in my heart. The heart that begins with a lump in the throat and a heaving of the chest. Then a wet swelling of the eyes and a blubber lip.

The poem was called "Elegy For A Dead Labrador," and written by a Swede, Lars Gustafsson.

The lines flowed through me. Then I started saying them aloud, something I'd never done before:

...You had knowledge
I would have given much to have
possessed: the ability to let a feeling—eagerness,
hate, or love—
run like a wave through your body
from nose to tip of tail, the inability
ever to accept the moon as fact.
At the full moon you always complained
loudly against it.
You were a better Gnostic than I am.
And consequently
you lived continually in paradise.

I was crying now.

I couldn't remember the rest, save one line—"In my world most things were hidden behind something else."

No wonder Zeke's a better Gnostic. My world was bullshit.

***

I started to think about little Jonas. Then immediately about what sort of tortures Carol or other women in his life would be putting him through. I didn't want to think about that. I closed it off.

"Let's see what the next act is," I said cynically, my hand on the book. I was giddy. I felt that I was on a gigantic Ferris wheel and though I was presently falling, would soon be back on top again.

Life wasn't a puzzle anymore. Just stints between nightmares.

"What'll it be—what'll it be?" I muttered, looking down at the black-covered book. I had just about decided that whatever I found in the place where my fingers were could be my—what?—destiny?

Different books of the bible flashed in my mind's eye. The titles all in heavy Gothic script, the first letter of the text very ornate, the printing tiny and the wording arcane. Was this bible a King James version? A Revised Standard Gideon? The giddy idiots, as a self-proclaimed agnostic friend used to call them. Was it suitable for Catholics?

I sighed heavily. No sense putting it off. I opened the book to the place—my place. I didn't look down yet. I wished I had a cigarette.

I looked down, but instead of a biblical passage there was pasted in its place a page cut from another book. The printing was different and everything. It was glued right to the page.

I could see the small print of the original bible on the edges. This threw me, and I shuddered, like when a cloud passes in front of the sun on a chilly day.

I began reading.

I remembered the passage. It was from Antoine de Saint-Exupery's *Wind, Sand, and Stars*:

You, Bedouin of Libya who saved
lives, though you will dwell forever in
my memory yet I shall never be able to
recapture your features. You are
Humanity and your face comes into my
mind simply as man incarnate. You, our
beloved fellowman, did not know who we
might be, and yet you recognized us
without fail. And I, in my turn,
shall recognize you in the faces of
all mankind. You came towards me in
an aureole of charity and magnamiminity
bearing the gift of water. All my
friends and all my enemies marched
towards me in your person. It did not
seem to me that you were rescuing me:
rather did it seem that you were
forgiving me. And I felt I had no enemy
left in all the world.

I didn't know what to make of it. I quickly turned the
leaves, and in many places there were passages from other
works, other books and writings. Some were simply news
articles:

Miami—The state dropped
murder charges against William Paul
Hembree, the only white accused of
killing a black during the May 1980
Miami race riots. Defense attorneys
convinced the state that it was a
case of mistaken identity.

Others were cut from magazines, and some pages were covered with cartoons. There was a Doonsbury; a Peanuts; a Blechman I remembered chiefly from a big ad on the New York City subway.

I couldn't read anymore. It was getting too dark. I straightened out the many curled pages.

When I finished I was numb. I picked the book up and walked out of the hut.

The sand still felt warm from the departed sun. It was twilight, and the western sky glowed a coral pink that reminded me of so many winter sunsets I'd experienced on the Great South Bay on Long Island. I used to work right up until the sun dropped below the horizon. The air was clearer in the colder months. There wasn't that horrible temperature inversion, caused by the smog from New York City, that ruined the sunsets all summer long.

Sunsets were always pleasant in the winter if the wind dropped, as it did now. There was nothing to interfere with the glory of the ending day.

In the east the waxing moon had already begun to climb. A few stars were already in evidence. They foreshadowed a very clear night.

I began feeling the little cuts and bruises that I had in various places on my body. What I was doing here, I still didn't know, but I was already paying a price.

I was still on the north side of an island. Whether it was St John or not I couldn't tell. I walked up the beach a bit and quickly realized where I was. Le Duc, off the southeast end of St John, was straight out from the beach, from what's known as Hurricane Hole.

It was completely dark now. There were a few boats at anchor way up inside Coral Bay, one of the secluded harbors on

St John's east end. Then I saw a prick of light bobbing about on the swells that swept past between myself and the main island. I soon heard the whine of an outboard engine. One coming my way.

I could see someone in a Zodiac inflatable now. They were coming for me, I knew it. Whatever bullshit Randy was yammering about the night before was about to begin again.

Things weren't going right. I seemed to be spending most of my time knocked out and having nightmares. I was trying to straighten out my life, not twist it up into a one-way ticket to the loony bin. I'd already *been* there; I'd be fucked if I was going back.

I planted my feet in the sand and waited. Damned if I was moving. I'd just stay here until another boat load of regular people showed up. Fuck those lunatic creationist types up on the hill.

I wanted to shake my fists in the direction of Taylor's house, but then I noticed that I was still carrying that ersatz bible. And I really didn't know what I was mad at.

I held the bible out in front of me and clasped both hands over it. However strange it seemed to me, all the changes—the cut and paste job that someone had laboriously done, and over quite a long period of time—was relevant somehow.

I had just really glanced through it, but there was nothing—in all the articles, passages, or cartoons—that I wasn't familiar with. I recognized them. They were a part of my life, my intellectual being.

Certain responses were triggered in me that I had not felt in a long time. The additions, or changes, or whatever you want to call them had meaning for me in an emotionally and psychologically compelling way. I was drawn to each and every one.

I suddenly felt that whoever did do it, whoever had gone to all this trouble to restructure this bible, for whatever reason, was a kindred soul. It had to be someone like me, someone with the same intellectual tastes and desires.

The Zodiac ran up in the shallows about fifty feet away. The outboard was kicked up in the air by running aground so abruptly it screamed in protest. Whoever it was didn't know jack about beaching a dinghy or outboards.

The engine continued to scream. The prop being half out of the water made a fine spray which the Zodiac's occupant was trying to ward off as he tried to shut the thing down.

I heard a few well-thought-out curses, and had to smile in remembrance.

I mean, something like "cock-sucking glyptodont" you don't forget when you've heard it before and know what it is. A glyptodont is an extinct armadillo-like creature with fluted teeth.

There was only one person in the world I knew who swore with such imagination: Cal Franks.

I suddenly thought of that Judy Collins song where she sings, "You're like a rainbow coming 'round the bend."

I *was* really glad to see Calvin Franks—he was about as strange and as mystical as a '67 Pontiac. He may have fucked me over by leaving me for dead after I was arrested, but wasn't that the American way? And, for the moment, even though I knew the words would be clawing to be let out of my throat, I wasn't going to ruin things by questioning his motives in being here.

I liked Cal. He was a weird son of a bitch sometimes, but only because people usually let their own paranoid bullshit get in the way.

He *was* out to fuck ya—plain and simple. Nothing much

more than that. But when he wasn't trying to do you dirty, he was the best of friends. He had that all or nothing American aura about him that suggested straight shooting, whether from the hip or the heart. He might sell heroin to fifth graders, but he'd sell it to them at half price.

Cal was an American original: Right out of a Norman Rockwell done over by Ralph Steadman. If I was going to be really had, it might as well be by him.

The outboard engine had finally seized up and quit, the pistons melted to the cylinder walls, and Cal was slogging through the water to the beach like MacArthur returning to Bataan.

Cal looked like a military man—wearing a many-pocketed khaki jacket, a billed hat, and a fuck 'em all swagger that I know he always acquired when presented with anything he didn't really understand.

He wore the same outfit every summer. I remembered it from the Oak Beach days. He thought it made him look like Hemingway. A young Hemingway: dark hair, mustache and all. And Cal did. A fact, however, that was lost on the young female victims he chose to impress. But Carlos Baker would have come in his shorts.

"*You fuck!*" I greeted him with affection.

He started in on me right away, as was our custom: "I'll have you know, you bastard, that I left an important conference in Bucaramanga to be here tonight."

Then, from out of each great side pocket, he pulled sweat-beaded bottles of St Pauli Girl. With a churchkey that hung around his neck on a rosary chain he popped the caps off and handed me one. It was cold, too.

I was in a high, excited state. Like I'd done a handful of bennies or a potfull of *Bustelo*. I almost didn't want to drink the beer. I had the incredible thought that the bubbles would get into my bloodstream and I would explode with them as they burst...

"Your shrink is worried about you," Cal was saying as he lit two Camels in his mouth.

He passed me the cigarette. The glowing end in the darkness seemed comforting. I hadn't had a smoke in quite awhile and drew on it a little too quickly. It was harsh. I almost choked. And it made my head spin.

"Oh, yeah?" I answered him. I took a pull on the bottle. Fuck the bubbles.

I'd forgotten that I hadn't eaten in a long time. The beer seemed to pour down in me like a misty waterfall, filling my whole torso with a strange tingly sensation. I was completely empty, save that one swallow, which served to make me aware of the fact, and I felt great.

I took another puff from my cigarette. Thank you, God, for nicotine and alcohol...

"She seems to feel you ran away a little too soon," Cal went on. "Why the living fuck she got hold of *me*, I don't know. I guess you told her everything, you weasely prick. But she wants you to know that she's *concerned*. And..." He shuffled around in the sand a bit, drank some beer, then said, "And she wants me to say that I'm...I'm concerned too."

"Oh, yeah?"

"Is that all you can say? What am I supposed to do, go back and say, 'That's all he said, Jeannie. 'O yeah.'"

"Oh, yeah—" I couldn't help it.

"You're like an endoparasitic, you know that, you prick? You plant your shit inside somebody and then sit back and watch it hatch. Like that fucking monster in *Alien*."

"What?" I said, almost gagging on another swallow from my bottle. I was in store for another lecture.

"Well, it's good to see that your vocabulary's improved. You know, you look like Hell. You oughta get something to eat." He looked around, like maybe there was a deli or a Burger King right around the next corner. "But there ain't much here, is there?"

He pulled out another bottle and opened it. The empty he tossed to the sand behind me.

"You got another?" I asked. My own bottle I'd quickly drained also.

Cal smiled one of his snake-charming best and opened me one, too. We sat down in the sand.

"*Endoparasitism.* It's when a parasite enters your body and slowly eats its way out. The classic is the ichneumon fly, which really isn't a fly, but a wasp. *The females – of course*—locate an appropriate host and then convert it into a food factory for their own young. They pierce the host with their ovipositor and deposit eggs in it. Usually, the poor bastard doesn't know what's happened. At least until the eggs hatch and the ichneumon larvae begin their grim work of interior excavation. They usually choose caterpillars for this. But on the human scale you can draw an analogy with the insatiable desire of women—and men—" nodding at me, "to inject insidious ideas and feelings in someone. Until these turn into emotions which eat their way, growing all the time, through the pitiful host's psyche."

He paused, savoring his abrupt classification.

"And so?"

"And so? What's the matter with you, does everything have to be spelled out?"

"Yeah. Oh, yeah."

"Aw right. This leaves a void, a spiritual death—where the host feels a nothingness, an emptiness where there was once substance. A fucking void that once created needs to be filled, only to be emptied, again and again. But that's pretty far out in left field."

"What do you mean, then?"

"Look, fuck-face. I'm sorry about cutting you loose down in Charleston. O.K.?"

So there it was. An apology. From Cal. Anything could happen now. I found myself wondering how much they'd paid him to come here and be buddy-buddy with me again.

Cal had mentioned Jeannie. Was she here, too? Had Cal seen Nadine? Where was Julian?

A month or so ago—it had to only that long, though it seemed like forever—I used to think my life was like a country and western song. Now it was getting to be more like a soap opera.

I looked over at the big island of St John. They maybe had that telescope on the south deck trained right down here now. If nothing else, maybe I could get some answers from Cal. He liked to talk. For once I had some real questions.

"Are you one of them, Cal?" I asked. Might as well jump right in with both feet. I was feeling pretty good now, a little buzz on.

He poured down his beer in one long gulp. Very macho. I knew I'd hit a good button.

"I don't know what the fuck you're talking about," he said.

"You know. They're up there now, waiting for you to soften me up. For whatever reason."

"You're a paranoid fuck, you know that? But I'm not a creationist, if that's what you mean."

This was my opening. "Tell me about it, Cal."

"Yeah," he said slowly. Then: "Jonas, the things we do

in this life are unexplainable and inexplicable, enigmatic and inscrutable. You know, even ole Charley Darwin there thought there seemed to be too much suffering in the world. He even mentioned the ichneumon fly when he wrote that he couldn't persuade himself that a beneficent and omnipotent God could create such a thing. Or that a cat should play with mice before killing them, for that matter. But he never tried to find any anti-religious ethic in nature, much as your friends would like to believe."

"They're not my friends! I don't know what the fuck is going on," I blurted out angrily, then stopped. Who knows how much Cal knew, anyway? He was looking at me with that half-drunk arrogant leer of his that was usually reserved for eighteen-year-ole girls and slow bartenders.

"They're *not* your friends," he said strangely, as if I was a child, and caught in a lie.

"NO."

He started to say something, stopped, then started to say something else, as if he had made a decision: "It doesn't matter anyway. Things'll either work out, or they won't."

All right. "What about Darwin? What were you saying about finding an anti-religious ethic in nature?"

"Charles Robert Darwin. *The Origin of Species.* Supercargo on the good ship *Beagle.* He said, in effect, that all species of plants and animals developed from earlier forms by hereditary transmission of slight variations in successive generations. This means," and he pulled out yet another bottle of St Pauli Girl, opened it, and drank heavily. "This means," he went on, "that we've evolved from other forms of life, as it were. And these *present* forms of life, including thee and me, are those which are best adapted to their environment."

"Well, that's pretty obvious. There's always the winners

and the losers," I said, though it was depressing to me, seeing where I stood. "It's a theory, though, right? What's the problem with it?"

"The *Problem*, Jonas, is today. Right now, the modern creationists are accusing the evolutionists of preaching a doctrine called secular humanism. They're demanding equal time for their views. Which holds that man was created in the image of God, and so on. They think Darwin doesn't account for *evil* in his theory. And we all know that there are two sides to everything, don't we? Black and white? Good and—"

Cal stopped suddenly, as if the fillip to 'Good' wasn't adequate enough.

"You know," he went on just as suddenly, but speaking measuredly, thinking it out—"There are *four.* There have to be. Jonas—we've forgotten the nuclear age. There are four sides to everything, just like there are four basic forces in the universe."

He'd be really off and running now. I was lost. "What're you talking about? It's always been a dichotomy. Good versus Evil. That's the basis. Us against them. Whatever you want to label the other guy doesn't really matter. Like you said."

Cal had a strange grin on his face. He was a lot like Julian in many ways. Only he was a reader and thinker instead of a doer and maker. I had to like him. He made me wonder and dream.

"Energy, Jonas. Fucking energy. 'E' equals mass times the speed of light—squared. Einstein had it. Inert mass is simply latent energy. When Bob Oppenheimer and the boys on the Manhattan Project split the atom they unleashed into nature—as we know it, earth-bound assholes that we are—the basic energy of the cosmos. Like all that garbage up there..." He included the universe above us with a wave of his beer bottle, now empty.

"You got anymore of those?" I asked him.

"In the boat."

I waded out to the Zodiac and retrieved a sodden cardboard case of St Pauli Girl. He had style, Cal did.

"This energy, Jonas," Cal went on, "this fantastic power, is held locked in the nucleus by a force known as the strong force, which is the glue that holds the nucleus together. And there's also what is called the weak force, which is manifested in radioactive decay. You following me so far?"

He was shouting at me as I humped the case of beer through the shallows. "Yeah," I shouted back. "The strong force and the weak force—"

"These forces are chiefly responsible for the static properties of nuclei. These are nuclear forces. But there are two other forces outside the nucleus, which, until the explosion of nuclear weapons, had been responsible for virtually all life and motion on the earth since the goddamn beginning four and a half billion years ago."

Cal paused to pop open a bottle each. We were getting cooked, and it felt good.

"Yeah. The electromagnetic force, which is responsible for, among other things, all chemical bonds, and the gravitational force, which is the force of attraction between masses."

"So much for the physics lesson, professor—" I saluted him with, putting my bottle bottom up.

I knew that Cal would keep on going no matter what I said, or did. It didn't matter what I already knew. He always covered a subject thoroughly, especially when half-sloshed, like he was now. My roll was to play the still-wet-behind-the-ears freshman, suitably awed, but allowed to snicker now and then. Such was our relationship.

He went on: "Nineteenth century science never knew about

the nuclear forces. They believed in the law of conversation of energy and the law of conservation of mass. They thought that they were two closed systems. Another dichotomy, as you would say. But there's more to it than that. No wonder Darwin was mystified! The whole subject of evil he felt was just too profound for the human intellect. He put it very succinctly: 'A dog might as well speculate on the mind of Newton.' And a dog, like us, will get no further as long as he stays there, locked into that two-sided cage. Newtonian physics was human-scale physics. It wasn't until twentieth century physicists, pursuing their investigations into the realms of the irreducibly small and the unexceedably large, examined the properties of energy, mass, time, and space in the subatomic realm that mass and energy were discovered to be interchangeable entities."

"So *what* does that all *mean?*" I asked. I felt we were getting pretty far away from what I wanted to know. And now I wasn't even sure what it was that I did want to know, or if it even mattered. Detailed analysis did that sometimes.

Then I answered my own question: "Good and evil are just part of the same equation then."

Cal grinned. I had an *A* so far.

"Somewhat," he said. "The problem lies in that either the closer or the farther away you get to or from something the more realms become apparent. We stumble alone until *Aha!* We think we have the answer. The trouble is that the whole train of human thought and action you've been climbing on to reach this pinnacle becomes inverted. You are put in the position of then convincing this monolithic culture, that now lies heavily on your tired shoulders, that you've opened a new door. And beyond that door lies something *more*. But, just like Atlas, Ayn Rand notwithstanding, you can't shrug the world off. And it's gonna fuck you."

"But what about Einstein and Darwin? They made those quantum leaps, and they weren't screwed. They had to deal with a lot of bullshit, at first. But so did the Wright brothers, and everybody else. We're gaining on it, aren't we?"

"That's just it, Jonas. It's not the individual that gets punched in the balls. It's us. *All* of us. To get back to the mathematics of it—remember Hiroshima? The amount of mass expended in that city's destruction was about a *gram*—a lousy twenty-seventh of an ounce. It just takes a little bit, Jonas. The equation is woefully unbalanced on one side, and this monstrous disproportion between the basic power of the universe and the poor bastards by which and against it was aimed in anger defined the god-awful predicament that the world has tried, and failed, mind you, to come to terms with ever since. It's the same sorry story over and over again.

"There's another equation here, if you will, that's analogous to Einstein's: Make E stand for evil, M stand for good, and C—"

He traced out the equation in the sand with the tip of an empty beer bottle. "Make C stand for the mind of man. I won't honor it by calling it intelligent."

"Wonderful analogy, Cal. With that sort of reasoning I wonder how you ever got so far—if you got anywhere at all. Stick to anthropology or biology or whatever—"

"Christ, don't you see? Inert goodness, like inert mass—the type that people profess, but don't really *do*—the yea sayers, the knee-jerk liberals, the bleeding hearts, the rapacious industrialists 'making a better world,' the phony preachers with their fire and brimstone sermons and their new limousines, the politicians with one hand patting the poor man's back and the other in his pocket, any type of government welfare that ends up in a corrupt morass—all the good intentioned busybodies with their plans to rid the world of pain and suffering by making it safe for democracy or socialism or name your own tune—any religion, including Dr. Taylor up there with his Second Coming bullshit. It's just another scam, Jonas. It's called 'let's take a *phenomena* and capitalize on it.'

"Something weird and strange happens and all the operators want to get in on the act. And they're all full to the gut-busting point with good intentions..."

"'Good intentions mean sloppy shit,'" I said, laughing into my bottle.

"What?" Cal said.

I had him there for a moment. Julian and Cal were like two particles from the same atom. One had just been in school too long.

"You're right, you know. Just like the paving stones on that well-known road. Inert goodness is simply latent evil."

Cal said the last like a final pronouncement. But I wanted to hear more. Especially what he'd let drop about 'Doc' Taylor. All the freshman theorizing aside, I knew I was being groomed for something. Cal was a friend, of a sort, and I wasn't too sure I could trust him. But I was rapidly reaching the point where I had to let loose with a few ideas of my own. The only trouble was the usual: I had the dreaded habit of either saying too much too soon, or too little too late.

It seemed that whenever I reached a point where, as Frost put it, the path diverged in the wood, I choked; inevitably I always ended up on the wrong path. And I still didn't know this late in the game whether I was letting myself be pushed down that easy road to Hell or I was subconsciously following some inner impulse to fuck myself.

But for the first time in my life I felt clean and empty inside. The beer just made it more apparent. I was blasted, but in a way that made sense. I was clear.

"*What* is scientific creationism, Cal?"

He looked at me from the corner of his eye, a bottle at his lips. I know he was thinking that I was a stupid asshole for asking such a question. I had the feeling that to him it was like St Peter asking, "What *is* Christianity, anyhow?" He'd humor me, though.

"A pseudo scientific version of the story of divine creation told in the Old Testament Book of Genesis," he stated sarcastically.

That's what Nadine had said, only without the 'pseudo.'

I had to know how Cal really felt. He was a good bullshit artist, and maybe he was just stringing me along.

"Why does it have to be scientific? What's the matter with plain old down-home faith? People believe. They don't have to be pumped up with 'facts.'"

"Maybe you *don't* know that much," Cal said, lighting another Camel. He looked at the burning cigarette for a moment, like he expected an enigmatical answer from it. "These aren't too bad—not my brand, but what the hell."

"Give me one," I asked. He tossed me the one he'd just lit and stuck another in his mouth.

The night was warm, and the air still. Our smoke rose straight up into the clear sky toward the moon, which was at its zenith now. We sat there awhile in silence, just inhaling beer and leaving my question alone.

It was a night for sempiternal lovers and peasant poets; I found myself wishing there were still some around to enjoy it. Hell, I wanted to enjoy it—and maybe I was.

The bottles lay around us like the trees around Mount St Helen's. Cal got up to piss. I was watching the sky, and a few meteors came crashing through the atmosphere. One zigged straight across from east to west. I watched it fall somewhere in the northwestern sector.

I had to blink a few times for that one. Usually this time of year the Geminid meteors provide quite a show. Sometimes fifty an hour when conditions are right.

But not like that last one.

I stood up, trying to see where it had gone. Maybe it wasn't a meteor. Maybe another man-made satellite was biting the dust somewhere in North America right now. Then I saw something that I really couldn't explain...

A star was rising in the northwest.

"Cal? Come here—or stay there. Look to the northwest, just over the tip of the mountain on St John."

I heard him come up behind me. "Ahh—the *phenomena!* She rises!" He grunted as he bent down to get another bottle.

"It's *rising*, Cal. There's a goddamn star, or planet, or something, rising in the goddamn northwest."

"You want one?" Cal asked from down in the sand.

"Cal—"

"Sit down, Jonas. I've been thinking..." He sat down heavily, or rolled over, and with one hand dragged me down alongside him.

"Cal, you *see* that?"

It was definitely rising, and getting brighter. Maybe it was Darth Vader in the Deathstar—

"Yeah, I see it. And I see something else. Jonas, you may be a pariah—a King Midas in reverse, turning everything you touch into shit—but I'll be fucked if I'll let you be a sacrificial lamb."

There was a new tone in Cal's voice that I felt comfortable with. Like the overly dramatic sarcasm that comes with truth.

"Let's start at the beginning," he said. "We may do this dialectically if you'd like—for I only know what I think at the moment I know. You get me? Sometimes the Socratic method leaves a lot to be desired."

"But what about…" I began to say, gesturing towards the 'phenomena,' as he called it, coming up bright and strong on the wrong side of the sky.

"Inscrutable phenomena we'll leave out for the time being. Let's start with something I'm more familiar with. Freud, for one."

"Freud? What the fuck does he have to do with this? I'm already in the midst of a nervous breakdown, goddamn it."

"Exactly."

"…I'm probably dreaming…"

"Could be."

"…I'm drunk…"

"Me, too."

"'Gestalt! Gestalt!'" I suddenly cried out, bleating goat-like, gesticulating—mimicking some poor bastard I'd seen freaking out on acid almost fifteen years before.

"You got it, Jonas! It's unanalyzable. You just gotta go with it."

I shoved the 'bible' at him. "What's this?"

"That's *your* life. I've got one too. So does everybody else. We've all got our own copy. The only thing different is…"

He laughed crazily then, and so did I. It was lunacy. Two losers on a moon-struck beach on a hot night in a purgatorial paradise.

"…is the text!"

I started scraping the bottom of my bottle with its cap. The sound reminded me of crickets on a long forgotten summer night when I was a little boy, and the sweet honey-suckle smell of the hedgerow growing on our back fence seemed to come with the sound, and how entranced I was then by the texture of the night and its all-enveloping fullness.

That's why I liked that sound. If Cal wanted to take the cap away now I'd make him eat it.

I felt the same now as I did then as a child. It didn't matter where I was. I just didn't want to wake up under starched white sheets with US Public Health stamped on them.

"So start with Freud," I said.

"It'll be easier that way," Cal sighed. "According to the master, man has received two major blows from science. And all, mind you, in a relatively short period of time. One is that the earth is *not* the center of the universe. You must remember from history all the bullshit *that* caused. Talk about trauma!

"Every child goes through the same trip. The ego suffers an irreplaceable loss. And you know the problems that ensue on an individual level—we have to deal with it every day of our lives—whether within ourselves or with someone else. But we dealt with it. Rather society or civilization did. Whether we ever really *believed* it is another matter."

He shut up for a couple of minutes, as if he was trying to believe it himself. Or wanted to and could not.

"What's the second? You said there was two," I asked. But I knew.

"The second blow—yes, the second wave, so to speak—maybe the last," he began contemplatingly, as if in ruminating on it he saw something that shouldn't be broached. But that was my opinion. Cal's compunctions were rarely my own.

"The second was Darwin's baby. And he wasn't alone in it, much as Galileo and Copernicus weren't either in *their* hypotheses. But *this* blow we're still reeling from.

"It's with us now, and the sting is almost unbearable. Think of the child, Jonas. The child who not only finds out that he's not the *all* that he thought he was, but also that he's just another orphan. Like all the other poor creatures who share this cold alien world.

"Basically, evolution tells us that not only does Man not

have a privileged place in creation, but that he's descended from the animal kingdom. He's kin to the rest of the beasts whom he's trampled on and domesticated and beaten down in the name of civilization..."

"*But so what!* We're on top!" I cried. "I mean, we *won*, didn't we?"

"Interesting that you put it that way. We won, huh?"

"Yeah."

"I wish it were that simple," Cal said. He sighed. "Let me tell you something. Or ask you: Do you think there are any winners in a nuclear war? No, of course you don't. We've *had* this discussion."

He wasn't going to get off that easily. "But you're a biologist. A scientist—of a sort. *I* know that you are just another dope dealer. But isn't the central principle of modern biology evolution?"

"Yes, it is," he answered slowly. "But Darwin's theory of evolution remains an outrage to millions of people...perhaps *because* it's an inescapable inference, and *not* a raw datum...who knows? It's not what *is*. It's, rather, what *appears* to be."

"You're losing me again," I said.

"Look, do you know who Louis Agassiz was?"

"Somewhat. I think so. Nineteenth century scientist who defended slavery, I think—one of Darwin's detractors."

"He was a great man, in many ways," Cal said. "Even though his views were...but anyway, you know, of course, of the Galapagos. The *Encantadas* of Melville?"

"I know," I told him. "I read the poetry. I know that Darwin did a lot of work there."

"Did you know that, just before he died, Agazziz went there? He was so intent on disproving his famous adversary that he had to check it out for himself. And do you know what he found? Nothing. And do you know why?"

"No, I don't know why. It amazes me that he'd even go there. The man was a terrible bigot, not that I remember."

"That's besides the point, but it meshes in, I guess. Agassiz was simply too committed and defensive to be receptive to the signal that Darwin—young, restless, searching—was attuned to. Hell, Darwin was still in his twenties when he went there, of course. Agassiz had a year to live when he first saw the islands, but that was it! The man just couldn't *see!*"

I felt like that I probably couldn't see it either. "Like what? I read the *Voyage of the Beagle*."

"So did a lot of people, but I'll give you an example: There are birds there called masked boobies. Their egg-laying areas, on bare rock, mind you, are strewn with appropriate bits of twigs and other nesting materials that adults gather for their mutual displays. And that's all it is. A display. Once they lay the eggs—or before, I forget which—they sweep the stuff out of the egg-laying area to lie unused upon the ground."

"So what?" I asked.

"Don't you think it's curious? I mean, a nest is used to protect the eggs. But the boobies gather all the makings and then just kick it away when you'd think it was needed most. This change in function is a primary proof of evolution. Their actions only made sense in the light of a previous inherited history."

"I can see that," I said. "I remember the boobies now. No wonder they're called *boobies*...but how do the creationists see that today? There's enough evidence, isn't there, on the evolution side to prove it—or at least make a logical assumption."

"Logic!" Cal snorted. "Hah! How the sweet Jesus can you sit there and talk about logical assumption! There's *nothing* logical about it! Evolution is an *inference*, not fact! In a sense it's almost like religious faith. You have to weigh the evidence and choose."

Now he was being confusing again. "Whose side are you on, anyway? Where do you stand—or, better yet, just *what* do you stand *for?*" I demanded.

Just because he had obviously been thinking this over for himself out loud didn't matter. I considered Cal to be amoral. Or nonmoral, like the evolutionist's conception of nature.

He laughed, and answered me: "For truth, justice, and the American way!"

"And I'm Yoda," I countered. "Come on, this is serious."

"Hoo hah," Cal sighed, bringing himself down. Then he started singing: "'Drinks before dinner, and wine with dinner, and after dinner drinks...'"

He was really drunk now. Once he started singing the lecture was usually over. But I was no closer to my part in this thing than I was before. Maybe I was dreaming all this.

I grabbed Cal by the shoulders and started shaking him. The son of a bitch. He knew a fuck of a lot more than I did, and I told him so. For a dream he felt pretty solid and after awhile I got tired of trying to get him to come around. I sat back on the sand and then just lay back, my arms stretched over my head.

Damn it.

I wasn't getting anywhere. Evolution—creationism. What the hell did I know? I was a clamdigger at best and a scholar at worst—but I read the papers occasionally, and had subscribed to various magazines, at different times—from the Atlantic Monthly to the New Yorker to Popular Mechanics and Newsweek. Whatever subscriber coupons that came my way and one didn't have to send any money in with, I sent in and got that rag for however long they thought I was good for. I got all the slicks at one time or another, including High Times, Screw, and Mother Earth News.

I liked to read. It filled in the gaps between depressions.

It made me forget how alone I was much of the time. Movies and the tube did the same thing, but then I was stuck to a timetable again; besides, with the video media I couldn't flip back to catch what I'd missed when my mind started wandering.

I did know something about evolution—fundamentalist Christians were making it a public issue once again. Their head was that the view of man as a direct genealogical descendant of lower beasts spawns a materialistic, antireligious ethic and that teaching it in the schools is responsible for the rise in crime and general moral decay of society. The big interest seemed to be focused on these ethical implications.

Good and evil, again.

I remembered talking with Nadine about it that night in Key Biscayne. We were talking about the schools, and the inroads the creationists had made.

"You know, Jonas, that as far back—recently, I mean—as 1969 we…"

That Nadine considered herself to be one of them was a fact I didn't fully realize until now. I knew it, but just didn't *realize* it.

"…got California to teach evolution and creation as competing theories."

I had read something about that, and to impress her I mentioned it: "But wasn't that revoked? Isn't creationism looked upon by the courts as religion? Don't you think it's ironic that scientific creationism is based on the untestable, unprovable act of a *creator?* Which should disqualify it as a science anyway."

"Don't be too sure," she said.

"Sure of what?"

"Untestable and unprovable."

"What?"

She got up and went to the bathroom or someplace. But now I remember the look on her face: supreme confidence.

I'd always known Nadine as cracked. She'd done enough mushrooms and other mind-blowing chromosome re-zoning chemicals to unhinge the august heads on Mount Rushmore. She didn't seem to be proselytizing as hard anymore, like she'd done with her better-world-through-cosmic-awareness-through-chemistry trip. Maybe because she wasn't alone now in her quest. She was easier to talk with, anyway. But everytime I did talk with her I seemed to lose my senses. Like just being around her was soporiferous.

Maybe from all the drugs she'd done she just exuded their special properties into the breathable atmosphere, affecting everyone near her. I know Julian sure had changed.

But what was happening to me? Nadine was a catalyst, I was almost sure of that. What'd she say, just before I'd passed out, or been drugged possibly, by inference or osmosis, in the midst of the Gulf Stream?

"Do you know why you are called Jonas?" she'd asked.

Jonas. Jonah. Nineveh. What *did* I know?

The biblical story was straightforward enough. The reluctant prophet fleeing from the Lord's command: 'Go to Nineveh and tell them they got forty days or else.'

But he didn't go. Jonas ran away, causing a lot of hardship for those poor bastards on the boat. Finally they ditch him. He even admits to being the cause, forever after creating in folklore and literature the Jonah stigma.

God sends Leviathan to gobble Jonah up, and Jonah repents, and then goes to do his duty. But even then he balks. He wanted to see some action, but God cuts loose the city of Nineveh from destruction when the people heed His messenger. They put on sackcloth and sat in ashes...

Sackcloth. Whenever I see that word I think of clams. And the burlap bags we'd put them in to sell. I used to love the smell of those bags. Most of them were former potato sacks, and they had such a solid rich aroma. You hardly see those burlap sacks anymore. Most of the bags that are used for today for holding clams are synthetic, and formerly used for holding onions instead of potatoes. No smell at all, just a few old onion skin flakes.

Why *was* I named Jonas?

I never could figure out any significance to the name for me. I may have wondered about it, but I just let it go. My father named me, I suppose. All the Coffeys had biblical names.

My father was Amos, my son Jonas, my dog Ezekiel. And we weren't even Jewish. But speaking of that, Jonah meant 'dove' in Hebrew. I'd been born a war-child, while my father had been a liaison officer with the British forces in Palestine. I'd first seen the light of day in Cadiz, my mother on the run—I don't think she saw the States or my father until after the war.

The symbolism of the Book of Jonah I'd delved into before, while still a 'student.' For a while there I'd been interested, but had run into a block whenever I'd remotely broached the subject with my parents. They wanted me to be an engineer, something which I had no proclivity towards whatsoever.

Jesus refers to Jonah in Matthew and Luke. The three days and three nights Jonah spends in the whale's belly Jesus used as a symbol of his own death and resurrection. And that the people of Nineveh repented at Jonah's preaching was a means for Jesus to reproach the Jews of his time for their unwillingness to repent.

It seemed that one could view the story as history because there is a reference to a prophet Jonah in II Kings. It's better as a parable, but there are those who allege that to challenge the historicity of Jonah is to set in question the whole idea of the resurrection.

And round and round it goes...

CHAPTER TWENTY

I lay there going over things that I hadn't thought of for twenty years. Maybe I was just going into male menopause...

I heard a rumbly sound. It crashed into the quiet night like a low-scaled quake. I looked over at Cal, but he'd stopped singing to himself and staring towards the point at the tip of Le Duc where it points toward the little bay called Hard Labor on St John.

It wasn't an earthquake, though I wouldn't have been surprised. The sound came from a pair of engines; powerful engines.

I sat up.

I could hear them better now, though they were still some distance away.

"Where?" I whispered.

Cal cleared his throat and said, "The point. Just coming around."

I squinted in that direction and could just make out a sleek-hulled monster of a boat heading our way. They'd probably figured Cal had spent enough time with me...

I looked at Cal again. I had an instinctive sense of danger; I knew it was getting through to him. He knew as well as I did that he'd come as a Trojan horse. But I hoped they'd miscalculated. I had an inkling of what was going on. I wanted to know more, but not at the hands of Randy—Dr.

Rand—Nadine, Taylor, the *Devin*, and the rest of the crew. And Cal was still a good pump, if I could just keep him primed, bullshit and all.

"Let's Go!"

Cal got up and stumbled over the beer bottles after me. Those damn bottles made such a hedonistic sight on that pretty beach. I almost wanted to clean up. No time now—

We got in the Zodiac and started paddling. There were some mangroves on the other side of Le Duc, and if we could make it there in time we'd be safe until daylight. It was an extremely small place, not well known at all, but somehow a colony of mangroves had started here in amongst the hard rock and hard luck of a desert Caribbean island.

The mangroves. I hated swamps and anything to do with them. The idea of all those roots and branches and dripping leaves gave me the creeps. Especially in the dark.

We made it in time.

We had to squeeze the Zodiac into them, pushing and shoving until we were wedged in there, almost impaled in places. I hated it; it was sticky and slickly wet. Paradise flip-flopped.

"Shit."

"What's the matter?" Cal said.

"I *don't like this*," I hissed. "Reminds me of the jungle."

"It is the fucking jungle. You were in Vietnam, right? You oughta be used to this."

"I wasn't a grunt. We flew over this shit. I never had to wade through it."

I wanted to tell Cal to be careful. There were poison trees in here, like in Palua, in the Republic of Belau in the South Pacific, where the trees exuded a black sap that blisters the skin and would swell your eyes shut. I don't know why I thought of that now—Palua. But I'd been there once, on a diving expedition in my early days. Palua was a paradise, too. And all I remembered was the poison trees.

The big speed boat had made directly for the spot we'd vacated. They were carefully sweeping the beach with small flashlights, remaining just far enough off the beach to avoid running up like Cal had earlier.

I almost felt like giving in. I really didn't know why we were hiding; there didn't seem to be that much danger. No one had tried to hurt me, and as far as I was concerned, I was still in some crazy dream.

It seemed that way. Only I couldn't quite make myself believe it.

The current kept our pursuers—I imagine they were our pursuers—moving along the beach. We could see them through the tangled growth. The boat I recognized as a high-speed Magnum—a half million dollar sixty-knot rich man's toy. When their weak flashlight beams picked up the pile of empty St Pauli Girl bottles the engines growled loudly, stopping their forward motion. Then the boat backed up with a great churning and thrashing of the water.

"Uh-oh," Cal whispered.

I didn't say anything. We'd be all right, I figured, if they didn't land on the beach. On this side of Le Duc, there wasn't enough water for them to stay in close.

The Magnum seemed to hesitate a moment, then pointed directly at the beach towards a spot where the bottom dropped off quickly. She came straight into this spot, and her knife-like bow pushed gently up on the dry sand.

"Jesus—"

"Yeah—"

Three got out, jumping down off the high bow. The

helmsman stayed behind, keeping her in gear so the current didn't loosen their hold. Two of them made quickly for the hut where I'd awakened just before sundown. The other stopped at the pile of bottles.

"*Immonde pourceau,*" he grunted angrily.

I wanted to giggle. I had the sudden thought that these guys were Park Rangers, and we'd be hauled in for littering. But why the French? We may have been pigs, like he said, but something else bothered me about him. A bit too familiar.

The others came back from the hut. "Nothing," one of them reported.

"They're gone then. That Jew son of a bitch!"

He kicked the bottles, and a couple of them broke. The sound muffled on the sand.

"They can't be far. They only got the dinghy," one said, his voice and body outline familiar also. I knew they weren't Park Rangers, unless one of them answered to the name of Klaus.

"We should have finished programming him first. If that Hebe got him drunk it could wipe out everything!"

The leader, or so it seemed, ordered the two others to search up the beach. They split up, each going to opposite ends of the island.

It was dark, but now I knew who the Frog was—Randy. I never liked him. There was always something wrong there. As if his quick-change act and multi-tongued ability was inherently...evil.

Le Duc is a small island. It's more like an appendage that was cut off from the mainland of St John millennia ago by a rising ocean. The whole thing can be circumnavigated by dinghy in twenty minutes. Randy's henchmen—I didn't know what else to call them now—were back very quickly.

Seeing Randy in this way made me feel cold, as if I'd been roughly awakened from a pleasant day-dream of verdant summer hills and dales to a flat landscape of ash-gray emptiness. I was scared.

Pieces of my dreams—that merciless night on that Vietnamese river bar with Scott Shaw; other nightmares came bombarding back, certain images—those of impending doom; dread; callous guards and hooligans; wanton destruction and fiendish manipulation—all were cascading on me like incinerating showers.

I couldn't stop it.

I began shaking. Flushes—hot and cold—came over me in waves. I felt my teeth chattering. I feared for my lips and tongue. It wouldn't do to bleed now. Suppose I had some of that poison sap on me?

Cal reached over and put his arm around my shoulders. His touch was immensely reassuring. My palpitations stopped as suddenly as they began.

"They're leaving," he said.

"Thanks."

"They're leaving, I said."

"Yeah. Thanks, Cal."

He grunted. "Don't mention it."

The fuck. He had to be macho even in the clutch. But I felt a lot better. The fear was gone. I owed him.

I thought of what we talked about before. Of Einstein, and Cal's crazy rendering of $E=MC2$. I remembered reading once where, in a discussion on the coldness of scientific method and thought, someone said that scientists seemed determined to reduce the mystery of the universe to a few equations. Einstein just laughed, and said, "It's conceivable they will. But don't worry. It would be forever inadequate. Something like representing a Beethoven symphony by air pressure curves."

Darwin and Einstein. What a pair they would have made if they could have worked together. And had a nut case like Cal Franks as a lab assistant. With Freud as department chairman.

The Magnum was searching the stretch of water between Le Duc and St John. I could see their pitiful flashlights working the edge of the reef along Hard Labor, and then down to Johnson's Bay. Whoever was at the wheel knew the waters here.

They kept heading down into Coral Bay. I wondered if the *Melchoir* was still on the north side of the island, in Leinster Bay. I was a little worried about Julian—Randy sounded definitely menacing.

"You know those guys?" I asked Cal.

"You mean the *Nazi* and his boys?"

"Interesting that you should put it that way. Why don't you start leveling with me? Who is Randy—Dr. Rand—and what are you doing here, anyway?"

Might as well get down to it. It was going to get light pretty soon. We'd have to make a move before then. And I didn't want to do anything yet until I knew the score. At least as much as Cal knew.

"Well, this is another fine mess you've gotten me into," he said.

"Come on, you bastard. I'm just one of the idiots around here. Probably half a robot by now." Those words, 'We should have finished programming him first—' rankled deep within me, like a steel ball in a slow-moving pinball machine.

Cal sighed. It was one of his late-night-drunk sighs, but one that usually signaled a retching up of true insight, however painful.

"Rand's banging Nadine," he said.

"What?" He *would* be thinking of his cuckolded cock, no matter how ridiculous that notion was now.

He turned toward me with a strange look of triumph. "So, you think your great friend Julian's so wonderful? Ha. From the way I see it, your Dr. Rand's been getting in her pants for quite some time now. Your buddy's just a stooge—they're keeping him around until they get *you* all finished."

I grabbed him, almost tossing us both out of the Zodiac.

"You fuck! Why the Christ have you been bullshitting me all goddamn night with your philosophic crap! What'd Randy mean by 'programming?' Huh? You son of a bitch!"

We struggled back and forth; then I got one of the paddles across his throat and held him down. I felt like crushing the life out of him right there.

"Jonas!" he rasped. "Stop. They said it was too late. You were one of them. I didn't believe them until I heard the tapes!"

Tapes?

"What're you talking about? You fuck—"

"Let...me...go," Cal pleaded.

Why not? Maybe I'd learn something. I had the feeling that I still had a chance. At anything. Whatever Cal was, I knew he was human. There was too much pain and anger in him to be extinguished.

I let up on him. He slipped back down the rubber side of the Zodiac and lay exhausted in the bilge.

"What's the matter?" Cal asked, whining. His voice was hoarse and breathless.

The question struck me at first as asinine. How was I supposed to respond to that? I was the one who should be asking. Not him. And I had a lot of other questions that I couldn't seem to get answered...

What's the matter.

It suddenly came to me that Cal was innocent. Of a sort. He was a bastard, but he truly needed to ask the question. He wasn't the masterly improviser of evil deeds who already knows the answer—like Iago out to screw Othello. No, he was another dupe. Like me and Julian.

Maybe even Nadine was too—all of us lost in an incomprehensible world and prodded along like simple cattle who think because they have the run of the pasture they have it made.

I remembered bits and pieces of things that, if taken together, should have probably made sense. That there was something wrong; something to watch out for, whether immediately or in the future. I always seemed to retrospectively chide myself for 'not picking up on the vibes,' as Jeannie used to tell me.

Like Julian asking, "Do we really need it?" or dropping something about 'Nazis everywhere' in that phone 'conversation' we'd had so long ago.

Nazis everywhere.

I remember Nadine, late at night, as we drove non-stop through the South to that fateful disaster outside Charleston, reciting from Sylvia Plath, her voice in a child's singsong:

Every woman adores a Fascist,

The boot in the face, the brute

brute heart of a brute like you.

I could picture her now, her long yellow straight hair swinging in the shadows as she rocked to and fro in the VW van, keeping time with the rhythm of the highway—

But they pulled me out of the sack,

And they stuck me together with glue.

And then I knew what to do.

I made a model of you,
A man in black with a Meinkampf look

And a love of the rack and the screw.
And I said I do, I do.

She had Plath's meaning all skewered. This was no
lament for her. *She liked it*, that hard brittle bite of Freudian
self-knowledge.

Saps like Cal and Julian were only way-stops between
Auschwitz and Dachau. And I was another, only now we were
all going along for the ride. If such a thing as Evil existed, or
be inherent in something, then this was it.

The resistance of experience to meaning was something I
had to overcome somehow, no matter the bizarre circumstances
I chose to begin with. It didn't matter what I did, so long as
I ceased pounding away at intractable barriers and stepped,
climbed, or flew over them—

Psychopathic reality, here I come!

I felt exhilarated in that moment. I didn't know how long
it would last, or gave a damn. I was purged. But like the man
who only knows he's hungry when his stomach's empty, I had
a yen to fill myself again. But if I did, it didn't matter—I'd
had the feeling.

That was enough.

"Everything—" I answered Cal.

"What?" he panted, still getting his breath back after I'd
choked him.

"...and nothing. You got another cigarette?"

CHAPTER TWENTYONE

It was mid-morning by the time we'd made it up the mountain through the undergrowth to just below that cantilevered, multi-leveled, imperially situated house of 'Doctor' Taylor's.

If nothing else, I felt they wouldn't be looking for us around here.

Plus, I was on a mission. I had to hear those 'tapes' Cal had mentioned. He'd elaborated some, and told me that some of them were translated transcriptions made of the ancient scrolls that Leigh had pirated out of Jerusalem. And I wanted a look at the real thing, if they were there.

But I really wanted to hear the recordings of my own babblings. Probably while I was on the *Melchoir*, and perhaps on Le Duc while I was 'asleep.'

I'd put a few things together on my own and with what Cal told me. Nadine's intensive knowledge of hallucinogenic and other mind bending drugs was at the top of the list. Julian's and my own strange behavior and dreams were typical of a type of deluded psychosis prevalent among paranoid schizophrenics—exactly *how* I didn't know yet. Nadine certainly had the background and was crazy enough.

And she knew about me. My already tender emotional state and previous traumatic experiences; including the breakdowns I'd weathered through. Or at least I was pretty sure she knew. I couldn't remember what I'd told her about myself—I was closed about it with everybody, including my family. There was a lot of stuff I never shared on the 'couch' either. It didn't matter, I suppose. She could have found out using simple sodium pentathol.

But the thing that really blew me away was that 'bible.' I carried it with me—my own personal talisman.

The wealth of related experience, moods, and simple knowledge of my taste in reading material reflected a persona like mine remarkably. It had to have been put together in such an erudite manner by someone very much like me, else it had been sucked up from my mind like an Army Corps of Engineers dredge digging channel and depositing its effluent on a spoil island.

Fucking eerie.

Cal told me he'd been invited to St John by an organization called the Scientific Creationist Research Institute, ostensibly to hear his views on field biology. He had quickly grabbed the opportunity. A free week in the Virgin Islands in December was fine with him.

He even had enough material to tell them what he thought they wanted to hear—the whore.

Of course, he never stopped to wonder why they chose *him* to come. It wasn't until he saw Nadine that he knew something wasn't kosher.

Still harboring a grudge, Cal wasn't about to trust Nadine. And he didn't like Randy right off. They compounded things right away by offering him money. Nadine still saw Cal as a money-grubbing little Jew-boy, and treated him as such, no matter how hard she tried to slickly cover over her real feelings. Of course, Cal wasn't about to turn down a buck, especially if he could work things around to get a little revenge.

But why him?

Cal had an idea that they were having a difficult time 'programming' me. Sometimes researchers found it was helpful for subjects undergoing intense analysis through hypnosis to have someone there they respected or felt extremely comfortable with. Therefore, Nadine and company thought a pep talk from Cal might help, even though we'd had that little 'squabble' a few years previous.

And the fact that we'd been seeing the same shrink—who may have mentioned a few things pertaining to me, while in the sack with Cal, may also have had something to do with it. But I had the definite idea that they fucked up with that scheme. Cal immediately got me drunk, and I'm sure they cautioned him against that, though he said he doesn't remember any rules like that one.

Cal was also smart enough to figure out his role in the charade when they told him I was undergoing a nervous breakdown due to intense biblical study. They really screwed up there. Cal knew I was a reader, but intensive research or study, never—especially on religious lines. It was the one subject that we'd stayed clear of in our countless drunken discussions. Cal said that I'd totally clam up, ending the evening, no matter the time. *That* was something I didn't remember...

Cal made them tell him more, leading with his own line of bullshit. The 'Hey, maybe I can really help you guys—this is really interesting, etc.' rap. I guess they thought he was easy, too.

But Cal was convinced, almost, that I was a goner. He followed through only to stick around to gum things up for his own insane purposes.

"Second Coming, my ass. You know what else?" he was saying, as we sat on the steep hillside, a few hundred feet below the northside deck of the house. "They're not even real Scientific Creationists. There's a couple of bonafide organizations that profess the creationist line—but they never heard of those guys. The others put out a number of books and support a nationwide movement to influence school boards. I checked a *little* before I came down here. I wanted to know something before I shot my big mouth off. When Nadine and that character Rand met me at the airport I almost shit. I haven't seen her—in what? Five, six years? And suddenly there she is, blathering something about you, and how important you were to the organization, blah, blah, blah."

"So they really thought they had me, huh? I'm still in the dark with a lot of this. The only Second Coming I know of is J.C. They can't be serious…"

"They are serious, Jonas. I think that stolen scroll has a lot to do with it. Maybe it's another whole Book of the Bible. Some sort of prophecy."

"But what about me?"

He snickered. "You're part of the backup, I think. But you gotta hear the tapes, Jonas. It's you, all right. It sounds like you, and it's goddamn convincing. If I didn't know you so well—and I didn't think that I did—I would swear that you were the prophet Jonah himself. You sounded *very* good."

"What was I saying?"

"Oh, a lot of garbage. 'Behold, I am the Lord's prophet…' that sort of stuff."

I felt slightly crestfallen. I guess I wanted the big role. "But if I'm part of the backup, as you say—if their 'Second Coming' doesn't happen, as planned—then who is the star?"

"Your guess is as good as mine. It wasn't until you told me that Rand had mentioned the Second Coming that I could piece this whole act together myself."

"Yeah, but we don't know how, or why now, and we don't know when, or any details."

We both looked up the steep incline to the house. It stood positively temple-like in its magnanimity. 'Why' was a question almost too simplistic. 'How' was better. Who was going to believe them? Who was going to believe *me* as the reincarnation of Jonah?

"You know, this is some shot they're taking, if we're reading this right. Who in Hell would believe them? There's got to be proof of something for them even to be taking the chance. I mean, they're fucking around with my goddamn life!"

"They're big bucks people, Jonas. They want control, no matter what. Religion's as good a vehicle as any. You know, a lot of people around Stony Brook and other places——- the whole scientific-educational community—say that the creationists misrepresent science, destroy education, and debase religion. All the creationists say is that they want equal time for their views. But the trouble is that behind this nice democratic idea—equal choice and all that shit—is something else: the old power trip again. It's a much larger campaign to establish a more authoritarian and religion-based society. Hell, we've been feeling the backlash from the Sixties for some time now, and this is the epitome of it."

"I thought you said that these people aren't creationists?"

"Who knows? Maybe they are. I just know that no one's ever heard of them. Yet. Maybe they're a secret group, like the *Prieure de Sion*...holy shit!"

"What?" I said. Cal looked like he'd just swallowed a fruit fly.

"I'll bet ya that's it, Jonas. That's why Rand speaks in French when he thinks no one is listening!"

"What are you talking about?" I said, not wanting to discourage him. I wouldn't doubt anything about Randy, but I was sure that he could speak in any language he wanted to.

Above us we suddenly heard voices. Someone was out on the deck.

The morning was clear, with little wind yet. We were a distance away, but we could hear snatches of conversation and the tread of their feet. I grabbed Cal by the arm and we started climbing some more, being very careful not to make a racket.

One of the speakers above us was a woman. I was pretty sure it was Nadine.

CHAPTER TWENTYTWO

I knew it would come to this.

Robert Louis Finkel

The hillside directly below the deck had been cleared from when the builders were there. It was just rubble—dirt clods, chunks of cement and other debris. For us to scrabble over it without causing a major landslide would be tough.

Right now we were at the edge of the underbrush. Cal was panting by my side, the sweat streaking the dirt on his face.

"This is it, Jonas. We can't get any closer."

"That's Nadine up there," I whispered.

"I know, I know. And Rand, too."

It was frustrating. We could hear a little more, but not enough to make sense of it.

Damn it! I felt like making a head-long rush for the deck, springing over the parapets Marine-style, grabbing the both of them, trusty commando knives at their throats, and...

Cal could always sense the craziness in me, as I could in him. "We'll never make it, you dumb ass. It's a hundred foot of straight climb over all that shit. They'll have their goons on us before we made it to the base of the house."

He looked around us, then motioned for me to follow him.

"Come on, fire-nuts. Let's make along the edge here. There's some cover a little closer on the far side."

I followed Cal and we worked slowly through the dry brush, trying not to make noise. It was difficult going. Heading straight up a thickly over-grown hillside is one thing, but traversing it is another. The stickers and branches of the scrub growth that covers much of the Caribbean islands is brutal to finagle past. It doesn't like to let one go by easily.

We weren't halfway to our destination when the speakers on the deck were joined by others. We hesitated a moment, listening intently. Then, looking up, we saw Nadine, Rand, Leigh, and Taylor staring down at us.

We were easy to spot. That type of vegetation doesn't afford much cover.

We could hear them plainly now.

"Paulo! Klaus!" Taylor shouted. "Down below!"

Taylor turned away, and we heard more orders.

"Roberto—the carbine."

The bastards. Now they were playing for keeps. I knew it would come to this.

We made a break for it, skirting the vegetation along the clearing, stumbling over the clumps and debris like frightened children. The group on the deck were pointing at us and shouting instructions to the men sent to round us up.

One of them up there had a rifle pointed in our direction.

"You can't get anywhere, Jonas!" Nadine yelled shrilly.

We were just below them now, almost to the denser growth on the far side of the clearing. There was a lot of commotion going on just beyond the house to our left. I could see a few men scrambling through the trees there.

Above us I heard Nadine plainly say, "Shoot the other one."

Three shots in rapid succession: the slugs ticking chunks of dirt and concrete just in front of me and ringing Cal. We just made it to the larger trees.

On the deck someone, it could have been Randy, angrily growled, *"Give me that!"*

Anther bullet passed over my head, breaking a branch Cal had just grappled by.

The trees didn't last long enough. We burst through onto a road.

Waiting there for us were three of them, all armed with light machine guns.

They brought us back up on the deck, the one called Klaus pushing menacingly into Cal's back with his weapon.

They were all there.

"Well, Jonas. You had your chance," Randy said, as if Cal and I had just been bested in a set of morning tennis. He was remarkably poised for someone who had a minute ago tried to end Cal's life. He still held the carbine.

I glowered at him, and he passed the weapon to one of the goons. Even now he appeared peaceful and at ease, though he showed a slight chastisement at being caught with the smoking gun still in his hands. I wouldn't have bet on him to miss.

The others were quite agitated, Taylor and Leigh particularly. Nadine was as cool as Randy. She stood in front of us, her hands in her khaki trouser pockets.

"You're lucky Roberto isn't the shot he's supposed to be," she said to Cal.

Where was her milk maid dirndl now, I wondered.

"Or your boyfriend, bitch," said Cal out of the side of this mouth.

I had to admire his temerity. I could see Nadine's leg flinch, as if she had all she could do to stop herself from giving him a good one in the balls. I looked down her leg to her magenta-painted toenails, visible through her sandals, then back up to her face.

She was still beautiful, even with the hate-mask she had on now for her ex. I had the incredible desire to throw her upper torso over the deck railing, rip off those creased khaki pants, and violate her anally with the telescope. I couldn't help smiling at the thought.

"And you, Jonas. I see that you find this all very amusing. You were about to be made famous. More famous than you'll ever imagine. This is the big time." Her voice was almost a purr.

"Maybe he can still be useful," Randy said to her, coming up alongside and placing a steady hand on her hip. "You were a great prophet, Jonas. You were the herald. One who would tell the world of their...Lord's coming."

"Fucked up again," I said, shaking my head, looking downward.

I suddenly realized who the 'Lord' was going to be—

"It's to be you, isn't it?"

I looked up at him. He smiled a beneficent smile. One that looked so smooth and practiced that it could have been real.

I wanted to say, 'You'll never get away with it, motherfucker.' But I held it in. He *did* say maybe I could still be useful. There was still a chance, slim maybe, but a chance.

"How is all this going to happen, Randy? If I may ask," I said, as nicely as possible. After all, they had us now. Why not let us in on the big plan?

Randy was beaming. I could tell the old con-man in him was anxious to impress a pigeon. It didn't matter that Cal and I were, had been, little more than shills. Taylor and Leigh weren't as happy, however. Neither was Nadine.

"Let's get rid of them," Taylor put succinctly.

"Very good idea," Nadine seconded the motion.

Leigh nodded in agreement, but Randy—good ole Randy—looked theatrically aghast.

I really think he liked me. Plus, he really wanted to convince himself—as much as anyone else—of whom he was supposed to portray.

"I don't think we really have to resort to such...*final* measures," he said.

Go Randy!

"I think that part of the trouble we've had with Jonas, here, is that we haven't been entirely open with him. We know how susceptible he is to suggestion. We know his...*background*."

He walked over to the edge of the deck, placed his hands on the railing, and gazed out towards Virgin Gorda.

I couldn't help feeling a little uncomfortable—besides the guns pointed at us and our immediate circumstances—Randy's choice and emphatic use of certain words was un-nerving. He reminded me now of various venal characters in William Burrough's *Naked Lunch*. And besides the Sunday school garb and beatific countenance, Randy still reeked of the greasepaint. There was a carnival atmosphere about this whole thing—

All the stock characters were here. The Magician (Randy), the Beautiful Girl (Nadine), the Manager (Taylor), the Barker (me), even the exotic backdrop—all just waiting for an audience, which was to be the entire world, I imagine.

I wondered now whether it all started this way. A few characters get together, set up some razzle-dazzle to spoof the local yokels; all in the guise of doing it for *them!*

Maybe it wasn't the prophets, but those who came after. Those who could see from a higher aspect the true ramifications of the absolute power of faith...

Something inside me was struggling to get out, and I found myself saying, "I want to believe, Lord. I want to believe in your Power..."

"'If it was not so, I would have told you so,'" Randy said, turning from the railing at the sound of my voice.

He approached me with open arms.

His voice dripped honey as he began reciting—it was Psalm 51, and I followed him, though there began a strange tug of war inside me as I did so:

"'Have mercy upon me...'"

I felt as if I was being sucked through an open portal, like in a jet airliner that had lost its pressurization. There seemed to be a tremendous force pulling me out into the open sky.

"'Against thee, Thee only, have I sinned...'"

But I was holding on, frantically it seemed, though I somehow was also a bemused bystander watching all this take place.

"'Hide Thy face from my sins and blot out...'"

I tried being the bystander, something I felt that I could never do before—

"'Create in me a clean heart, O God, and renew a steadfast spirit within me.'"

It became apparent that Randy was the force I was struggling so hard against—

"'...then I will teach transgressors Thy ways.'"

But I couldn't understand why I was so desperate to stay where I was—

"'Deliver me from bloodguilt...'"

The feeling wasn't comfortable, and I felt as though I was an empty shell—

"'...then shall bullocks be offered upon Thy alter.'"

Then we stopped.

Randy looked radiant as he said, "The sign, Jonas. The star our Father has sent for us to follow: It rises in the West—over wicked Gotham—and heralds my coming. Ye shall be my harbinger..."

He went on, though I was locked inwardly. I had the sudden feeling that something was going to give. I felt really good. Something like the night before in the mangroves when I'd felt purged. It didn't matter now which way I went. I knew I was going to...

Suddenly—

Randy was flat on the deck, and Taylor was shouting for some of his boys. Cal had grabbed Nadine and was slapping her – *one, two*—probably something he'd been wanting to do for a long time.

Leigh was stupidly holding the carbine now, pointing it first in one direction, then another.

Roberto was out like a light, slumped over a table. Klaus was just getting up by the railing, the machine gun gone.

I didn't know what I was doing. It was like seeing a movie...

Somebody hit Cal from behind, and he fell forward on his face. Randy was getting up, saying, "Don't hit him...don't hit him! She'll take care of it!"

Strange—who is he talking about?

I smelled something really peculiar then. Greasepaint? And I felt the needle's prick.

A sudden flash—

CHAPTER TWENTYTHREE

Julian was pecking away at the cement between two concrete blocks with a piece of wire lathing.

The angle of the sun left his head bathed in light, but below it was too dark to really make out what he was up to. I could tell, though, because—well, Julian was Julian, and that's what I thought he'd be doing. Plus I'd been watching him now for at least twenty minutes—ever since I woke up—and the dirt floor I was lying on was littered with ferro-cement material, of which iron wire lathing is a part.

I would have said something earlier, but it had taken me this long to figure out *what*—never mind who yet—the image across from me just was. The sun helped: as it rose (it was morning, then) more and more of Julian's grimacing features came into view. I first could only hear the steady scratching and see the concrete block wall. Then, Julian's tousled dirty hair came into sight. A few minutes later, his sweat-streaked skin and facial features.

It was fascinating to watch.

In my still groggy state I imagined myriad forms and monsters were being revealed. A thousand hours seemed to go by in those few minutes. I relived countless horror movies and other morbid vehicles that I'd cluttered my mind with.

The rest of the place we were in was black. The only light came in through the one avenue over my head. It was either a vent of some sort or a defect in the building itself. I hope it was the latter.

Everything came back to me in great gulps.

The coolness of our prison made me shiver also. I never did like the cold. We must be under the house—where else? It could be worse. At least Julian was all right.

"Do ya think it'd be easier to attack that vent or crack up there, instead of the wall?" I asked. No sense in amenities. Julian always appreciated the direct approach.

The scratching stopped.

Julian let out an audible puff. "Too high to work at steady. And that's the driveway out there. They might catch on," he said.

The scratching began again.

I sighed contentedly. If nothing else, Ju-boy was in command. It was a relief to fall back into familiar patterns.

"Take over for awhile," Julian said.

I started to crawl over there, but Cal's face shown in the sunlight, and the scratching resumed.

"Cal?"

He grinned. "Who'd you expect, the *Devin?*"

"Not so loud," Julian whispered. "All we need is another couple of hours or so and we're the fuck outa here. So let's not let 'em know we're getting restless." He spoke from the darkness to Cal's left.

"Where we going after that?"

"Who knows? Away from this loony bin."

"Is the *Melchoir* still in the cove? There was—or were—another couple of boats down there the other...what day is it, anyway?"

"I got no idea what's down there. I've been here a week. I was beginning to go bat-shit when they tossed Cal in here."

"What about me? When did I show up?" This bothered me. I hated being singled out.

"I guess they had plans for you, motherfucker," Julian said, a tinge of bitterness in his voice.

"Take it easy on him, Julian. That fucking hyena bitch got him so pumped full of shit he doesn't know who he is. Plus, I don't think they would have tossed him here on the dung heap with us if they thought he was going to work out."

"Ah, shit. Sorry, Jonas. They had you saying and doing some weird shit—me, too, I think. They got some really weird revival going on here. Jesus Christ, bible-talk, stars rising in the west, omens, prophets—"

"And machine guns," Cal added.

"Yeah—that too."

"You got any idea of their time-table, Ju?" I asked.

I had to know. I was still in this whether I wanted to be or not. Whatever the others did, I was determined to get this whole thing doped out. It wasn't going to leave me alone.

I'd already spent far too much of my life as a dummy. One of those at the end of the aphoristic chain that begins with those that 'make things happen' and those at the end who always have to ask, 'What happened?'

"No, and I don't want to know," Julian answered me.

"But didn't they tell you anything?"

"Look—all I know is that for the past couple months or so, before I drew solitary here, I was some kind of zombie. All I did was what Nadine or that fucking Randy character wanted me to do. I've had some fucking nightmares that I don't even want to think about."

"I had them, too."

"Well, maybe you did, Jonas. Maybe you did. But I saw you up there with them. Playing press conference."

"Press conference?"

"Yeah. Reporters and all that shit. They had cameras and everything."

"The tapes, Jonas," Cal said from the wall. "I tried telling you about them."

"Fucking *video* tapes?"

"Yes."

"But where—of what?"

"They made them right here. I knew there was something funny going on. Those same dorks who captured us were the 'reporters' on the tapes. It's all a set up. They're probably going to beam it up to a CATV satellite from somewhere and then present it as real—unrehearsed, live from Heaven: *He-e-ers Jesus!*"

God.

The real God. They're really going all the way.

"What about me? What do I do on the...the *show?*"

"You're some act, that's for sure," Julian said. "You're convincing, that's all I know."

"Cal?"

"You're the Prophet Jonas—formerly Jonah. They got you and the *Devin* up there in the lights and microphones like you're serious—and damned if you aren't. The reporters throw questions at you like gunfire, and you handle them all. You don't seemed drugged or fucked up in the least. It's *you*, only...it's not. It had me convinced, though."

"What do they ask? What do I know about anything? Jeannie used to say I was like a jack of all knowledge, with none of it mastered. I fuck up on really deep questions."

"You got the *whole* creationist rap *down*, Jonas. You got all the answers. Even J.C. himself is stepping back to reclaim the throne."

"I give a date?"

"No. I don't think you're trusted with that info yet. You sidestep the question brilliantly. Soon, though. Soon."

"I don't think I'm trusted with shit, anymore."

"After that act on the deck I'm surprised we're both still alive," Cal said. "You were really something, like a mountain gorilla backed into a corner."

"What'd I *do?*"

"You totally freaked. After that little recital with Rand—whatever that was all about..."

"Psalm 51."

"Yeah. Well, you blew 'em away, long enough for me to get my licks in—" Cal's eyes flicked quickly to where Julian was, then away again. "But then they regrouped and I folded. Next thing I knew I was down here. Only it was night. Very uncomfortable here at night. Worse than being out in the bush. There's no light at all. Only that little bit from up there in the morning. Thank God Julian was here."

He continued scratching.

"Isn't there a way out?"

"No," Julian said. "They dumped us in by a trap door way above our heads. I checked the whole perimeter already. It's like a tomb."

"Must be dug right into the mountain, too," added Cal. "We can hear a car or something start up in the morning and come back later through the crack there."

I turned to look up the wall behind my back. The crack must be a good fifteen feet above us.

I had a sudden thought.

"How do you know that the block you're working on isn't way below ground?"

Julian answered. "The slope. This is the north wall. And by my calculations we should be able to go straight out. I hope."

CHAPTER TWENTYFOUR

Later on it got dark. Dark dark. Like all the nightmares of the pit.

The only sounds were our breathing and occasional conversation. And some scurryings and scuttlings that gave the dampness and dankness of our prison added dimension. And the ubiquitous scratching.

We worked in shifts. The pieces of wire we used wore down almost as quickly as the cement. As the night wore on it became hard to tell whether my fingers were sweating or bleeding. The scratching gave us a purpose, anyway.

I told Cal about Newton's aphorism that I'd connected with the evangelists sitting on the prophet's shoulders at Chartres.

"There was a book about that. Merton wrote it, I believe," Cal told me. *"On The Shoulders of Giants."*

"Who's that?"

"Robert K. Merton. Sociologist big-wig from Columbia. He traced the metaphor back to Bernard of Chartres and thinks that the windows are an explicit attempt to capture that idea. I remember it now."

"I wonder what he'd say about his whole act," I said bluntly.

"Who, Merton? He'd probably prove that your friends upstairs aren't the only ones with this crack-pot scheme."

"They're not my friends..."

"All right, Jonas."

"Tell me about Merton."

The darkness and cloying damp was easier to take with live conversation. I needed a backdrop to collect some of my thoughts on anyway.

"Merton's spent most of his time showing that almost all major ideas arise many times, usually independently and virtually at the same time—"

"You mean that things happen simultaneously all over the world. I've heard of that. Things are in the air, and people just pick up on the vibes, so to speak. Like in the Sixties—the movement, or movements, whatever. Kids all over the world were suddenly tuned in to sex, drugs and rock and roll."

"Well, yeah. But Merton's talking about *great* ideas. Multiple discoveries in science, for example. Take Darwin and Wallace. Darwin developed his theory of natural selection was back in 1838, but it wasn't until twenty years later, when he got a letter and a manuscript from Wallace, that he moved on his own *Origin of Species*. He had it doped out years before, so it was nearly ready to publish. But the thing is that Wallace had the same idea, natural selection, coming to it independently while sick with malaria. Darwin was stunned by the detailed similarity. Wallace even claimed inspiration from the same non-biological source: Malthus' essay on population."

"Darwin must have been pissed to get almost ripped off like that—"

"No. Wallace revered Darwin. He was consistently deferential. They disagreed on a few things, like sexual selection and human origins. Something which brings us to the present, matter of fact..."

Cal trailed off. It was irritating in the pitch darkness to have someone to do that. At least in the light you can often read as much from the expression on someone's face—

"You know," Cal started again. "It's funny how all subtle ideas—*great* ideas, that could be giant stepping stones for man instead of islands of ideology to bicker over—can be trivialized and otherwise messed up in the minds of people when these ideas are put in uncompromising and absolute terms."

"Wow," I said, though I wanted to blow him off. His bullshit was getting smelly, considering our circumstances. But I remained a gentleman. "What do you mean? Like what?"

"Well, I'm talking about Darwinism. But look at Marx—he felt compelled to deny he was a Marxist!"

My turn. "I know," I said. I knew something about this. "Marx even supported the feudal system. He was against the dissolution of the family. Which the feudal system was, and what Marx was really against was the rapacious middle class. He thought that the bourgeois would destroy the family unit, and that the Industrial Revolution was a catastrophe that man could do without. I remember reading a critical essay on *King Lear*, of all things, where the author, an avowed Marxist, went into it."

"Yeah. Look at it. A Marxist today is considered anti-family. And Einstein. He had to deal with the serious misstatement that he meant to say, 'All is relative.' And Darwinism is often considered as the belief that each function or behavior of an organism lead to a 'better' organism. That's almost like the creationist idea. That belief in nature's 'rightness.' It's like substituting an omnipotent force of natural selection for a benevolent deity."

I was lost. "What about the survival of the fittest idea? Didn't that make a 'better' organism?"

"Maybe. But there are other processes at work. Adaptive change in one part of an organism can lead to non-adaptive modification in other parts. Look at the dinosaurs and how big they got. And don't forget that just because something is developed for a specific duty doesn't mean that it can't be used to do other things as well.

"The hyperselectionists, particularly Wallace, had the idea that *all* modification had a *specific* purpose and *none* could exist that did not have a specific purpose at one time. This simply is not valid. It's a caricature of Darwin's subtler view: natural selection may build an organ 'for' a specific function, but this organ can also perform many other tasks as well."

"Reminds me of Dr. Pangloss. Remember? 'All is for the best in the best of all possible worlds...Our noses were made to carry spectacles, so we have spectacles. Legs were clearly intended for breeches, and we wear them.'"

"Right. And we have a giant brain for hunting, that's why we have limits on our thoughts and emotions..."

"'Things cannot be other than they are...Everything is made for the best purpose,' says Dr. Pangloss," I sang on.

"And that's just *it*, damn it!"

Cal was suddenly agitated.

"It's a myth. A goddamn myth," he said.

"What is?"

"Natural harmony, Jonas. The idea that all structures are well designed for a definite purpose. That is what hyperselectionism *is*. And it leads right back to the basic belief of an earlier creationism that it was meant to replace. This faith in the rightness of things, the idea of a definite place for each object in an integrated whole."

"'We just want our place in the sun...' *That* sound familiar to you?"

"Same shit," Cal agreed. "The old rap that we're here because we're *supposed* to be here. We deserve it, it's ours...and if you don't go along with us, *we'll kill you*."

"Right," I agreed. "It seems that no matter what, people are determined to believe in their own uniqueness. Whether from their ancestors before them or from other men. We're always 'better' than *them*."

"But you know the funny thing? About Wallace, I mean? He was a hyperselectionist, right? But he stopped at man's intellect and morality. Whatever *that* is. He was convinced that the human mind could not be a product of natural selection—and, therefore, since natural selection is nature's only way, some higher power—*God*—must have intervened to construct this latest and greatest of organic innovations."

"So there it is. *Faith* wins. Wallace couldn't take the big step. How did Darwin see it?"

"He admitted Man fully into the natural system with all the quirks, big brain included. But don't confuse Wallace's rejection of natural selection for the human mind with being inconsistent. That's exactly how many view Darwinism today. Rigid selectionism versus Darwin's pluralism."

"Pluralism?"

"Yes. There are other factors to be considered besides just selection. Like I told you before—things are made because there *may* be a need. And once it works one way doesn't necessarily mean that it'll keep performing the way it was supposedly designed to. Hey, there *is* a harmony in nature—but structure has its latent capabilities. Life is flexible, man—it may be messy and probably *always* unpredictable, but it's all we got. No sense in pretending anymore about it."

I believed him there. I thought about an old Jimmy Buffet song where he sings about a pirate turning forty:

Mother, mother ocean, after all
these years I've found

My occupational hazard being my
occupations just not around.

And my favorite lines from that song, speaking of Mother
Ocean:

And in your belly you hold the
treasure
That few have ever seen,
Most of them dreams,
Most of them dreams.

I started humming the song, and said, "But there are
scientists who believe otherwise, correct?" We were getting
somewhere, and I didn't want to lose Cal.

"Sure," he said. He was listening to me hum also, and
added, "Buffet, right? Mother Ocean?"

"Yeah," I said. Close enough—

"Always liked that," he mused. Then—"A lot of them,
scientists, play right into the hands of the crazies like we got
upstairs. Faith is fine, but I don't believe in anything that
has to have a machine gun backing it up. Look, evolutionary
biology is in a dreadful funk at the moment—some call it a
scientific revolution—I know, because I'm surrounded—or I
used to be, anyway—by people who live and breathe evolution.
Every learned journal and scientific meeting is sprinkled with
papers bitching about Darwinism. Jeremiahs and iconoclasts
are jumping onto their soapboxes and accusing their
fellow evolutionary biologists of circular reasoning, hollow
explanations, baseless assumptions, and general all-around
bullshit.

"Some say evolution isn't gradual, as Darwin says, but

comes in bursts of relatively rapid change, interspersed with long periods of little change in established species. There are other theories: genetics based on French anthropology, systematics rooted in Viennese philosophy, dialectical paleontology..."

Now he rung a bell. "That reminds me of something. What was that you said—whenever it was—about Rand's French. You said something about a secret society, or something."

"*What?* I said what?"

I had him stopped cold for a moment.

"You said," I told him, "something like maybe Randy and his friends are from the...Sion society or...?"

"Right. Right. The Prieure de Sion."

"That's it. When you said 'genetics based on French anthropology' I thought of Randy. And the Prieure de Sion. What is it?"

"You know, Jonas, that's really interesting," Cal said, almost to himself now.

He was quiet for awhile. Julian must be asleep. I couldn't tell—but no one was picking away at the cement between the blocks. I felt guilty that I was not.

I remembered a movie I saw called *Escape From Alcatraz*. Clint Eastwood was in it, and in one part of the movie he gets thrown in 'D' block for fighting. 'D' block was a row of cells where you were put for 'solitary.' No light at all, and you got washed once a day by a guard with a high pressure water hose.

Really pleasant conditions. We have it easy compared with that—

Eastwood portrayed a con named Frank Morris. And he *does* escape. The movie was based on a true story. Morris chips away at the rotten concrete around the vents along the back wall of his cell. Morris steals a nail clipper—right from the warden, too—and makes a digging tool out of it. He actually welds part of the tool together in his cell using matches.

Some of the dialogue was good. One of the other cons says to Morris, "I turned thirty-five today. When's your birthday?"

"I don't know," Morris (Eastwood) replies.

"What kind of childhood did you *have?*" asks the astonished con.

"Short," Morris answers.

They never found Morris after he escaped. Less than a year later the government closed down Alcatraz.

Maybe if we waited here long enough...

***

"There's a book out called *The Holy Blood And The Holy Grail,*" Cal said. "In it the authors claim that Jesus married Mary Magdalene and fathered a child; staged his crucifixion and resurrection; lived into old age."

Thing were clicking for me now. "And his descendants still can be found in Europe," I added.

"You know about it, then. The Prieure de Sion was..."

"The secret society formed to protect the royal blood, which, mistranslated, was taken to mean Holy Grail! I never saw the book, but I remember something about it from the Times review or somewhere."

"Well," Cal went on, "the book was shot to pieces by the Church, of course. The authors say that Jesus was descended from the royal house of King David and could literally claim to have been 'King of the Jews.' After the contrived crucifixion and resurrection Mary Magdalene and her child fled to what is now southern France. And the bloodline was ultimately extended into the noble families of modern Europe...just think of the uproar and mad grab for power if it could be proven!"

"But who's going to care about J.C. getting married. It doesn't matter. It's all faith anyway."

"Don't you see the reverberations? It means that—possibly—there's a chance that Jesus was a normal man. that it's *true!*"

"So what?"

"*So?* If you were the most powerful institution on the face of the earth, and your authority, based on a questionable event two thousand years ago, is being challenged with irrefutable evidence..."

"What kind of evidence?"

"To begin with, proof. Such as Leigh's purloined scroll, from the tomb of David, mind you—that now only does the sanctity of the Holy Ghost not hold water, but that also the earth wasn't formed in less than a week only ten thousand years ago."

"So," I said, "the thing to do is contrive a Second Coming to boost attendance on Sunday."

"Right. Look at a few things: modern creationists are biblical fundamentalists going under the banner of *science*, not religion. They claim that God created the world in six days and that this notion is supported by *scientific evidence*—just in case your average slob has gotten bored by standard bible rhetoric—and they also claim that *evolution* is not science at all, but disguised theology. They're attacking on all fronts. Everything's covered!"

"And here I thought that evolution and creationism was just a classic test of the American principle of separation of church and state."

"You know it's more that that, wise-ass, or we wouldn't be here."

"Sorry, professor. I'm just having a difficult time swallowing this."

"Well, I'm going to tell you something. Just before I flew down here—maybe it was on the plane—I read of an Associated Press poll which showed that over 76% of the American people think that public schools should teach both evolution *and* creationism. You know what that means? It means that people are ready to accept just about anything if it's put in the proper format. Got a problem with the masses believing in religious dogma? Call it *science!* Hell, it's a high-tech society we live in. Everything oozes science today. It's hot stuff. Just look at the slick magazines that are out now just for the layman—all with a science and technology bent. And I'm not talking about *Popular Science*, either. There's *Discover, Science, Omni*—and a whole shitload of nature magazines. *Scientific American* may still be too high-brow, but..."

"I know, I know. They all send me complimentary issues."

"And they're filled with articles that titillate readers into thinking they're really *learning* something. They got articles in them like 'Things Your Body Never Told You About Fat' and 'Fusion Power: Why Nuclear Energy is Good For You.'"

"I know," I tried to tell him.

"It's all simplified *pap*! But Joe Schmo doesn't see it that way. He thinks that he's in the know! Science used in this way is better than heroin. Look at how video games have taken over the kids. They're fucking computers, just like daddy has...everyone is into them. Ever since Sputnik everybody's imbued with scientific technology."

Cal was off and running again, describing mankind going to the dogs.

I envisioned a giant computer terminal, with some fiend

playing Pac-Man, the little monsters closing in on mankind as he desperately tries to gobble up all the knowledge he can before they get him, Wagner's "Emulation of the Gods" blasting in the background...

Cal went on for quite awhile there in the blackness, touching on just about everything, just rapping away like a berserk encyclopedia. I think the darkness was getting to him.

I was at the wall and felt like scraping a bit, but I didn't want to intimidate Cal. I wanted him to keep talking. It was important to me to have that steady drone; he could have been reciting the alphabet over and over again for all I cared. It was easier to think like this.

It was funny how Cal described people who read all those magazines; their thinking that they knew something.

I was like that.

My father used to tell me I was like a bumblebee, going from flower to flower gathering pollen. I really kind of liked that image of myself—but the old man would always punctuate the metaphor by saying, "Trouble is, Jonas, you never pick up enough pollen to amount to diddly-squat."

Oh, yeah—

What happened to me? I couldn't seem to remember anything. Some of my dreams, but nothing in them about press conferences, or the *Devin*, or Jesus Christ. Maybe it had all happened to someone else.

What did I know? What had Leigh really found, or stolen? Maybe he did find it. Who knows? What was it that Randy said when he came in us that night?

Something about a well.

"Cal?"

"...and look at people like Philip Gosse. He was a

contemporary of Darwin's, and was convinced that creation burst forth complete with false records of a non-existent past..."

He was still going strong.

"Cal," I asked loudly, "what was so special about a water well in Jerusalem?"

"...these things were called *prochronic* objects—pre-time, mind you. And some of the other theories are equally bizarre... what?"

I got him stopped.

"I remembered something," I said. "About where that scroll came from. Randy said something about a well."

"In Jerusalem?"

"Yes. At the site they were digging in. An ancient well."

"Oh—yeah. They had a big water pipe there. Still have, rather. Called Warren's Shaft. Charles Warren was an archaeologist who discovered it in the 1860's, I think."

"Randy quoted something from the bible...there was just something about it. It's bugging me."

"Well, from what I remember Warren's shaft has been there a long time. Before the bible. It wouldn't be unusual for one of the old prophets to have mentioned it."

"'Go up,' Randy said. 'Go up through the water tunnel into the city and destroy those lame and blind Jebusites.'"

"Yeah," said Cal. "You got it. Sounds like the old testament. The Jebusites held the city before David did."

"'Go up,' he said..."

"Right. That's how they snuck in. Yeah, leave it to the Jews to think that one up..."

"God told them."

"Right...right, right, Jonas," Cal said disgustedly, probably thinking that I'd cracked.

"On the shoulders of Giants..." I had it now. It was a chance, another one, but it beat chipping away at the cement. "Cal, is Julian near you?"

I stood up.

"Yeah—" Cal answered me.

"Wake him up, I..."

Julian's voice came out of the gloom. "I'm awake. You don't think it's easy to sleep with motor-mouth here, do you?"

"What's the matter, afraid you might *learn* something?" Cal said, but his manner was easy.

"You never know, do you?" Julian replied.

I heard him stir, then was groping alongside me.

"You want me on top, right? I'm the lightest, I think."

He'd picked up on the same idea. The ceiling above couldn't be much more than fifteen feet away from us.

"And I'm the heaviest. Maybe. Cal, come over here," I said, squatting down. "Now. You get up on me until you're standing on my shoulders."

"All right," he said. I felt him behind me.

"I'll stand a little. You just climb up on my back."

I was smaller than Cal, but I knew that he'd have he could do to hold Julian up. And Julian had to go. He was the only one of the three of us—maybe besides myself—who could somehow get back up into the house from the hatch opening they'd dumped us from.

I could feel Cal teetering already. Julian was alongside me guiding him.

"Get alongside the wall, Jonas."

I maneuvered closer to the wall; Cal made it up fairly easily now. I felt some gritty dirt fall down inside my shirt from his shoes. It was cold dirt and made me shiver.

Julian grunted as he then climbed over me also. I spread

271

my feet out a little more, feeling the weight. I was holding up well over three hundred pounds. The anchor man on a human ladder.

From above in the darkness Julian whispered hoarsely, "Shit! Just out of reach."

"Can you feel anything?" I grunted.

"Just the fucking wall."

Damn it. I could almost taste being out of there and into a place with some light.

"Work along the wall a bit," Julian said. "Maybe we'll come to something."

I started edging along, scraping my feet slowly through the dirt.

The pressure was becoming somewhat unbearable. My middle back felt as if someone had lain me prone across two spaced chairs and then started dropping cinder blocks on me.

Maybe this was Hell. An apt punishment for a hedonist: total darkness and a lot of pain.

"Did I die?" I croaked. Maybe levity would help.

"*You?* I guess I shouldn't complain," Cal replied.

My breathing was getting shorter and hoarser-sounding. Maybe I'll black out. Boy, that was a joke. You would think that after hours of darkness you would be able to see *something*. There was always a little light somewhere. But not here. Maybe I'd gone blind...

I felt that I couldn't talk anymore. Just breathing was way too difficult, but I wanted to ask Cal what he would think if someone suddenly shined a big spot light on us, or we stumbled out onto a stage in a burlesque house, or I walked off the end of a cliff...

I suddenly had an image of little Jonas, and he was crying. I saw his tears first, then his big brown eyes and those wonderfully long lashes he had. The tears dripped off the lashes, splashing on his little round cheeks, which I saw next. Now his whole head was in view and he was bawling to beat the band, one little fist ground up in one eye, the other hand held up in the air, as he'd just thrown something.

He seemed to be alone. My guts ached for him. Where was Carol? Why wasn't she right there?

Jonas was blubbering something. Was it 'Daddy?' Was he crying for me? Oh, Jesus—please, please, please...

I could see Jonas more clearly now. He was in a sand box it seemed, seated up high on a little hill like, and crying harder.

Damn it! My goddamn life was such a piece of shit. I would be glad to end it right now if it wasn't for those other two losers on top of...

The mound!

There was a mound where they'd dumped us. Cal mentioned it earlier. He'd said that we were lucky nothing broke when we were tossed in here. Even with the built-up mound there was always a chance of fracturing something or other.

I started moving directly away from the wall

"Whoaaaa—" Julian cried out.

"Da-a-a mooun," I groaned, trying to tell him to hang in, or on, rather—I had hardly a breath left.

And now it felt like someone was dropping 100 pound bags of cement on me.

I just got to the edge of the mound. The dirt was looser there. My feet were caught and wouldn't budge.

Strange. I suddenly came to the realization that I hadn't eaten in a long time...

I could hear Cal's voice but I couldn't see him. I'd fallen asleep on the deck of my clam boat in the middle of the day.

Cal had just come up alongside in another boat. Why couldn't I see him?

"Jonas—Jonas! Wake up, you're O.K.?" Cal said.

I rolled over. No boat. Hell again.

"Julian's up there," he said.

"What? What happened? Sorry, man. I just pooped out. I guess."

"It's O.K. Julian is up in the house. He grabbed a cable or something just as you crumpled. The hatch pushed up."

Above me I could see a sliver of light. Holy moley. Out of the frying pan and into the dogshit!

My ribs ached and my back ached as if I'd been used for stomping practice by the Hell's Angels. It hurt to breathe.

"Cal?"

"What, Jonas?"

"Let's not do that again ever."

CHAPTER TWENTYFIVE

The hatch slid back a little bit more, shedding more light. A rope slithered down through the opening.

"You want to go?" Cal asked.

Did I ever! But I thought he might need a boost.

"You first," I told him.

"All right," he replied without hesitation. Smart man.

Cal humped his way up. It was pretty far. I don't think we would have done it even from the mound.

Then, in the scant light there was—it did seem like a lot, but it was night, and no lights on in the house—I could see the cable Julian must have grabbed. It dipped down in just one spot. It was an extra loop that an electrician didn't feel like trimming. Sloppy intentions mean good shit—for us, anyway. I'd have to tell Julian.

The rope was empty.

Cal was on the floor above, peering down at me. I grabbed the rope and hung my weight on it. But for the life of me I couldn't pull myself up. I just hung there swinging a bit.

Christ.

What now? I'm to be trapped here forever? Serves me right. The only asshole not to escape.

"*Come on!*" Cal whispered frantically.

Can't the stupid fuck see that I can't make it?

I felt like dropping back down on the mound and just curling up in a little ball. I think I would have but Cal suddenly brushed some dirt down from the floor above. It sprayed me in the face.

"God damn it—"

The same shitty cold dirt I'd felt before. I started climbing the rope.

We were in a hallway. The doors off it probably led to bedrooms. But I felt that one of the doors was the one to that office-like room where I'd talked with Taylor, Randy and Leigh.

Julian appeared out of the midnight gloom. "There's a light on in someone's room in the other wing," he said quickly.

I wanted to ask him where he'd found the rope. It was perfect for climbing, like the heavy thick ones in high school gym. No sense making small talk, though.

He was breathing heavily. "You wouldn't guess where I got the rope," he said.

I let out a heavy breath, almost a chuckle. "Where?"

"It was part of a big block and tackle out by the driveway. They were using it to load a trailer there. Matter of fact, the whole thing was attached to the trailer so it wouldn't roll down the mountainside."

"What's holding the trailer now?"

"You'll see."

Good old Julian.

"Which way out?" Cal was anxious to make tracks.

I didn't blame him, but I wasn't through yet.

"Look, I'm going to have a look at those tapes, if nothing else," I said.

Suddenly we heard a door open.

Someone might be coming our way. I dumped the heavy line back down the hole. For a second there I thought of leaving the hatch cover off. It was dark enough for someone to fall right in. Cal and Julian must have had the same thought—we all looked at each other for a moment.

It was a split second in our lives, but one that you lock away to pull out again at an easier time.

We silently slid the cover back in position.

Whoever was down the hall said he'd be back in a minute, and he was coming our way. We pulled back down another passageway as the figure approached. He headed right for the room at the end of the hall. That was the office, I was sure of it.

The room was locked, but whoever it was produced a key and entered, leaving the door open behind him.

Julian was right alongside me. "It's Morowitz," he hissed.

One of the astronomers I'd 'met.'

He'd do just fine. We moved silently into the room after him.

The first thing I noticed was the window I'd jumped through. It was covered over now. Without the stupendous view the room and its artifacts were cheapened somewhat. Maybe it was just the crappy plywood over the window. The raw-looking veneer with CDX Boise Cascade stamped on it just didn't fit. I had an urge to pry the plywood back a bit to see how far down I'd leaped.

Morowitz was digging through some files in the corner, alongside a large television console I hadn't noticed the last time. Maybe it wasn't there then. We came up on him suddenly and his glasses fell right off his face.

Morowitz told us a lot, but a lot he didn't know. Mostly were things we'd guessed already. Taylor and Leigh had recruited him and the other scientists much as they did Cal— an open invitation. Later they'd come to the truth—which that

Taylor had in his possession certain documents that detailed the Second Coming. These documents giving time, date, and certain astronomical data.

Exactly when, however, Morowitz had not been told. I believed him. I could tell that he was uncomfortable around the 'rough element,' as he termed the armed goons hanging around the place lately.

I asked him who the *Devin* was.

"He's from Israel. The *Netorei Karta*," Morowitz said. Anymore he didn't know.

I turned to Cal.

"It's an anti-Zionist group," he said.

"He's anti-Jewish?"

"It's a little more complicated. They're extremely orthodox. Like Hasidics. You know, the little guys with the hats and the curly stands of hair from Brooklyn—"

"Yeah, I know what Hasidic Jews look like. But what's this Netorei Karta. Another secret society?" I made a mental note to ask Morowitz if he knew anything about the Prieure de Sion.

"Well," said Cal, "I really don't know that much about it. But they believe that only the Messiah can establish a Jewish homeland. The *true* Messiah, that is."

I pondered this, and realized that if the 'real' Messiah was coming back it would mean quite a bit to a group like them.

"Another thing," Cal put in quickly, seeming to just catch his intellectual breath. "There are a lot—and I mean more than a few—eminent scientists in the world that are Jewish. I think Morowitz will back me up on that, right?"

"Yes. Without a doubt," Morowitz said.

"So, what I'm saying is, is that we're also dealing here with anti-Semites. I'll bet you that Morowitz and I are the only Jews in the house right now. That's why I'm getting more and more suspicious..."

Christ, Cal could be paranoid. "What?" I asked. "The Nazis? You think Taylor and Randy are Nazis?"

"What'd Julian tell you on the phone?"

"'There are Nazis everywhere—' Right, Ju?" Julian was standing right there. Cal could have aimed the question directly.

Then Morowitz said, "I'm not Jewish."

"See?" cried Cal triumphantly.

"Will you shut up?" Julian ordered.

The door was shut, but there was good reason to be quiet.

"Thanks, Julian," I said quietly. We were getting loud. Then I added, "What'd you say it for?"

"Say what?"

"About the Nazis..."

"Because they are," he answered simply.

I turned back to Morowitz. "What'd they want from you? Specifically."

"Well," he began. Morowitz had a way of saying 'well' that came out in a Western-type drawl that was annoying. It sounded like 'wa-a-a-all,' and highly nasal. Like a kid with adenoid problems. I wanted him to get right into it, and that peculiarity of his was irritating.

"Come on, dammit."

Morowitz sniffed once, like I'd made fun of him. He'd probably been chided about it before, maybe even as a kid. But I wasn't going to let that bother me now.

He went on. "I've been working with Bruce Margon and some other people on SS 433 since he first discovered it back in '78."

"Whoa," I said. "Who is this Margon guy?"

"He discovered it."

"What?"

"SS 433."

"What's that?"

"A star. Unlike any other previously known and..."

"*What* do you mean by that?"

"Will you just let him tell it?" Julian said with an air of finality.

I guess I did get carried away in the interrogation game.

Morowitz looked at me and I just nodded at him.

"Wa-a-all," he began again, "we've been watching SS 433 for awhile now. It's been studied from Mount Hamilton, Palomar, Wilson—and Kitt's Peak, where I'm from.

"In Arizona," he added quickly.

"Go on," I said, nodding approvingly. Times, dates, and places I liked to know.

"The most striking thing about it—making it noticeable—is that its spectrum is *pairs* of emission lines."

Morowitz said this with increasing excitement. He reminded me of Cal when he got wound up—

"Instead of single ones, this star has huge blue and red shifts. Now the blue shift—" He paused here a moment, probably thinking about how to explain all this. "The blue shift indicates matter approaching earth; the red shift, matter receding from earth."

"An emission line," Cal suddenly added, "is a characteristic spectral signature of an element. It appears as a bright, thin band in the spectrum. Am I correct, Doctor?" Morowitz assented. "The spectrum, of course, is the array of colors, or *wavelengths of radiant energy,* that we see when white light passes through a prism."

"Anyway," Morowitz went on. "SS 433 is the first known case of a large blue shift in any celestial spectrum. We found that the red and blue lines were shifting back and forth with a cycle of 160 days and..."

"Well, what the hell is it?" I blurted out.

I didn't have to know that much. We could be here all night. Suddenly it occurred to me that Morowitz had told his companion or whoever he'd left down the hall that he'd be right back. Even now the whole cabal could be on the other side of the door, listening in.

"Wa-a-a-all," he drawled, "there are some—from all over, not just the States—who say SS 433 is a giant black hole, with a mass of a hundred thousand to a million times that of our sun."

Cal whistled softly. "Is it getting closer?"

"Just for the record..."

Turning to me, Cal rejoined, "That's equivalent to something smaller than you can see with a microscope that can hold as much matter within it as Mt. Everest."

Right—

"Wa-a-ll, yes it is, to answer the one question. But there are some others who say that *maybe* it's something else, and that..."

A moment before I'd noticed that Julian had drifted over to the door. He was right alongside it now, flat against the wall, when the door opened.

***

"A piece of it is here already." Dr. Leigh filled the open doorway.

From looking foolish with that carbine a day or so before he now looked very comfortable with the pistol he held stiffly in one hand.

Julian looked like a mischievous school boy about to do a dirty deed. Exactly what, though, I don't think he knew.

Tackle Leigh? There didn't seem to be anyone behind him. But one shot would blow it for us.

"The phenomena—rising in the west—is *from* SS 433, I believe. Wouldn't you agree with me, Dr. Morowitz?"

I instinctively looked at the astronomer. I was still deep into the conversation we'd been having, so I missed Julian's initial leap. He must have batted Leigh's gun hand just right, for the piece came flying across the room and hit me on the foot.

Morowitz just stated at the gun, and for a split second I thought he might even go for it. I didn't want to bump heads with him. My innate politeness would follow me into the grave.

I scooped it up, and with the gun in my hand I told Julian to let Leigh go.

Cal had prudently shut the door and stood with his back against it, a smug look on his face. Julian got up, grinning foolishly still, and sat on the desk. I felt a little wicked myself.

We had the upper hand for the moment and it felt pretty good.

"All right, Leigh. Tell us about it."

"It's near dawn, you fools. Where do you think this will get you? We're on the threshold of a new age..."

Cal cut him off. "I wonder about that. What is SS 433, Leigh? Where does that tie in with the documents you stole?"

Obviously, Leigh didn't like being called a thief. he seemed to throw a hard mask over his features when Cal accused him. But if it was all he seemed to think it was, then he was correct in his previous statement. Hell, I'd be shouting to the rooftops—but then there was always the burden of proof.

"Wherever you got the scroll doesn't matter now. Or the time. We already know that we're worthless to you and your buddies. Otherwise we wouldn't have been tossed in the black hole of Calcutta down the hallway there—" I pointed past him with the gun.

I felt deliciously powerful at the moment, and kept the weapon prominently aimed in his direction. I really wanted to impress upon him the fact that 'new age' or no, he might not ever *see* the dawn.

"Now, why don't you tell us about it. This *phenomena?* This 'Star of Wonder?'" Strange that I could speak of it so, but why not?

"It's true. It's the same phenomena the three wise men followed from the East. And all the astronomical data is the same as that moment two thousand years ago. I have proof."

"Bullshit!" Cal cried. "Maybe there was something in the skies then, but we know it was a comet, or a meteor, or something—just like now."

"And that wasn't the first time a Messiah appeared," Leigh said quietly. There was an intenseness in his voice that seemed to verge on hysteria. He *wanted* to tell us. "The same event has occurred before. With the same results."

"Right, right," Cal said tiredly. "Every time we get a rare grouping of planets or something, the astrologers, whether self-ordained priests or university degreed, decide that *something* is going to happen. Ha, ha...*ha!*"

"What else is happening up there, Morowitz?" I asked.

"Wa-a-all," Morowitz began.

"What does he know?" Cal said irritably.

I couldn't understand what was upsetting him now. "Will you let him talk, Cal?" I asked easily. Maybe it was just Morowitz's voice. It *was* hard on the ears.

"Go ahead, Moro," I said.

"There is a close alignment of planets pretty soon. They'll all be located within a relatively small arc on one side of the sun. The effects of such an alignment can vary from a possible nothing to the catastrophic. It depends. It's happened before, you know."

"When?"

"Wa-a-a-all..."

Leigh smiled grimly. "Two thousand years ago. And before that. But it's not going to matter. This time will be different. Mankind won't have another chance. That's why we've taken so many precautions."

"Including setting up phonies, like Randy and me, in case your predictions don't come out as planned?"

He stared at me derisively. "*You* were a poor choice, indeed, Mr. Coffey. You had the necessary, shall we say, *background?* But you failed us. And, I'm sorry to say, you most miserably failed yourself. Something you seem to be quite proficient at..."

"Shut up, you fuck," Cal said, moving towards him. Leigh cringed.

There was something more between these two than I'd imagined. Or hadn't thought of. I was feeling very ill-at-ease with Leigh myself. He seemed to know *too* much.

"What about my background that everybody seems to think is so important? Huh?" So what? What'd I have to hide anymore?

Cal sighed.

"The breakdowns, Jonas," he said resignedly. "Your past mental history. Nadine knew about it. Studied it. They plugged your profile into a computer and figured you were a likely candidate."

"But why me? Just because Nadine knew me?"

I was just a guinea pig.

"What about Randy? Is he programmed too?"

Leigh and Cal shook their heads.

"Why don't you tell him the rest, Dr. Franks?" Leigh said.

"What?" I said.

"About where they got you..."

"*Shutup*, Leigh——" Cal growled.

I had the feeling that I'd been had again. All the bravado I'd had earlier was leaking away. Was Cal in with them too? Just '...playing those mind games, together...' as John Lennon used to sing it began running through my head and I started fingering the little gun in my hand.

A pretty little thing. The gun. Tight and small and wicked and deadly. So much more business-like than the .45 revolver I used to shoot or any of the service weapons I once handled. This one had a very small diameter barrel. Probably .22 caliber.

Make a nice round hole in someone.

I wondered what it would do to that small lump of bone just behind my ear...

"Jonas, look, I..." Cal began saying, though for once he was tongue tied, tripping over his words like an inept lover. "I didn't...I couldn't know..."

"Why dontcha just *tell* him, Cal?" Julian suddenly burst out with.

He was down off the desk and stood facing me.

Cal didn't say anything. Morowitz looked bewildered.

I felt like Morowitz looked.

And Leigh had a smirk on his puss that meant disaster for all hands.

"I told her, Jonas," Julian said. "She asked, and I told her."

"But...but I never really said anything to you about... about..." I stammered. It was true. We had never talked about it.

"You told me enough. The service...Resthaven in L.A. Sketchy, but Nadine had the credentials to get records. I talked to her over a year ago about you."

A year ago?

"She's nuts!" I cried. But I felt she wasn't so nuts. I was the fucking nut. I'd told her stuff, too. I felt betrayed. But not by Cal anymore. I told everybody things about myself. I had nothing to hide, and what I did, I never thought would matter...

"So what?" I said. "Some people have prison records. I've been in the nuthouse. Sorry, Leigh. Nice gambit, but you lose. Now I want to know something, or rather *see* it. Where are those tapes? I want to see my act."

I was feeling a little hyper—

A *little?* Hell, who likes their psychic laundry gone over by their 'friends?'

But at least Leigh was a little more cooperative now. He dug out a tape from a whole library of them underneath a row of shelves. Julian set it up on the machine.

While Julian did this, Cal told me that somehow I must have fit a personality type that Nadine or the others felt would be easily led. Especially under the influence of certain drugs that Nadine was very familiar with, and she was familiar with most of them.

And though there were probably thousands of people like me that they could have used, I was the most convenient: I was known to be a dreamer; to take chances; have suicidal tendencies (in case they had to dump me); I was a sailor (dramatic effect?). And a lot of background legwork was avoided by just asking mutual friends about me.

But exactly *why* me, there didn't seem to be an answer in present company.

I regretted dumping the rope back down the hole.

I didn't want Leigh to do anything fancy, while Morowitz was another unknown. But then Julian turned the monitor on—the show was ready to go.

There I was, right alongside the *Devin*, just as Cal said. It was a press conference arrangement and reporters were asking questions. I recognized some of the 'reporters' too. The whole thing was a phony setup—but could have been just a dress rehearsal.

Either way, I had trouble seeing myself like that. I spoke in biblical parables, sidestepping questions that the *Devin* wouldn't answer.

At one point I was explaining, on the tape, that the "sons of the kingdom will be expelled into outer darkness. There will be weeping and grinding of teeth there." I was quoting the Master. I sounded so utterly serene and looked so calm I could have been Randy.

I never knew that I could be that much at ease.

I kind of liked it. My new presence, so to speak. But the message was harsh. We spoke much of fire and damnation to be visited on those little of faith.

The piece wasn't that long. Less than a minute, it seemed. Enough of a teaser, though. We played it through and were about to cut it off when it came on again. Everything was the same, except the language had changed. German now, either our lips perfectly synched, or we were actually *speaking* another language. Hard to tell.

I had Julian run the machine fast forward on a hunch— same act, different language. Again and again. The tape seemed to be a master of some kind.

Even Cal was impressed. "I've got to hand it to them," he said. "It's goddamn amazing."

"Why?" I asked Leigh.

He didn't seem to want to answer.

Cal did. "For worldwide distribution, of course. Isn't that right, Leigh?"

"In twenty-five languages. The message, this time, will be truly universal."

"But how do you hope to pull it off?" I asked.

"Oh, He's coming," Leigh said calmly, with a touch of reverential lunacy. "We just want to make sure He gets—"

"The proper news coverage," Cal finished for him. "Don't you see, Jonas? They're making the Second Coming—the *proposed* Second Coming—a media event! It's all engineered, right here from mission control. Who even needs Jesus with everything they got here. They don't even need *you* anymore. They already got you on tape, in twenty-five goddamned languages, no less, spreading the Word like some kind of electronic..."

"Prophet," I put in.

"Yeah. These yahoos don't believe in Him either. They just want everybody else to believe so *they* can run the show."

Leigh spoke up, and his voice, redolent with latent fanaticism, brought to mind that carnival side-show image: "You're right, Dr. Franks. But think of it. This time the Word will be truly *universal!* All the signs are here for a spiritual awakening the world has never really seen in its entirety. Human history is marked several times by the coming of a savior. But has it made any difference? No. Mankind has gone on in the same tired way, working along towards his – *and the Earth's*—destruction! There's a chance here. A real chance for Christian values to be upheld, for God's precious Word to be abided by, for all to know the..."

BEHOLD THIS DREAMER

"Lord Jesus Christ as their personal Savior." I finished if for him this time. Leigh's rhetoric was bible-belt fanaticism all right, but with *auto de fe* hovering in the background. It was just a feeling I had, one that this whole scheme reeked of.

It became very quiet for a moment. All of us, Morowitz included, wanted to know just what Leigh was proposing. He looked us over like we were all doomed anyway.

"I might as well tell you," Leigh sighed. "I brought back from Ophel Hill more than evidence of a Second Coming. The astronomical signs were the most pertinent, of course. I found proof that the same conditions have occurred at least twice before, in different parts of the world, at different times. Giving rise to legends or myths of a recurrent Messiah."

"But what are you saying? There is no *real* Messiah?" I asked.

Leigh faced me directly. "Jesus was a *man*, Jonas. Just like you and me."

"You have *proof* of this?" Cal asked quickly.

"Yes. Not irrefutable, I'm afraid. But..." He hesitated, as though being sure about anything was becoming increasingly impossible. He went on in a low voice: "That's why we must act *now*, while conditions are right, just as they were then."

But why the conspiratorial tone? What was he afraid of? Was it a deep-rooted, maybe even primeval conviction that was so hard to buck? Or was he just crazy...like they all probably were...

"You're fucking crazy," I said.

It was the easiest thing for me to say, but I knew a nut when I heard one. That's why *I* was here. "Where are these Scrolls, Leigh? Show them to us."

"They're not here," Leigh haughtily replied, as if we'd asked him to show us his underwear. "We're not a small organization, you know. We have enclaves all over the world."

289

"The *Prieure de Sion*," Cal whispered.

Leigh chuckled. "No, but you are close. Those fools and their book have done us no harm. It doesn't matter. We're too close now, and we're fully prepared for anything."

"You said the 'conditions,' as you call them, have been the same twice before. What do you mean by that?"

Leigh looked at me. He seemed to be almost trying to gain something from me, as though I held something over him. "You know of the last time. There was another before that—thousands of years and miles away from the Mideast—another fertile area where civilization reached a peak, then began to crumble, to decay into a morass of moral turpitude and over-indulgence. The idea of the Messiah, in somewhat of the same form, came to the ancestors of the Incas."

"The Heavenly City. *Macchu Picchu*," Cal said.

"Yes," answered Leigh, nodding.

"You found such evidence there?"

"Among other places. Dr. Taylor and I found some extremely interesting artifacts near the source of the Amazon and a peak called *Ojas del Salado*. Relics that would astound biblical scholars. But this is besides the point. It has happened before, though."

"What about the markings? The ones that can only be seen from the air—out in the desert?" Cal asked.

"At Nazca? There's some sort of tie-in there. We've found other evidence of that. Probably due to the astronomical events, which seem to play such a large part in the whole procedure."

Leigh seemed to be able to blithely switch from proselyte to disinterested engineer. Whatever seemed to suit his needs at the moment. He would have made a good consultant to the Inquisition. But I wanted to change the subject. There was something about the Indians...

"How are you going to get all the tapes out? Just send them to the networks?"

"We have access to a transmitter where the taped interviews will go out simultaneously all over the globe," he said smugly.

"They'll just bounce it off a satellite. Or satellites," Cal added. "That's what the set-up is for on St Croix, isn't it?"

"Interesting that you should know that," Leigh said carefully.

"I don't know how you ever expect to get away with this."

"Ah, we will. It's destiny. The time is ripe and the time is ours! Do you realize that throughout history man has always struggled to become *more* than he is—"

I thought of the classic line in a movie where a mad scientist—German, of course—explains to someone that human life was just the scum on somebody's dirty pool.

"—and in the process he creates the idea of a *God*. An all-powerful entity that, being omnipotent and omnipresent, emulates the good side of man. This in turn makes man a *copy* of the god, ennobling him and uplifting him, enabling the poor half-beast that man *really is* to overcome life's innate brutalities. And, of course, pretend to ideals and morals."

Leigh paused, his eyes searching all of ours.

"Yes," he went on. "The time is now. We have need of a new religion. The old ones, dinosaurs that they are, have become stale, outmoded and out classed. The people turn away from them, looking for solace in drugs and electronic marvels. And just as Jesus and his followers saw the need two thousand years ago, and others in antiquity before them, *we* are now taking the great step to lead mankind back into..."

"The fold, Leigh? Is that what the creationist line is all about? Do you think people are really going to buy it?"

He laughed. "They've *already* bought it! The evolutionists can't decide whose theory to pit against ours. The public always wants a good show, and we've given it to them! That machine right there—"

He pointed to the monitor.

"That machine has mesmerized the earth. What people see there they believe as *gospel!*"

"You're giving them an electronic Christ," I said.

"And why not? You would rather we stuck with parchment and stylus, and live oratory, reaching *maybe* a very small percentage, who would undoubtedly just turn on channel seven the moment they got home anyway just to see what's happening on *Cheers?* Such is the age we live in!"

"It's just another soporific," Cal argued. "You bastards are just in it for the power."

"On the contrary," Leigh countered. "We *all* could have been in on it, as you say. But you choose not to. That's to your own detriment, not mine. The path we have chosen for man is at least uplifting."

There was a small space where the plywood covering the broken window didn't cover. I'd been watching it, and I could see the ocean far below the house now through that space. It was getting light. We had to move. Somewhere.

"We've got to get moving," I said anxiously.

Leigh just smiled that sly serene smile of his.

He reminded me of a picture I saw once of the head of a Beluga whale. The same bulging baldpate, squinty eyes and unflappable grin. I could have blown his smug head off.

"One thing, Leigh. Where's it to be this time? I mean, we had Macchu Picchu and Jerusalem."

"Follow the star, Jonas. The Star of Wonder!"

He was really cracked.

I turned to Morowitz, shaking the little pistol in what I felt was a menacing way. "What about it? You're the astronomer."

"Wa-a-a-all," he said.

There was a knock on the door.

We all froze. I wondered if the door was even locked. Whoever it was must have heard our voices—hopefully a servant. Who else would be up this early?

It was Roberto, the falsetto-voiced houseboy. Julian pulled him in quickly.

Now we really had to go.

My first inclination was to dump them down the hole. Instead we tied them up with some TV cable. Leigh smiled through it all.

We crept through the main room of the house. I hadn't really noticed it before, but I should have.

It was an immense room, at least thirty by sixty feet, with a high ceiling. A Persian rug covered most of the floor. Flanking an entrance were two huge elephant tusks. A rhinoceros horn hung on one wall. There were African shields and drums here and there, a number of stuffed animal heads, some more of those ceremonial masks like there were in the office, a bronze bust of a Masai warrior, even a totem pole.

On another wall were some antique rifles and long knives. In a corner was a strange-looking horn that appeared to be made of copper. It was at least eight feet long.

"What the hell is that?" I whispered to Cal.

He looked at me with annoyance.

"It's a Tibetan temple horn," he told me quietly.

We crouched by it. It had been my idea to go this way, mainly because I wanted to see this room. Julian had already gone outside to check out a possible escape vehicle.

"Its sound is supposed to represent the void."

What?

"You mean *nothing?*"

"No. There is a sound. Kind of low, very hollow sounding."

"You've heard it, then?" I had an urge to take it with me. I wanted to hear it.

"Yeah. There's one in New York. At the Explorer's Club. This room reminds me of it." He looked around as he spoke. "Come on, Jonas. Let's go!"

"We should take one of those tapes with us," I said.

I was holding back for some reason. Perhaps for the *Fehlleistung* of blowing the temple horn right there. And I wouldn't have minded a little *tete a tete* with Randy. Or Nadine.

I still had the gun. But it was probably impossible to even find them now in that big house, if they were even there.

"Maybe on St Croix we can get one of the tapes," I said, placating myself. "You're right, we just better move now."

"They don't have anything on St Croix," Cal said. "I just wanted to see how much Leigh was lying. Everything's probably right here. Julian told me when we were in the pit that there was enough electrical power in this place to light up a small town."

"Well, dammit then! Let's not let them get away with it! No one will believe us once this shit gets out. Let's find that transmitter room."

I started edging back towards the way we'd come. I was hot now—

Cal grabbed me. "Hold it, you dumb cluck. We can go to the cops right here if you want. There's a number of charges we can level. Kidnapping, for one."

I looked at him.

He was serious.

"Yeah, sure. They're really going to believe a couple of convicted dopers. And if you think they'll believe *you*,

you're crazier than I am."

The large room faced north, and the rapidly lightening sky filled the windows with a soft grayish glow which seemed to reflect the sea so far below. The polished copper horn shone eerily in the gray light.

Time was wasting.

I was going, Cal or not. I almost knocked over a small table in my haste. Something fell to the floor and I automatically picked it up.

It was a tiny boat, made of reeds.

I looked it over, turning it slowly.

The boat was made of rolls of thin reeds bundled together, the bundles coming to a fine point at each end.

"I used to make these when I was a kid," I told Cal. "It was the only thing I could do that impressed the old man."

Cal grimaced. "You used to make them like *that?*"

"Yeah. I could have made this one." I turned it upside down. "Where's it from? You know?"

"It's a copy of the reed boats the Uru Indians made. They lived on islands of reeds that they made on Lake Titicaca."

"Titicaca? That's in South America, right?"

"Peru."

Something was trying to click on inside me. It was a curious feeling, as if I was mentally stuttering. I had to know more.

"What were they like?"

"Who?"

"Those Uru Indians—"

"Jonas, this isn't the place!"

"Come on, Cal. We've come this far, we'll get out. Now *tell* me," I begged him, holding the little boat in my hands.

He sighed. "I don't know that much, but the Incas treated them with a mixture of awe and contempt. They were said to have certain powers, but lived a lowly existence...I don't know...they seemed an anomaly. The name itself, Uru, meant 'light of day' in the Aymara language. They're the Indians who live on Titicaca today."

"What happened to the Uru?"

"They're gone. That's the other thing. In the Inca language Uru meant 'vermin.'"

"Macchu Picchu is in Peru, too, isn't it?"

"Just north of Titicaca. Come on," he said impatiently.

I wasn't satisfied. "Where's Ojos del Salado?"

"God! I don't know, Jonas!"

I decided to leave off the questioning. I was groping, but there was something about those boats—

"Let's talk to Randy," I said calmly.

"*What?* Are you crazy?"

"Too?" I added. Then I said, "Wait outside with Julian if you want. Or take off. That'd be better. The two of you split. I'll get out of here myself."

"You're being an asshole, Jonas. They don't *need you* anymore. You'll end up in the hole again, or worse."

Cal sounded really sincere; I wanted to snicker at his melodramatic tone. I had the feeling he was right, though.

"Do me a favor then. From one asshole to another, O.K.? Everybody's going to be up in a little while. Let's give them something to do. Julian said he got the rope from a trailer or something out there—"

I had no idea what to tell Cal, but Julian would know what to do. I went on:

"Just tell Julian we need a *diversion*, O.K.? And I'll meet you guys at the seaplane base—Julian knows where—tonight. Let's say at eight o'clock. Got that?"

"Yeah," Cal said resignedly.

"Go," I told him.

He hesitated a moment, then left. I was alone now. Strangely enough, I felt relieved. What ever happened now would fall on me alone and I wanted that.

It was almost fully morning now. I hid behind a huge ottoman as a servant passed through the room. People were getting up.

CHAPTER TWENTYSIX

As soon as it seemed safe, I made for a connecting hallway. As I turned a corner I heard Roberto shouting in his ringing falsetto.

Damn! That meant they were loose. I never could tie certain knots.

I skipped down the passageway, looking for—what? Randy? The transmitter room?

People were hot-footing it all over now. I ducked into a little alcove that had a door off it leading somewhere. I cracked it open as quietly as I could.

Labored breathing met my ears. I could then hear little cries of delight and deeper-sounding grunts.

Somebody was getting laid.

I hoped it was Nadine and Randy. I pictured myself bursting in, with them in coital embrace, and then registering double shock when they realize that it's me—

"Something's happening," a deep male voice said.

"Yes! I know," another voice replied breathlessly.

"No. I mean outside. In the house..."

It *could* be Nadine, but I was pretty sure her partner wasn't Randy. But I was curious to see just *whom* she was fucking if it wasn't him.

"Don't get up yet," the voice pleaded. It must be Nadine.

"You like it like this," he said, his voice slightly familiar now, guttural sounding. "Don't you?"

Like what?

"Let me…get…up on my…knees more," the voice croaked in a husky whisper, the words coming out in little bursts, sounding an increasing rhythm. A musk laden scent, redolent of sex and bitch-in-heat, surrounded me.

It *had* to be Nadine. I could tell that sex-voice anywhere. The smell seemed to clinch it.

I could be wrong though: women in the throes of passion, like their partners, seem to reach a universal level where they become one—indistinguishable from each other or anyone else.

Suddenly there came a terrific crash from outside the house. There was a window in the bedroom I was eavesdropping on. I could see the daylight on the carpet through the slightly opened door. I chanced a look, pushing the door inward.

The bed was off to one side, the participants crouched in canine position. *Coitus interruptus,* and intent on the action just beyond the window.

They had a side-long view of the hillside which tumbled down to Leinster Bay. I had to enter the room to see what they could. I kept the pistol erect in front of me as I softly treaded by the foot of the bed.

It was a wonderful sight.

The trailer Julian had purloined our escape rope from was charging merrily down towards the water, equipment flying out of it at each bounce, tearing a ragged path through the brush.

A gaggle of house servants and a few goons were gesturing and shouting from the now empty spot where the trailer had been. They were suddenly enveloped in a cloud of dust as a Jeep roared by them, scattering a couple down the hill in the general direction of the impetuously released trailer.

At the wheel was Julian, dark hair flying as he maneuvered the Jeep expertly—at full bore—up the twisting dirt track away from the house. Cal was alongside him, looking back; right at me, it seemed. Goodbye, amigos! *Adios!*

There were a few scattered shots, then a steady spray of machine gun fire as the goons realized they'd been beat. The Jeep was getting out of range, but then the windshield erupted in spider-cracks and a tail light exploded, the red and chrome plastic pieces reflecting the morning sun as they drifted back down to earth through the brown dust.

For a few seconds the Jeep was invisible. I felt as if my guts had fallen out and been replaced with a large cold rock.

"*Ach!* De got dem now!" cried the rearward figure on the bed.

Klaus.

He had his naked back to me, his hairless ass pinched tight, but I could tell him by the heavy folds where his neckless head met his shoulders, the prickly bristle hairs there coated with sex-dew.

I was directly behind them, and Klaus had his partner's hips tightly grasped. Klaus, excited now, rammed it home; a painful-sounding groan, not exactly a *complaint* though, came from below him.

I thought suddenly of the line, 'Every woman adores a Fascist.' How fitting. Cal would've enjoyed this. I hoped I'd be able to tell him about it…

I looked down towards the bay just as the trailer, minus most of its cargo, hit the water. It made quite a splash. I could've added my own pleasurable groans to those on the bed.

I didn't want to look up the mountain; the dust would have cleared by now and I'd made the decision to almost empty the pistol immediately into the figures atop the bed, saving one bullet for myself.

But we got a reprieve—

"*Dumkopfs!*" grunted Klaus.

I caught his Mussolini-like profile, lower lip bulging, heavy brows twitching. Then followed his scornful gaze out the window.

The Jeep was further up the hillside, perched on a small bluff. Julian and Cal were leaning out, having impishly stopped to watch the trailer's demise.

The group on the road below were still randomly firing at them, and I blurted out, "*Get going you dumb bastards!*"

My sentiments, of course, were somewhat differently directed than those of Klaus—

It has always amazed me, though by now it shouldn't have, just how *fast* large beings can move. I really shouldn't be surprised; after all, a boat's speed is a function of its waterline length, at least with displacement-type non-planing vessels, such as most sailing craft. The longer the boat, the faster it'll go.

This equation also holds true for large animals. The elephant and the hippopotamus are among the swiftest when aroused, as is the whale. And every kid on the block can tell you how close to nine seconds their favorite pro halfback, bending the scales in the 100 kilo range, can do a hundred yards.

Anyway—

Klaus spun half-way around, dragging his limp human reservoir with him. He pulled loose as he recognized me, moving very fast; though he made a ridiculous sight, phallus still erect and slick, he was almost on me before I could blink twice. The gun he seemed to disregard as does a bear a gnat, slapping it away with one monstrous paw as the other swiped at my throat.

I had instinctively backed off just enough. Klaus's flight

ended with a crunch as his head hit the window shelf. I couldn't help noticing that even though he'd split the thick wood shelf with his chin, his eyes, still on mine with a robot-like intensity, never blinked.

Perhaps it's strange that at moments of extreme stress or trauma many people focus in on details that seem woefully incongruent at that specific moment, but later on the most insignificant flash or minor event experienced, if remembered and reflected upon, leads to greater understanding of our actions in the split-second decision making process that can mean added time to our lives *or*—and this is, maybe, what it is all about—one's swift extinction.

I'm speaking of whatever influences us to turn either right or left, to hesitate or go forward, to focus in on one detail to the exclusion of others—the survival instinct that some develop because they know it is there, and others just follow almost unknowingly.

Being in the latter group of survivalists, I don't really know what made me dive for the opposite side of the bed—versus towards my gun, which had slid conveniently near the door.

There was only *one* way out, and I'd just leaped in the other direction. Maybe it had to do with the 'vibes,' as my shrink would say, that were in the room. There was a difference in the sexual air here that I was unaccustomed to.

At any rate, in the micro-seconds that I'd avoided Klaus, I had focused in on two things. One was a flash of color, a red silk scarf that Nadine was fond of wearing and the other thing was dark hair. A profusion of it.

Both impressions suddenly appeared where I wouldn't expect them to be. This, plus a furtive movement from the figure on the bed, which I picked up out of the corner of my eye, probably accounted for my aberrant maneuver.

I was in mid-leap. A bright flash, then a shock wave stung the side of my face. No sound, though. Strange.

I knew what it was: I'd almost caught a bullet in the teeth, and had just missed the oblivion express...

I bounced on the sweat-drenched mattress, feeling a small heavy object bounce along with me. Someone had lost their grip, and I was glad it wasn't me yet. But I was still on a roll, and grabbed the still bouncing object—a weapon—and came off the bed and onto the floor in one uncanny movement.

I felt like Steve McQueen, Charles Bronson, and Clint Eastwood all rolled into one—

The red scarf I had just glimpsed outside on the road below—Nadine was wearing it. The dark hair covered the posterior of one of the lovers on the bed. Where women don't have any.

It was just sunup, and the room was still in shadows. I righted a small lamp I'd knocked over when I'd come off the bed. I was still on the floor and hesitated a moment before switching the lamp on.

The agitated smoke from the gunshot hung in the air above the bed, the sky beyond the windows a simple gray. There was no sound or movement from the foot of the bed where Klaus had been.

The figure on the bed sat up; the face still in shadow. I said, "Don't move," but I couldn't hear myself, so I said it again, trying harder. Something was wrong. But the figure froze. I switched on the lamp.

"...have to shout," he said.

It was Taylor.

I stood up, my hearing suddenly back. There was more shouting outside, and the sound of vehicles trying to start. I smiled at the continuous cranking noise—none of the engines were firing.

Julian had covered his escape well. For the first time I felt I should have been with him and Cal.

Taylor was wearing a sickly-sweet smile, his nakedness obscenely grotesque in the yellow lamp light. I felt somehow contaminated just being in the room with him. He'd almost blown my face off for catching him *inflagrante delicto*...

Klaus was just a big mound of bloody flesh now, thrown against the wall like discarded refuse. A mis-calculated moment in time, a cerebral mis-flash, and our worlds collapse.

Taylor's eyes were wet; his breathing taking a load. I felt for him, suddenly realizing that the enormity of death, with which I had been so familiar, he had probably never experienced. I had had the 'experience' to the point where I'd become essentially incapacitated mentally. I had always been at the effect of death; never the cause.

This feeling of helplessness, always being at the effect of death, angered me now. I felt cheated. I realized also that it had never been worth the nuthouse—the degradations, the explanations, the incredible loss of self. The feeling of endless ruin and emptiness of days with no end spent wandering...ah, self-pity! How well I know thy bitter-sweet kiss!

I felt like saying something cute, like "You happy now, Doctor?" or something equally Bogartish, punctuating the line by poking him with the barrel of the gun.

Turning to face me, Taylor suddenly spit out, *"You scum!"*
What!?

"How dare you disrupt this most momentous historical and religious undertaking! It's scum like you that forced the Messiah underground. You, who have no conception of responsibility, no sense of propriety, no feeling of respect for your betters!"

I couldn't believe what I was hearing. "What are you

talking about, Taylor?" I shouted at him. "You just blew your...friend...away. How can you...?"

I was getting upset again. I had to control it. I was getting quickly into a rage, and I knew now where *that* led me: To either one end of the emotional spectrum or the other—incomprehensible rage or total docility. And that always put me back in the cage. A game I could never win once started.

"'Be submissive to every human institution for the Lord's sake,'" Taylor intoned, ignoring my outburst. "That's from the first epistle of Peter, Jonas. Listen! 'You domestic slaves should with unqualified respect be submissive to your masters, not only to the kind and considerate but also to those who are harsh; for this is meritorious, if with consciousness of God one endures the pain of unjust sufferings. For what merit is there in standing a beating for doing wrong? But if you bear patiently with suffering when you are doing right, this is pleasing to God. To such experience you have been called!'"

So Taylor was cracked too. That same smell, one that seemed to permeate the house now that I thought of it, was especially strong here. I'd noticed it in Key Biscayne and on the *Melchoir* also. I finally realized what it was.

Ayahuasca. The hallucinogenic the Peruvian Indians are so fond of. I should have remembered.

I *did* remember a cocaine dealer friend of Cal's who brought some back from Lima. He touted it for a few weeks, turning everyone on. It wasn't very pleasant, though. Nothing like coke. But he really got into it; so much so that he stopped dealing cocaine. Everyone said he was a changed man after that. The last I heard of him he was in Creedmoor, the massive state mental hospital in Queens, just outside New York City.

Taylor droned on: "'...for he who has suffered physically has gained relief from sin, so that he no longer lives by human passions but for the rest of his natural life he lives by what God wills...'"

The gunsmoke was stratifying in the middle reaches of the room. We had to be having visitors soon. A servant or somebody would be in telling the boss what had happened.

"*Taylor!*" I grabbed his bare leg and yanked him around.

He shut up.

"Is it the Ayahuasca that Nadine's been using? Is that what she's used on me?"

He blinked. I could see his eyes now, grayish pools that were startlingly clear. "It is more than that. Much more. Do you think we're just a simple cult? Brewing potions with the bark of a jungle vine? Every culture had their elixirs, their poisons, their stimulants. *We* are forging a new culture—a *new* religion!"

"But I can smell it! This place reeks of it!"

"Yes. But there is more. The vine is not the only catalyst for talking with God!"

I had to get out of there. Taylor sounded like a sixties acid-head. He'd just killed Klaus instead of me, but the act seemed to have no effect on him. Charles Manson would have been proud.

"Where's the transmitter room?"

"Why? Do you think that *you* can stop us? Your friends won't be believed. I have the highest standing in these islands, if not the world!"

"Can it, Doc!" I waved the gun at him. "This toy of yours can stop *you!* Look what it did to your friend over there."

He shrugged as if I'd complained about the weather. "Sacrifices have to be made. Mistakes, also. Such as you, Jonas. I was against using you from the beginning. Your sociopathic background did not intrigue me as it did some of the others."

"Who? Nadine?"

"Yes. Dr. Griffiths was one in your corner. But Dr. Rand actually chose you."

"*Chose* me?"

"I am surprised at your astonishment. He knew so much about you. Surely, you..."

"I never laid eyes on him until Key Biscayne!" I was perplexed. Randy? "But Nadine could have filled him in. She had access to all the records. She *knew* me."

"Maybe," Taylor mused. He seemed to be suddenly looking at me in a new light, almost as if he'd had a revelation. "You were never a *patient* of Dr. Rand's?"

"What?"

My face must have answered his question for him. There was something else I wanted to know. I hadn't been getting the answers I wanted to until now, but then I never did. My questions always seemed to precipitate *more* questions.

I remembered Cal saying once, after a long drunken harangue, that all answers were self-evident, and questions merely man's excuse to bullshit. If that was what I was doing now, so be it.

There was a bible on the floor where it had fallen, from probably off the night table I'd knocked over. I picked it up. "Who did it, Taylor? Who set up the specialty edition just for me? What'd you guys do, a brain removal and then just wring it out like a sponge?"

He stared at me, his nakedness now as natural as the sunlight that filled one side of the room. The side where Klaus was lying, against the wall. "'Truly I assure you that he who listens to My message and believes Him who sent Me has eternal life; he comes under no sentence but has passed over from death into life.' Do you know who told me that? Or, rather, explicated the true essence of it for me? Listen! 'Double think means the power of holding two contradictory beliefs in one's mind simultaneously, and accepting both of them.' Sound familiar?"

I nodded. "The second more than the first. Orwell, *1984*. I know what you are talking about." I opened the book in my hands, but Taylor's bible, like my own, was—

"*Doctor Taylor!*" A voice screamed from the doorway. Sounded like Roberto.

It was. He came in and turned white at the sight of Klaus. I pointed the gun at him. He bolted.

"Fuck!" I cried.

Taylor hadn't missed it. I'd failed to shoot. Then, logically, I wouldn't shoot him...

Almost before I knew it, I was sprinting down the hallway.

I fetched up at the end of a corridor, where two large metal doors were shut tight and locked. I still had the big revolver Taylor almost parted my face with. There had to be a big room beyond the doors. They looked heavy enough to be sound-proofed.

I felt like Alice: I was alone in a strange place, a stranger in a strange land. And I was going all the way.

I stood back and blasted away at the door knobs, feeling like some movie hero. I was strong, invincible. With a single kick the doors burst open and I swaggered through.

Inside was a sterile-looking environment with twenty or so video tape machines, the big ones. There were as many screens, and a gigantic console contraption that dominated one end of the room. The floor was interesting—alternating squares of red and green. Christmas colors. How appropriate.

I climbed the steps up to the console. There it all was. A

plethora of switches and dials and blinking lights. It was unreal. Ultra-real. Star Wars or Mission Control. James Bond or CNN.

Yeah. Like being in a news room. Clocks were lined up on the walls, all set to different times. One for each zone. Of course.

Incredible, it was. And all true. It was happening. If there *were* any doubts, the flooding tide of television coverage would do the trick. What normal modern human being could deny a barrage of commercials *telling* you that *Jesus Christ* is here again?

Hell, TV commercials sell stuff that one couldn't *give* away live on the street. If it's seen on the tube people swear by it. Genius or insanity? Did it make any difference?

Would *I?*

CHAPTER TWENTYSEVEN

H ello, Jonas."
I wasn't surprised. I knew he'd be here.
"I know the whole scam," I told him. I displayed the gun with bravado, intending to give the impression that I was in 'control.' "Klaus is dead. Taylor shot him."

I wasn't saying what I wanted to say.

"He's lu-lu, and so is Leigh," I continued.

Randy moved closer, slowly mounting the steps to where I sat up on the console. He watched me steadily as I blathered on about everything but *what* I wanted to say.

He stopped at the step below me

(God, I was glad for that)

and stood listening, like a patient older sibling with a tired and nervous child.

I started telling him about the significance of the number three, beginning, of course, with the close association with death I had had, particularly the last occasion minutes earlier.

"It's always three, Randy."

"Yes, it is, Jonas. A frequently evoked image. *Always* a fateful choice."

"Three caskets in the *Merchant of Venice*, three daughters in *King Lear*, the Holy Trinity: Father, Son, Holy Ghost...but what do you mean by choice? *What* choice did I have?"

"Jonas, all human beings wish to believe that they have a *choice* when they have *none!* Things just are. As for three, well, it's simply a symbolic expression of the three fateful roles that the female plays in the life of the male. As mother, as lover, and, finally, as the symbolic mother, earth itself—to whom man returns when he dies."

"I've never killed anyone," I said with ineffable sadness. I felt myself slipping away. A struggle just to focus on the moment. "What was Morowitz talking about? The star—phenomena, or whatever. What's really happening?"

"Whatever you *want* to happen."

"*Don't bullshit me!* I'll blow your fucking head off, damn it!" Anger helped. I could hold on to that somewhat.

Randy stiffened, then relaxed. "You mean the Jupiter effect. The alignment of the planets on one side of the sun?"

He was playing with me. "SS 433, Randy. The chunk of it that's in the atmosphere now. Just like two thousand years ago. And before that. You know what I'm talking about! The 'cloud' that's been in the news, circling the earth."

"Ah, but *you* know, Jonas," he said solemnly. "You just don't *want* to remember. I've been trying, with the help of your friends…"

"Friends? What friends? They're gone by now. And you'll be lucky if they don't come back with the cops!" I felt really self-righteous saying that, but Randy just slowly shook his head, his dark dark eyes open and serene.

"You've read a lot, Jonas. And you've seen a lot of films. You're the epitome of alienated modern man. You don't know where you're going, *but*…I know where you've been."

"The book. That 'bible.' Where'd *that* come from?" I'd been wanting to ask that. It's all I really wanted to know.

"You still don't know." He shook his head, his long hair swinging back and forth. "Hoo, boy—" A western-style twang slipped into his voice: "Remember one time, when you was a little feller—"

He put an elbow on one bent knee, hand under his chin. All he needed now was a Stetson to push back on his head.

"You were making one of your little reed boats. A *balsa!*"

He watched me, a questioning look in his bottomless eyes, shiny flecks glittering.

"And you had to go. You know, to the bathroom. You were in the backyard, over by the lilac bushes, the ones covered with honeysuckle."

He was describing the backyard I grew up in, and as he did so my eyes welled up, and I could feel a tear in each tremble on the lip of their lids.

"You were standing in that little sand pit your father had dug. Where the wild bamboo grew."

Jesus. What was he doing? His voice was changing again, getting New Yorkish, Brooklyn, the Bronx—

"You had to go really bad, but your father was in the house, and you were afraid he'd ask what you were doing."

How old was I then?

"You were terrified of him, and felt more at ease going in your pants." He looked at me through half-closed eyes, then they closed more, becoming thin conspirational slits.

I remembered now. I must have been five years old.

"You waited until you thought your father was asleep. He normally took a short nap in the afternoon – *when he was home.*"

Another switch: Randy drawled now, slurring some words, biting others off in the peculiar manner of a California native. "But after you got in the bathroom he woke up, and followed your shitty foot prints there. It'd run down your pants and into your shoes…"

And caught me in the bathroom scraping the shit off my

shoes with the little boat I'd made from the reeds that grew in the drainage ditch just beyond the honeysuckle-covered lilac bushes...

***

"Get down off there, Jonas! Roberto, go tell the others we've found him." Taylor was standing in the doorway with Leigh. Roberto was trotting quickly back down the passageway, a machine gun bouncing on his back like a broken wing.

Randy didn't turn around, but stood watching me.

He reminded me of Bogart at the end of *Casablanca*. I almost expected to hear Dooley Wilson singing 'As Time Goes By,' and Randy-Bogart, as Rick, say, "It's over with, pal. Why dontcha give yourself up?"

But not yet. I knew that somehow Randy was everything I'd ever heard or known. He was that combinative *Uber-ich* of Freud's. The all-American superego, seeking to destroy or bury the guilty self.

At least I wanted Randy to be that. I began pushing buttons on the console.

There was a whispering noise as the reels began spinning. I pushed forward a switch, below which read *Speaker 1*. There were more than twenty others like it, and a big double yoke switch labeled in red: *Transmission*.

CHAPTER TWENTYEIGHT

It's like Guy Fawkes said: *Desperate diseases require desperate remedies.* Just before he was drawn and quartered.

I put my hand on the big red switch, feeling the contoured plastic under my grip. "Here we go, folks!"

I had them by the short hairs for once. Taylor and Leigh weren't moving a muscle. Randy stayed put. A few others showed at the door—Morowitz and some other 'scientists.'

There was nothing on the video screens, so I played with a few dials. Still nothing, then I turned one clockwise that said *Volume.*

A resonant voice came out of one of the speakers: *"Car Dieu a tant aime le monde..."*

I quickly spun a few more dials, then all of them—

"...dab er seinen eingeloren..."

"...Zoon gegeven heeft..."

"...affinche chiunque crede in lui..."

"...should not perish, but have everlasting life."

The room filled with the sounds of John 3:16 in twenty-five languages. The various tapes went on with the rest of the chapter, the cacophony of the world's languages strangely melodious.

Mesmerized by the sound, I was at ease for the moment. Then the tapes stopped.

"Why is there no video?" I cried. But those at the door were visibly relieved I hadn't pulled the big transmission lever. It was safe. For now.

Then Nadine came in, followed by Roberto. Another one of the gun-toting houseboys slipped down along the wall to the end of the room as Nadine approached me, her red scarfed head brilliant in the otherwise sterile surroundings. Except for the floor.

I noticed that she had one hand cupped and held close by her side.

I raised Taylor's revolver. "No closer, Nadine. I'm not playing anymore."

She stopped.

Taylor whispered something to Leigh, who then moved into the room behind Nadine. The others remained where they were. In a ludicrous attempt to be discreet, Leigh whispered to Nadine, "He won't shoot. Just get him down from there."

She was more beautiful than ever.

Her hair framed her face in a golden halo, and she was so innocently lovely I was inwardly glad that I didn't catch her in Taylor's position this morning.

"Jonas," she said, her voice even and cool. But strong. "I'm coming up there with you and Randy."

Ahh, I wanted her to come. I would have like for her to sit on my lap so I could fondle her like the little doll she was—

BLAM!

The one clock above the door, which must have been set to Greenwich time, exploded in shards. The hour hand remained on the face, however, pointed between two and three, then it tipped out of its broken case and fell to the floor.

The wonderful cocoa tan Nadine sported disappeared for the moment. She was stock-still on the floor, unable to even blink. The armed houseboys had their weapons at the ready, but were still cringing.

I watched the smoke ooze out of the gun barrel. "What's

the schedule, Randy? When does this show go down? When do we go on the air?"

"It's no show, Jonas. You *know* that."

"Someone else then," I called out. "Leigh! When...or better yet, Morowitz! When does it look good? When'll the stars be right?"

"Wa-a-a-all," Morowitz uttered as usual, then stopping and furtively looking around to see if it was all right.

It seemed to be. Everyone was still slightly shocked.

"By my calculations," he went on in his usual slow manner, "based on the March 10 alignment, touchdown should be..."

Touchdown?

"*Shut up*, Morowitza!" Taylor suddenly commanded, back in control. "Dr. Griffiths, proceed."

Nadine remained where she was just for a moment, then came a little bit closer.

"Hold on, Nadine," I told her. "I know you have me set up for a shot. What are you using? Ayahuasca and what else? Teonanacatl? Mescaline derivatives? Pure LSD? Sodium pentathol?"

I squeezed off another round.

The explosion didn't seem as loud this time, but the ricochet echoed weirdly. There appeared a ragged hole in one of the tiles near Nadine's left sandaled foot.

"Dr. Rand," hissed Taylor. "Get away from there!"

Randy turned from me for the first time since the others came in. "Go," he said to them. "Jonas is *with* me now."

"He's useless to us," Leigh argued.

"Step away, Randy," Nadine said softly.

Taylor raised one hand. The armed houseboys were already in position.

It looked like the end of the movie. And I still didn't

understand the scenario. "Randy," I said, "I know that it's you that's behind all this, that wrote that 'bible.' But I'm lost, buddy."

He turned back to me and said, "'Behold, I stand at the door and knock. If anyone listens to My voice and opens the door, I shall come in to him and dine with him and he with Me.' You have to *believe* now, Jonas."

"But I can't! I don't believe in anything!"

Nadine took a few steps closer.

"Not even in good and evil. There's more to it than that, you know. Cal explained it to me. There is the strong force and the weak force, the electromagnetic force and the gravitational force. Evil is simply energy created by a little goodness and too much intelligence."

I pulled the trigger again, this time the bullet burying itself directly into the red tile in front of Taylor. Pieces of the exploded plastic rained down with a slight pitter-patter.

"You believe in energy, then, Jonas. If evil is energy, would you believe in *love* as energy? Let us call it *spiritual* energy."

"All right," I said, swallowing. "Sure——" I was listening to him. I also had no shells left. No one seemed to know it yet.

"And this energy the human heart can pit against the physical energy released from the heart of matter...do you follow me, Jonas?"

Everyone remained stock-still, frozen in their positions, as if in a child's game of freeze tag.

"Love can create, cherish, and safeguard what extinction would destroy and keep in nothingness. The strong force and the weak force of the universe. The nuclear glue and dispersing agent that brought *us*—you and me, Jonas—here, to Earth."

"What are you talking about? *Brought us? How?*"

"'Truly I assure you that he who listens to My message and believes Him who sent Me has eternal life.' *Believe,* Jonas!"

"Don't hand me that Sunday school crap! You laid the same thing on Taylor. It's *you!* It's been you all along."

I was shouting now. I could feel the saliva building up in my mouth, flecks of it, foamed, flying out with my words: "Double-think! Contradictory messages! The oxymoronic fact of the *Word* itself—"

As I said this, I remembered something a doctor had told me long ago about psychoanalysis, and that a true comprehension of the shrink's art requires not only an intellectual realization but a simultaneous emotional response. Neither alone would do. And Freud said that only a well chosen metaphor would permit both..."

I stopped shouting.

A *well chosen metaphor.* Randy said that love was an energy that came from the heart, and also that it was the nuclear glue and dispersing agent of the universe. And Freud spoke of the soul as the seat both of the mind and the passions that remains deeply hidden. The soul may be intangible, but remains a powerful influence—

Metaphors for time and space. Enigmatic and inscrutable. Love, and the soul it is created in.

And there was always the conflict, within the heart or within the soul, making life seem to *begin* and to *end*—when it just *was.*

Einstein said that space was simply the arrangement of matter and fields. And time was just where you happened to be in that arrangement. A continuum. A mural on someone's wall or a geodesic structure.

Others stumbled on this idea. They could see that there was something more than what man's limited view permitted him. Something locked away inside us, waiting to be tapped, and only visible through occasional catalysts who came to earth from—somewhere.

But Darwin knew this, as did Freud, though they were on the periphery: They could view the mural, or geodesic form, and Einstein could even describe the structure.

Darwin, though he saw the whole spectrum, could not begin to fathom the seeming leaps in development of species, especially man.

Freud saw the soul as a battleground, though not between good and evil, but Eros and Thanatos. He wanted to integrate the emotional life into the intellectual life, preventing the destructive force, Thanatos, from taking over.

But death doesn't exist.

Except in the intellect. Leaving the emotional life, and the soul, as ever-lasting.

Randy said that *love* could create, cherish, and safeguard what extinction would destroy and shut up in nothingness... and that was *why* we were here.

The Power and the Glory forever...

Randy talked to me steadily and unswervingly. He described incredible intellectual vistas and sweeping emotional hells. I was losing most of it, like grasping at raindrops while drowning.

He said we, too, came from a place. We had a beginning as creatures, as men. There were worlds within us as there were worlds beyond us. But this was our world now. This earth.

And it was time again for the catalyst, for man to evolve more. Before extinction would destroy him and shut up in nothingness what he was.

This was *our* purpose, my purpose. Many times before had we come to do this—

The room was swirling around me. I saw a bright crimson slash of brilliance descending, felt a sickly cold pinch.

But still the words came, all part of a dialogue that

stretched across the universe and across time, all around and back to whence we began—

"Do you remember Challa? Where you were once born? The island of the Moon?"

"And you, *brujo*. Born on Isla Titicaca."

"Yes, *curandero!* You remember! The Island of the Sun. Remember now, in the deep lake, where we swam with Leviathan?"

I did remember. I knew who I was now.

"And in the Holy City, where we flew with the condor."

But still...still a doubt: The prophecy of the *parousia*, the advent of the anti...

CHAPTER TWENTYNINE

I was scuffing down Forty-Second Street, just west of Times
Square.

Cold out. Or, rather, I was cold. My robe was thin and
did not provide much protection against the chilling gusts of
early spring. I'd really have to talk to someone about getting
some decent clothes. But then, that would mean going back,
and I was going to avoid doing that for awhile.

The whores were out early today, and the other hustlers
were swarming around my regular corner. Passerby were
watching that electric sign giving a visual news readout:
...UFO STILL VISIBLE OVER THE NE US...SCIENTISTS
SAY PRESENCE STILL UNEXPLAINABLE...

I began my usual spiel. The attendants wouldn't be here
for awhile yet. They thought I was still in hydrotherapy. Well,
fuck them. They knew where to find me.

Ahh, New York sure wasn't Nineveh!

***

Two men watched the street scene that morning from the
comparative comfort of a Chock Full O'Nuts café. They were
in the news gathering business.

A dark green van pulled up to the opposite curb, and,
with almost one sweeping motion, two burly men, both
dressed in light gray tunic-like uniforms, got out and took
away the uncelebrated character who had been haranguing the
passing multitude for the past half-hour.

In the café, one of the observers remarked, "Now that was a nice clean pickup."

"Yep," his companion agreed. "Poor bastard comes back though. He's there at least two or three times a week."

The other man sipped his coffee. He noticed that the 'poor bastard' had left behind a single slipper. It remained on the sidewalk until, in a scant few moments, it has been kicked by the swiftly moving crowd into the gutter. "What was his act?"

"Hmmm?"

"What did he say? End of the world, that sort of thing?"

"No. Strange son of a bitch, though.

Quite lucid, actually. I caught a few seconds of it yesterday. He was going on about the *Third* Coming of Christ."

"The Third? Didn't know we'd had the Second yet."

"Not according to him."

A Danish was placed in front of one of the men by a dark-skinned waitress. He picked it up and began eating. Could it happen, he thought. Christ come again and no one give a damn? Interesting, but not very likely. Like the supposed UFO that everyone was so shook up about.

"Did you see that new book?"

"Which one?"

"Francis Crick. *Life Itself,* I think the title is."

"Didn't he do that book with Watson, describing the structure of DNA, or something?"

"Yep. But this is new. Interesting theory. 'Directed Panspermia,' he calls it."

"Yeah?"

"It's the idea that Earth's original life arrived as micro-organisms dispatched by intelligent beings who chose not to make the journey themselves."

"Outrageous! Somebody ought to make a movie out of it. Great idea!" But to himself he thought: Sounds like something that nut across the street earlier would be spouting.

"Isn't it though," his companion chuckled. "I kind of like the idea."

You would, just like any other flibbertigibbet, the man thought, but smiled at his colleague anyway. He watched an old bag-lady shuffle through the garbage in the gutter until she came upon the left behind slipper. She picked it up quickly, probably intrigued by its newness.

She sniffed it once, then tossed it away and continued down the street.

***

There is grandeur in this view of
life, with its several powers having
been originally breathed into a few
forms, or into one; and that, whilst
this planet has gone cycling on
according to the fixed laws of
gravity, from so simple a beginning
endless forms most beautiful and
most wonderful have been, and are
being, evolved.

—Charles Darwin